BLACK TRUTH, WHITE LIES

HAILEY EDWARDS

Edited by Sasha Knight
Copy Edited by Kimberly Cannon
Proofread by Lillie's Literary Services
Cover by Damonza
Illustration by NextJenCo

BLACK TRUTH, WHITE LIES

GROW THROUGH
WHAT YOU GO THROUGH

1

Forget Santa. Forget the live reindeer. Forget adorable kids dressed as elves.

Asa in a black silk top hat was giving me hot flashes.

The tidy cravat was weirdly sexy. Very Mr. Darcy. He wore his Black Hat-issued dress pants, crisp white button-down shirt, and polished dress shoes. The cane he carved from a downed limb on my property, and he knitted a scarf for the occasion. The town festival closet—and yes, under Mayor Tate, we had a costume department— provided a period-appropriate jacket.

His gorgeous hair was scooped into a man bun to give him a clean nape for the sake of his character, and I already missed his braids. Though I was slightly obsessed with the black post earrings, representative of coal, and the thick black bar piercing his septum.

The sunset bathed his features in a golden glow, and the scowl cutting his mouth made me want to chuckle. Since it was genuine, not acting, I behaved myself. Mostly. Except for the videos and photos I sneaked of him while he bah humbugged at the citizens of Samford, come to enjoy A Downtown Dickens Christmas.

He could Ebenezer my Scrooge anytime.

"Scrooge is hot." Camber fanned her face. "Good thing Mayor Tate skipped the fake snow machine."

"His hotness would have melted it," Arden agreed. "Puddles everywhere."

The glare I cut them would have drawn blood in my black witch days, but I was a white witch now.

And I got zero respect. Seriously. None. At all.

Forget the boogeyman I ought to be to them. I was more of a fairy godmother in their eyes.

The ding to my pride was enough to almost make me miss inspiring pants-pissing terror in my enemies.

But fear, as sweet as it smelled—minus the urine—had never made me as happy as the simple love from these two human girls. Girls with expensive, if impeccable, taste. Girls who had long ago memorized the shop credit card. Girls who, after years of practicing, could forge my signature with frightening accuracy.

Like the one Camber scrawled on the receipt for our Victorian-inspired dresses with modern hemlines.

Camber was a vision in pine-bough green, while Arden made a bold statement in cranberry red. I got the best of both worlds in a plaid pattern that incorporated both of their colors with light gold accents. Black flats, shining jingle bell jewelry, and matching updos pinned with the liberal application of faux-holly hair sticks lent us a uniform customers would notice when it came time to ask questions or make a purchase.

The extra expenses brought a tear to my eye, but this was our grand reopening. We aimed to dazzle new customers while reminding old ones we were still here, and we were back in business after the remodel.

Not that the girls, or anyone else in town, knew the truth. That a black witch wrecked Hollis Apothecary in a fit of rage. They all blamed my fictional ex-boyfriend, and I had no choice but to let them. I hated to lie to the people who had embraced me, but I had fabricated a life story when I arrived in Samford, and I couldn't edit the fine details at this point. They were facts in the minds of the townsfolk, and I was stuck.

Movement caught my eye where I stood in the doorway to the shop, welcoming in customers.

Dressed in ragged brown pants, a dirty white shirt, and ratty ochre jacket, Clay waved with his crutch.

His *crutch*.

That Asa, sucker that he was, carved to scale for him.

At seven feet tall, four hundred pounds, Clayton Kerr had no business dressing up as Tiny Tim.

Though I will admit, he was cute as a button in his newsboy cap covering his wildly curling brunet wig. He wore a gray scarf rescued from the bowels of my closet and a pair of fingerless gloves from the dollar store. His black suspenders, as mismatched as the rest of his outfit, strained to accommodate his height.

Those flimsy metal clips holding his pants up didn't inspire much faith, so I was glad he kept his distance. I did *not* want one to cut loose and pop me in the eye if he moved the wrong way. That would hurt like...

...the Dickens.

And the mayor would never forgive me if I made a spectacle that marred her winter extravaganza.

Never mind our town was so small that characters outnumbered shoppers two to one.

That was the only reason Mayor Tate agreed to let the guys pitch in. Arden's idea. Not mine. I would *not* have put Asa through this. He preferred to disappear into the background, not be thrust to the fore. Had I not assigned him Scrooge, we might have had a problem. His stark masculine beauty drew stares, and a middle-aged woman swooned at the sight of him. Granted, hers was a fear response, though she had no idea why gawking at him led to her collapse seconds later. His threat, his power, was a nagging prickle in the brain that warned prey to *run, run, run* until a thick door with a hefty lock separated them from him.

Not that either barrier would make a lick of difference to a daemon as determined as the one inside Asa.

Still, Arden had earned brownie points with the mayor for volunteering nonlocals to fill critical roles. She was hoping to sweet-talk her way into the second parking spot mentioned in our lease. I told her to save her breath, Mayor Tate had selective hearing when it came to me and my shop, but she was an optimist.

"Do you smell that?" Arden pinched me. "They're roasting actual chestnuts on an actual open fire."

"Hmm?"

"She's busy undressing Asa with her mind," Camber explained to her best friend. "I am too."

For the first time tonight, I was grateful Colby had elected to stay home to party with her friends online.

"Okay." I snatched a plastic holly sprig from the garland decorating the doorway. "That's it." I whacked Camber between the eyes. "Stop being a brat." I swatted her shoulder. "Bad shopgirl." Again. "Bad, bad girl."

"Hey." Laughter in her eyes, she danced back. "That hurts."

"You asked for it." Arden cackled. "You can't cry about it now."

"You started it." She pointed a finger. "You offered to lick the powdered sugar off his mouth for him."

Camber forgotten, I wheeled on Arden. "You did *what?*"

"He didn't hear me." She yelped when I smacked her. "He was already standing on the corner."

Keen as his senses were, he'd heard her. Loud and clear. Probably chuckled to himself about it too.

Me?

I wasn't laughing.

Thanksgiving had been a disaster.

Okay, okay, *fine.* Dinner hadn't been the problem. The meal was quite delicious, if I do say so myself. Asa and Clay, however, didn't know that firsthand. No sooner had I nailed down a mental list of bullet points on how to tempt Asa to cash in on his permission to kiss me, than a time-sensitive case hit his inbox with the *thud* heard 'round the world.

My world, anyway.

So, yeah, Thanksgiving had been a bust.

Two weeks later, Christmas wasn't looking much brighter.

Let the girls fantasize about Asa's lush mouth. I didn't mind. At least then I would be in good company.

With a final swat to both girls' bottoms, I returned the sprig to its garland and forced my eyes from Asa.

"We need to set out more sugar cookies." I did a quick mental tally. "We have about two dozen left. Can you refresh the cranberry punch while you're at it?" I aimed the question at Arden. "I'll get the cupcakes and napkins." Camber raised her eyebrows, waiting for her marching orders. "You can man the register."

With a twirl that showed off her frilly petticoat, she positioned herself behind the counter.

Arden slid her arm through mine and rested her head on my shoulder as we walked to the back.

Her trust was a gift, one I didn't deserve, but I was grateful each time she gave it to me.

"Two weeks until Christmas." She stared up at me. "Are Clay and Asa spending the holidays with you?"

Had the girls not brought a hefty plate of Thanksgiving goodies to my door after I passed on joining them for dinner with their families, they wouldn't have known I was sprawled on my bed, sulking with a book about a turkey shifter and a cranberry farmer that made me question if my dark tastes had gone too far.

Probably not a good idea to read a romance whose main characters made my stomach rumble.

I might have devoured those leftovers with a bit too much enthusiasm for a black witch in recovery.

"A lot can happen in two weeks." I bounced a shoulder. "I don't know. Maybe. I hope so."

"Is it weird that, like, they're a package deal? Clay could stay in town, give you two some privacy."

"We don't need privacy," I blurted before my brain caught up to my mouth. "Forget I said that."

"Aww." She patted my cheek. "That would explain why you've been so grumpy."

"I have not been grumpy," I grumped. "I don't know where I stand with Asa, that's all."

The hair bracelet said one thing, but the lack of ravishment said another.

"He looks at you the way Camber looks at a chocolate peanut butter cake."

Except Camber worshipped those cakes with her mouth.

Goddess bless, I was not jealous of a slice of cake for seeing more action than me.

"Thanks for the pep talk." I bumped shoulders with her. "Are you and Louis still talking?"

"No." She pinched her lips together. "He got weird, after..."

After David Taylor, the Silver Stag copycat, kidnapped her and Camber.

"I'm sorry." I brought her in for a hug. "Maybe he'll come to his senses."

"Maybe." She wriggled free and picked up her share of the treats. "Or maybe it's not meant to be."

The melancholy statement wasn't intended for me, but it hit home all the same.

"I didn't mean you and Asa," she rushed to assure me when my face fell. "You guys are different."

Arms loaded down with my half of the supplies, I shot her a smile that promised I wasn't upset.

Out on the sidewalk, she and I began restocking our table as the caroler troupe swished past.

A prickle of unease stung my nape, and I angled my head to scan the busy street.

Shoppers. Kids. Characters.

Nothing amiss.

Shaking off my paranoia, I dusted the table free of crumbs then straightened the cups and napkins.

A scream rent the night, frantic and desperate, and townsfolk rushed to the source.

"Rue," Arden breathed, her hand fisting the back of my dress.

"Stay here." I pressed my tray into her arms, ushering her backward. "Don't leave the shop."

"Okay." Eyes haunted, she inched toward Camber. "Be careful, Rue."

On my way out, I kicked the stop up and shut the door. Not that glass panes offered much in the way of protection, but until I knew what was going on, the illusion of safety was all I could give them.

Tiny Tim was jogging toward the action, his crutch forgotten, but Scrooge fell in step with me.

"Let's hope it's not food poisoning again." I kept my pace brisk. "Our festivals are earning a reputation."

"The mayonnaise isn't to blame for this." Asa pitched his voice low. "I smell blood."

As much as I wished for a mundane explanation, say, a hemophiliac slicing their thumb open at the gift-wrapping booth, I could tell this was more. And that was before the scent hit me.

Fear soured the sweet night air, amplifying the crowd's response to Asa. They shied away, uncertain why their hindbrains screamed at them to run when he was such a handsome man. So polite and helpful too.

A perfect predator.

"Everyone, step back." Clay waved Asa and me forward into a cleared space. "We need room to work."

"Oh no." I jolted with surprise. "It's Dasher."

The reindeer's throat had been ripped out, its spine all that kept its head attached to its body, and blood spread across the pavement. Massive jaws had torn off hunks of meat, moss and duckweed coated its soaked fur, and a distinctive fishy smell battled against the reek of its disembowelment.

Slime, algae maybe, floated in hand-sized puddles. Like footprints, or pawprints, they led away from the scene, but they were evaporating. Water dried fast on asphalt. Deep South winters tended to run warm, and today had been downright hot.

"The police will be here in a minute," I warned the guys. "Two officers are working the event."

Samford had a police force of six, including the chief, and they would have heard the commotion.

Clay used his phone to film the scene, and the gawkers, while I snapped photos. Asa knelt beside the body, scenting it while examining it for clues. He didn't get far before the crowd ejected two familiar cops who clearly weren't vibing with having their scene trampled by frantic locals or stolen by slick out-of-towners.

"What the hell d'you think you're doing?" Officer Waters bulled up to Clay. "This ain't your jurisdiction."

There went our best shot at tracking the beast responsible before the trail went as cold as poor Dasher's body. Waters was like a dog with a bone once he sank his teeth into a case, and he wasn't about to cede the limelight to Clay and Asa. We couldn't afford to have him tag along with us, so we couldn't afford to hunt.

"Officer Kerr." Officer Downy nodded to each of the guys in turn. "Officer Montenegro."

Ignoring Waters, which lit a fire under him, Clay shook hands with Downy. "Good to see you again, sir."

"We apologize for overstepping." Asa rose with inhuman grace. "Habit."

"You can take the cop out of—" Downy tilted his head. "Where did you say your precinct was again?"

About to spin another lie out of thin air, Clay caught my subtle head shake and buttoned his lips.

"We'll leave you to it." I hooked an arm through his and tugged him after me, calling over my shoulder to the officers, "Thank you for your service."

Asa took my hand, threading our fingers, but none of us spoke until we reached the shop.

The girls stood with their faces pressed to the glass, desperate for a glimpse of what was happening.

"Wait here." I parked the guys beside my table and entered the shop. "We're done for the night."

"What happened?" Camber clung to Arden. "Why is the news van parking by the diner?"

The news van was a soccer mom ride with honor roll brags pasted on the bumper, and the reporter was also often the camerawoman. When Casey Evans's husband was busy with the kids, she used one of those selfie sticks to record her pieces. She had already made her rounds down Main Street to cover the event. One of her sources must have had Casey on speed dial for her to have made such a quick U-turn.

"I'm not sure." I didn't want to lie, but I didn't want to scare her either. "The police are handling it."

And I planned on making busywork in the shop so I could keep an eye on their progress.

Arden tucked Camber against her side when her friend turned pale. "Will they need to speak to us?"

"No." I set a hand on each of their shoulders. "You two didn't see anything."

"I heard the scream," Arden countered. "Do you think that matters?"

"We all heard the scream." I nudged them toward the door. "I'll lock up tonight. Just get home safe."

Arden, this bolder version of her, was primed to argue, but she caved to Camber's desolate stare.

"Come on." She shepherded Camber onto the sidewalk. "You can stay with me tonight."

The look Arden turned on me demanded a promise I didn't want to make.

"I'll touch base if I hear anything." I offered her my pinky. "Text me when you get home, okay?"

Used to me fussing over her, she didn't put up a fight as we shook on it. "I will."

Once the girls were gone, I herded the stragglers out of the shop and helped Asa bring in the table. Clay, always eager to lend a hand —or a mouth—to a worthy cause, had already disposed of the baked goods. In his stomach. The punch met a similar fate. At least the long hours in the kitchen hadn't gone to waste.

With their help, I cleaned and stored the props until January, for the New Year's Eve Fireworks Show.

Fireworks weren't my thing, witches being flammable and all, but Mayor Tate had made it clear participation wasn't optional.

Ugh.

A storefront on Main Street was a much bigger headache than I ever thought possible.

Out on the sidewalk, I swept my area clean while stealing glances at the commotion. It was growing larger by the minute, not smaller. This kind of violence was a rarity in our town.

Giving up for the moment, I locked us in the shop, turned off the lights, and led the guys to my office.

"Well?" I plunked down in my chair. "Thoughts?"

"We have a dobhar-chú on our hands." Clay sat on the edge of my desk. "That's not good."

The wood groaned under him, and something popped, forcing me to shoo him away before he broke it.

"How can you tell?" I leaned forward. "I've read about them, but I've never seen one."

Dobhar-chú attacked adult humans, or other paranormals, but only when cornered on land with no water to aid in their escape. They were opportunists, for the most part, preferring to pick off stragglers. There were documented cases of bolder individuals, but usually in landlocked situations that forced them to hunt outside their norm.

"The smell." Clay tapped the side of his nose. "Rotten oysters and decaying fish."

Frowning, I rested my chin on my palm. "Now I feel bad for blaming that on Dasher."

"He's right." Asa tucked a hand into his pocket. "They have a distinctive scent."

"How did it get here?" I reviewed the hastily snapped images of the mutilated reindeer. "Tadpole Swim is the largest body of water in the area. There's a creek that cuts through my backyard, but it's shallow. Other than that, there's only the big fountain downtown." I set down my phone. "Why would it travel twenty-three miles from the nearest major water source?"

"A dobhar-chú wouldn't have traveled so far inland on its own."

"What do you mean?" I jerked my gaze to Asa. "Someone dumped it here?"

"'Tis the season for gift giving." Clay's smile was grim. "Too bad there's no return policy."

"It came into town." I drummed my fingers on my desktop. "During a festival."

That wasn't normal behavior for any wild animal, let alone a fae creature.

"Maybe it's sick?" Clay rubbed his jaw. "That could explain why it left the water."

"Might explain its hunting behavior too," I agreed. "It was drawn to people, not spooked by them."

Fae tended to leave humans alone, unless they were certain they wouldn't get caught having a snack.

"We're lucky it saw the reindeer first." Clay frowned. "That could have been someone's kid."

"It's here because of me." It needed saying. "This is my fault."

"It's the fault of whoever trapped a dobhar-chú and unleashed it downtown during a Christmas party." Asa circled the desk and crouched beside me. "Place the blame where it belongs." His hungry gaze roved my face. "You didn't do this." A smile tugged up one corner of his mouth. "But you'll make whoever did regret the day they violated your territory."

"Yes," I agreed with the first half, "but I don't have a territory."

Territories were for witches who could afford a home, a family, a life.

Until the director proved he was as good as his word, I couldn't get too attached to the idea of permanence. I trusted him about as much as I believed in Santa Claus.

"You do now." Clay chuckled. "Welcome to the big leagues, Rue."

"The sooner you claim it," Asa said, "the safer the people under your aegis will be."

The dark well of magic within me rippled to wakefulness as it considered the benefits of acting as judge, jury, and executioner for a region under my absolute control. Human laws would hold no sway over me. Paranormals would risk my wrath if they ventured onto my lands without asking my express permission.

Within Samford's borders, I would be its master, and that much influence filled me with sickening dread.

"I'm not ready." I pushed back from my desk. "I don't trust myself with that kind of temptation."

The eager, crueler part of me growled in disappointment then returned to its fitful slumber.

One day, it promised, I would be weak. I would say yes. I would embrace my birthright. I would *soar*.

And I would emerge from my ten-year chrysalis a monster who destroyed everything that she loved.

"Those who don't crave power," Asa murmured, "are the ones who should be trusted to wield it."

Oh, I craved it. I just didn't want it. I was an addict. Power my drug of choice.

"Maybe." I rolled my shoulders to shake off how much the notion appealed to me. "I'll think about it."

"For now," Clay cut in, giving me a break from the third degree, "we've got a reindeer to avenge."

"The holiday fun never stops when you guys are around." I heaved a sigh. "Goddess bless us."

Every one.

2

Pollen granules dusted Colby's hands and mouth, and cups that once held sugar water dotted her desk. I was too tired to fuss about the mess, so I ruffled her antennae and headed for the living room. Clay, Asa, and I already had our bureau-issued laptops out on the coffee table. We had been updating the software and emptying the caches and defragging the hard drives and…I zoned out after that, confused by the jargon.

Asa and I sank onto the sofa, and Clay took the ancient wingback Colby had insisted I buy for the weird perch carved into the wood trim at the top of the chair. All I could figure was the original owner kept a parrot. Whatever the reason, Colby loved to sit there. It was the best thirty-five dollars I ever spent on furniture.

Even if it cost me three hundred more to have it restored to its former, quirky glory.

"We need to call this in." Clay shifted his weight, and the chair protested. "Whoever dumped the dobhar-chú on your doorstep did so during a festival. It's a miracle no one saw it chowing down on poor Dasher. It's bad enough so many humans, with camera phones, got an eyeful of a mangled pet reindeer in an area where there are no native predators large enough to blame for that bite radius.”

“We have mountain lions, coyotes, bobcats, feral hogs, and the occasional black bear.”

“Rue.” His eyes saw too much. “We need to do this by the book.”

“We’re a team.” I gestured to the three of us. “This is what we do.”

“You don’t want to call it in,” Asa realized a beat after Clay. “What are you afraid of?”

“Samford doesn’t exist in the Black Hat database.” I checked, top to bottom, but its record was spotless. Only the Kellies, and the director, knew it was my new home. “This case would put it on their radar.”

“It would be the same as with any other town,” Clay argued. “There doesn’t have to be a link—”

“I’m a black witch, as far as they know, and I’m Black Hat. That makes me a threat, and threats get flagged on paperwork.” Standard operating procedure was to list paranormals associated with a particular area, including species and affiliations. “That would associate Samford with me *forever*. Any agent could access that information, and with the spike in rogue activity? I’m not okay with that.”

“You’re worried about Colby.” Asa cut to the heart of the matter. “You’re afraid for her.”

I was afraid for everyone in town, all my too-human friends, but her most of all.

“Old enemies would hunt me down.” I kept my gaze low. “That puts her in the crosshairs.”

Call me Rue Hollis, or any of my previous aliases, I had found one adage to be true.

The past always caught up to you.

“Forty-eight hours.” Clay used his senior agent voice. “I’ll give you that long to cowboy.”

Gratitude left me dizzy, and I sank back with relief.

“Past that,” he warned, “we reevaluate.”

Throat gone tight, I worked up a smile for the friend who had never let me down. "Thanks."

"You used the kid against me." He jerked off his newsboy cap and threw it at me. "Not cool."

The kid in question must have sensed the tension in the room and came to investigate.

A lush green blanket draped her cat-sized shoulders, a velvety shield against nightmares she held tight even during the day. Asa couldn't have given her a better, or more thoughtful, gift.

"How did the reopening go?" She lit on the perch above Clay. "Did you sell tons of product?"

"Hey, Shorty." Too late, Clay slammed his laptop shut. "How did your raid go?"

"What was that?" Her breathless gasp filled the room. "A *reindeer*?"

"A dobhar-chú got snackish." I attempted to divert her. "Hey, did you get that cursed-chalice thing?"

"That's so cool." Her antennae quivered. "It's here? In town?"

A smile threatened to overtake Asa as Colby refused to be distracted.

"Wrong answer." I pointed a finger at her. "It's not cool."

"Does this have anything to do with the blue guy hanging around on Mrs. Gleason's property?"

"What blue man?" A jolt of alarm shot me to my feet. "Where?"

"Down by the creek." Colby indicated the new curved monitor above her rig. "See?"

The past few months had taught me I wasn't as prepared as I would like when it came to security for the little moth girl in my care. I had stripped the wards to the bone, cleansed the earth, and then rebuilt our protections from the ground up with her help, using our combined powers. I had installed twice as many cameras, most of which I aimed at shared property lines, which meant monitoring the neighbors' yards.

After the wildlife photographer debacle, I wasn't taking any chances on the Nolan Laurens of the world.

"That looks like…" I zoomed in on the footage, "…Aedan."

The vibrant turquoise skin made him stand out where he sat in the shallow creek, his back against a tree, his arms propped on the roots. The picture he cut was a man of leisure on a throne nature provided him.

"That is Aedan." Asa set his top hat on the cushion beside him. "I'll handle this."

"I'll come with you." I didn't want him to go alone. "I'll run interference if Mrs. Gleason spots us."

For a woman her age, she was a spry thing. She also possessed an uncanny knack for sensing trespassers on her property. She might forgive me for toeing the line, but she remained suspicious of Asa. To be fair, she was suspicious of everyone. Except for the girl next door —*me*—who ought to ping as a threat on her radar.

"All right." Asa removed his scarf and the town-issued coat too. "This won't take long."

The day I had ringside tickets for challenges against Asa was coming, I knew that, but I hoped I wasn't on the VIP list for tonight. We already had one thorny problem on our hands without a daemon free-for-all.

"Stay put." I booped Colby on the proboscis. "No spying."

"Let's go slaughter some orcs." Clay ditched his suspenders and coat. "I want to see this cursed chalice."

Antennae aquiver, she vibrated with excitement. "It's a *doomed* chalice."

"As in anyone who possesses it is doomed?"

"Exactly." Her wings fluttered at hummingbird speed. "I knew you'd get it."

The pair returned to Colby's rig where Clay killed the overhead monitor and settled in to view her hoard.

Happy to have her distracted, bloodthirsty little thing, I exited the house and admired the starry night.

A swirl of warm air carried the scent of juicy green apples with a hint of cherry tobacco to me.

"You've been distant." Asa spared the moon a passing glance. "Anything the matter?"

Other than the kiss thing? The *no*-kiss thing? The total lack of lip-on-lip action? *That* thing?

"An aggressive paranormal creature is hunting in my town." I cut him a dry look. "Kind of stressful."

"Before the reindeer." He caught my elbow. "Have I done something wrong?"

"No." I heaved a sigh. "It's me." And my oral fixation. "You've been a complete gentleman."

Unfortunately.

"Is there anything I can do?" He circled around in front of me, and the heat from his body ignited a fire in my blood. "Anything I should be doing?"

The reminder he was new to relationships too shamed me for wanting to pressure him into more.

This wasn't high school, not that I had ever attended high school, but I had suffered through enough movies with thinly veiled peer pressure messages with Camber and Arden to decide for myself I didn't want to be the pathetic excuse for a person who had to liquor up her date so she could grope him under the bleachers.

"No." I pressed my hands against his chest to keep him at a distance. "You're fine. I'm fine. We're fine."

Black witches didn't do boyfriends. They had ritualistic sex, either to fuel spells or to grow the coven. The only time hearts were involved was if one or the other got snackish afterward.

Clearly, I was no authority on feelings or whatever that squishy sensation was Asa inspired in my chest.

Ugh.

Ugh.

Ugh.

Hearts were so much simpler to figure out when you held them in your hand.

To erase the line gathering across his brow, I redirected him. "Why do you think Aedan's here?"

"He didn't show for the last challenge," he said, which was news to me. "I assume he's made his peace."

And come to die went without saying when an opponent pitted themselves against Asa.

Hand in hand, I led him down the sloping hill. "Can he forfeit?"

"That is not the way of our world."

Our world could have meant his world, the daemon world in a broad sense, not *ours* as in his and mine, but the weight of my maybe-heritage pressed down on me more with every passing day.

"Hello, Death."

The cheery voice *almost* let me skip over the grim nickname, but I forgot both when I set eyes on Aedan.

For a daemon with blue skin, I picked out the pinkish-orange bruises with ease. Strips of his skin bore the telltale signs of claws, and his gills had crusted shut down one side of his throat. Sunset-colored fluids hit the creek and swirled in rainbow eddies that got swept downstream. His webbed fingers were wrong, as if the thin skin had been cut to separate each digit. He caught me cataloguing his injuries and chuckled in a wet and rattling way that told me there was worse damage than I could see.

Given his condition, he might have trespassed to guarantee immediate repercussions, but if so, he overshot the mark. A good six feet separated him from my side of the property line. We had to rectify that, and fast.

"Don't fret." He winked a black eye at me. "I'll soon be dead, and the dead no longer feel pain."

Jaw set, Asa glanced away at the other daemon's gallows humor.

"What happened to you?" I gestured to his, well, everything. "Who did this?"

"What does it matter?" A faint smile graced his swollen lips. "It was done and cannot be undone."

"Fine." Frustration set my teeth on edge. "Die with your

mysteries."

"Your sister did this," Asa murmured into the night. "The question is why bother?"

Word traveled fast about challenges issued to Asa. *Astaroth*. How could Aedan's sister not know?

According to Clay, daemons came from all over to watch, place bets, to see and be seen. Potential mates paraded in front of him. Potential allies courted him. Potential, in its hedonistic glory, was in abundance.

The spectacle appealed to the darkness within me, yet another reason I dreaded my inaugural bout. It worried me how much I might enjoy it when it cost Asa to end lives for the sake of preserving his own.

"There were things I had to do before meeting my demise," Aedan joked. "She was not pleased by them."

"Your younger siblings." Asa returned his attention to the moon. "You fostered them."

During the copycat case, we discovered one of our suspects was fostering a teenage troll from a wealthy family in exchange for a boon. Otherwise, the girl would have been hunted down by her older siblings to clear the path to their inheritance.

This had a similar ring to it, and it would explain why Aedan missed the last round of challenges.

"Does your honor demand I stand?" Aedan flicked water off his fingertips. "Or can I keep my seat?"

"You may remain seated." Asa cut his eyes toward me. "Are you sure you want to bear witness?"

"He's half dead already," I protested. "Can't you let his wounds finish him off?"

"That sounds painful." Aedan scrunched up his nose. "And it would pollute the creek."

Asa took a step forward, and flames licked over his arms as the daemon took control.

Slabbed with muscle, his daemon half towered over me. Skin

dark red, it was feverish to the touch. Black rosettes formed random patterns down his legs and over his bare feet. Thick horns in the same midnight shade as his long hair curled from his temples over his head. His pants, strained to bursting, were all that survived the shift. Asa trashed fancy suits by the dozens, and it warmed my heart to imagine the director footing the bill.

"We're on a case." I planted a palm on his chest. "You can't kill him until we close it."

Those were the rules, as Asa had explained them to me, and I planned to force him to stick to them.

This might not be official yet, but it was a case. Clay had given me forty-eight hours.

"Rue." The daemon tossed his head toward Aedan. "He challenge me."

"I know, and I'm not saying you can't fight it out later, but look at him."

Playing dirty, I raked my fingers through the silky length of his hair. "Give him a few days to heal."

"I can't decide if you're trying to help me," Aedan muttered, "or torture me."

"Do you really want to die that badly?" I glared down at him. "You're seriously begging Asa to end you?"

An uncomfortable pressure built behind my breastbone, making it hard to breathe without discomfort, and my eyes itched. Maybe it was that sliver of manufactured conscience wedged into my brain, forcing me to grow, but I could tell this was wrong.

It was *wrong*.

"Why does it matter to you?" Aedan cocked his head. "You're a black witch. I'll even give you my heart."

An unwelcome rumble in my stomach earned me a bitter smile from Aedan and made me double down.

"I've done a lot of terrible things in my life," I told him, fumbling to put my thoughts into words.

"That's hardly shocking." A smile sparkled in his eyes. "Black witch, remember?"

"What opened my eyes was finding myself the guardian of another person, a *good* person."

"Love truly is blind." His eyes widened to comic proportions. "Astaroth is hardly an innocent."

"Not Asa." I kept petting the daemon to keep him distracted. "A child."

Aedan opened his mouth, shut it, opened it again, shut it again, gaping like a fish out of water.

Once he got his jaw working, he asked, "Black witches foster too?"

"No." I had never heard of a single instance. "This was a special circumstance."

"I don't understand."

Setting aside his confusion, I worked to gain momentum for my argument to offer him some clarity.

"The child looks to me as a role model," I explained, keeping it vague, "a protector, a provider. I couldn't remain the monster I had been my whole life unless I wanted to extinguish a bright light by hauling the child into the darkness with me. To be what the child needed, I had to change. I had to do better. I had to *be* better."

Gaze sliding down to the rippling waters, he listened, which was as much as I could ask of him.

"You and I stood at the same crossroads, and we made the same choice. To show mercy. To care." As I said it, wiggly pieces clicked together in my head that explained my turmoil. "You have another choice ahead of you. Will you continue making the hard calls? The right ones? Or was that one good act all you had in you?"

"I've already issued my challenge." He peered up at me. "There's no going back."

"Why did you challenge him in the first place?"

"I needed Delma, my sister, to get comfortable." He rubbed his side. "She quit hunting our siblings when she heard I challenged Astaroth. She knew he would kill me, and our siblings wouldn't survive without my protection. She sat back and waited, and I used that time to spirit them away. She will kill me for making a fool of her, if Astaroth doesn't do the job for her."

"Then there was never any going back, was there?"

"No." He frowned. "I guess there wasn't."

"I'm going to send a friend down here with a poultice and some painkillers. You heal and think." I had an idea and ran with it. "Asa will give you until we solve this case to decide your own fate."

"And then?"

Absently plaiting the daemon's hair, I rolled a shoulder. "Then we'll see."

"Thank you." He twisted up his face. "I think."

Using the braid as a lead rope, I guided the daemon back toward the house. "You can shift now."

A rush of flames coasted over his body, leaving me empty-handed as Asa emerged with his hair loose, an always welcome sight, and shirtless. Out of the two, I wasn't sure which was my favorite post-shift quirk.

"That was sneaky." I tended to forget he was half fae—easy to do when his daemon half was so much more obvious—but then he pulled a trick out of thin air, and I remembered. "You let me help him."

His daemon allowed me to negotiate without any fuss in exchange for finger-combing his hair. Asa, on the other hand, had fewer options available to him. Protocol demanded more from him.

"I can't promise I won't have to kill him."

"I understand." I glanced back to see Aedan resting with his eyes closed. "How did you know?"

Until I set eyes on Aedan, I hadn't grasped the push-pull in my gut was a tug of war with my conscience.

"Your scent." His eyes were bright and sharp. "You were upset, and the confusion made you angry."

"Your nose is that good?" I cocked an eyebrow. "You can catalog my emotions based on smell?"

"I had to learn you first." He smiled at me. "Otherwise, it's too much sensory feedback to be useful."

Did that mean he could guess each time I conjured inappropriate thoughts about him, his lips, his taste? What if the holdup was actually...me? Was my confusion too confusing for him to unknot in the tangle of my uncertainty? Even if I didn't know what to do with him, I wanted him. But I also wanted him to figure it out without forcing me to order my jumbled thoughts into a cohesive whole I had to verbalize for him.

Emotions were hard. Gah. No wonder my ancestors had eaten their feelings.

Back at the house, I crammed oatmeal raisin cookies into a plastic bag then tucked them in a gift basket I had lying around from when I brought work home with me. A chicken salad sandwich, along with a bag of chips and two sodas, completed the meal. Then I added in the poultice and a pain tincture.

"Hey." Clay, who followed me into the kitchen, grabbed for the sandwich. "I was going to eat that."

"It's going to a worthier cause." I elbowed him aside. "I'm about to start dinner anyway."

We had time to kill before we sneaked back into town to try our luck hunting the reindeer killer.

"Who's the lucky recipient of your delicious charity?"

"Aedan."

"Hate to break it to you, but he doesn't need snacks where he's going."

"He's in the creek." I added a few more treats. "Actually, would you mind bringing this to him?"

"I don't understand." He helped himself to a cookie. "Why isn't he dead?"

"He got an extension."

"Ace's reputation will take a hit for this." He quit chewing and set down his snack. "You get that, right?"

"He's working a case." I shoved the basket into his stomach. "No challenges during cases.”

“You’re bending the rules.” A snort ripped out of him, and he glanced around. “I hope they don’t break.”

That made two of us.

Asa’s father, Orion Pollux Stavros, High King of Hael, Master of Agonae, employed lesser daemons to spy on him. Despite the attempted patricide that landed Asa in Black Hat service, Orion wanted his son back.

Eventually.

If I didn’t get him killed by showing mercy on his behalf first.

“While you’re at it,” I added sweetly, “can you help him settle on my side of the property line?”

The color of Aedan’s skin meant he had no hope of blending in. Unless he could use glamour, like fae, he was a sitting duck on Mrs. Gleason’s property. The poor guy had been through enough without buckshot in his buns as he tried to flee from her territorial furor. At least if he was chilling on my side, he was safe.

More or less.

“Can I go?” Colby zipped into the room. “*Please*, Rue.”

Aedan had earned my sympathy, yes, but I took zero chances with Colby’s safety.

“Sorry, smarty fuzz butt.” I snuggled her when she lit on my shoulder. “He’s too dangerous.”

“Rue’s right.” Clay patted her head. “This won’t take me but a minute.”

“Okay.” Her wings slumped down my back. “I’ll go wait at my rig.”

“You do that.” He tweaked my nose. “What did you say about dinner?”

To keep his goodwill, I shoved him toward the door and began prep for chicken parmigiana with roasted garlic crostini. Tiramisu required time I didn’t have, so I decided on an affogato. If I only had forty-eight hours, I wanted to make the most of them. A rich hit of hot espresso couldn’t hurt.

3

Downtown was as empty as Bob Cratchit's pockets when we returned, high on caffeine, to assess what remained of the crime scene after police, townsfolk, and the news crew had trampled it.

The reindeer had been carted off, and the area where its corpse had been found was hosed clean.

Including the mucky puddles leading away from poor Dasher, and, most likely, to his killer.

"So much for our trail." I turned a circle. "No signs are left of what happened."

Which, of course, was the whole point.

"They didn't preserve the scene." Clay hooked his hands on his hips. "Must be blaming an animal."

The great thing about humans was they didn't want to know. Full stop. Another world existed alongside theirs, and they were content pretending anything too unsettling was a hoax. Photoshop and CGI had come a long way in a short amount of time. It was better, safer, if any monster caught on film was fake.

I don't want to know was the single most powerful weapon in our arsenal when protecting the secret of our existence. Even in modern times, humans searched for wires, strings, glitching code, and zippers.

"Can you smell anything?" I aimed the question at Asa. "Without shifting."

I twirled a finger to remind him of the multiple security cameras the mayor had installed to bolster confidence she was serious about protecting the businesses and livelihoods of the people of Samford.

Another expense she laid at my feet, given that my shop's break-in had earned her so much bad press.

Usually, the Kellies would hack the system and email us the video, but the usual wasn't an option.

"They bleached the whole area." He carefully rubbed his nose. "I can't smell anything."

That would explain why Asa hadn't come any closer after pinpointing the location for us.

"Santa's village is open two more weeks," Clay reminded me. "I wouldn't be surprised if Tate brought the bleach from home and pressure-washed the area as soon as she heard the news. She'll sanitize the bad publicity too."

The village was little more than a few wooden cutouts to provide a backdrop for the enormous chair where the town Santa held court with the good girls and boys. Thirty-five dollars per snap of each kid with Jolly Old Saint Nick and a live reindeer, fresh from the North Pole.

Mr. Terfel, with his ruddy cheeks and round belly, reprised the role every year. He doubled as the Ghost of Christmas Present, which must have inspired him to bring the reindeer into town with him. Santa was excluded from the Dickens open house, since he wasn't canon, but Mr. Terfel kept fancy robes on hand for when he was booked for private events that required a less commercial, more Father Christmas vibe.

The mood tomorrow night, when shoppers returned downtown to discover a heartbroken Santa throned beside an empty pen, would be somber. I was grateful my part of the festivities had concluded for the year. Though the blame for this debacle would be laid at my feet as soon as the mayor had a spare moment to ream me out without being overheard by the revelers. Her dressing-downs made me regret I had given up eating hearts, but hers was usually in the right place.

Lives could be saved if people stayed home after dark, but that would also cost the town money.

The mayor was, despite her noble efforts, the *you gotta crack a few eggs to make an omelet* type.

A cracking noise jerked my attention to Asa, who had wandered onto the sidewalk.

He stood with one of the shiny new cameras in his hand, ripped from the soffit of a neighboring business. With a twist of his wrist, he snapped it in half and peered at its guts with a soft laugh.

"They're fakes," he told us. "There's a single thin cable for power, that's it."

"How did you know?" I scanned the street, picking out the others. "They look real to me."

"Colby," he said with a grin. "She's been curious why she couldn't access them."

That sneaky little...

"She hasn't mentioned them to me."

"You had enough on your plate, and it was idle curiosity. Until now." He crushed it into smaller pieces that would fit in his pockets. "I told her I would look it over while we were here." He lifted his phone. "There's even an app for detecting magnetic field radiations that approximate cameras or hidden bugs."

"Of course there is."

"Good work, Ace." Clay slid me a glance. "Hang on to that camera, Rue. It might come in handy."

Only one reason came to mind, and I cocked an eyebrow at him. "For blackmailing the mayor?"

"You said it." He grinned. "Not me."

"I want to tell you I'm above such things, but I'm not. Asa, make sure you hold on to those bits until we get home and I can stash them.”

“Fan out.” Clay picked three directions. “Walk one mile, then regroup here to compare notes.”

They wouldn't have cleaned far. Just enough to make the town sparkle again.

“Okay.” I placed my hand on my wand, through the material of my pants. “See you in, say, thirty.”

We couldn't rush if we wanted to ensure we didn't miss any traces of how the creature got here or where it had decided to den up for the day.

“Rue.”

I turned back to find Asa staring at me, his bright peridot eyes serious. “Yes?”

He swallowed whatever he had been about to say and tipped his chin. “Be careful.”

“Back at you.”

That the guys had included me, without fuss, meant they figured the creature would be too full to attack if I stumbled across it alone. Had Colby been here, they would have felt better. So would I. But she asked weeks ago for permission to stay home to raid, even at the cost of missing out on the open house. Many of her friends were leaving for extended holiday vacations soon, where their families would expect them to be present, and they had chosen tonight as their virtual feast night with raids galore.

I would rather peel off my fingernails than cost her a bonding experience with her peers, one that made her feel normal. Even for a little while. For that kid's happiness, I could handle this sans familiar.

Forcing my mind on task, I blocked out everything but the hunt and let my senses unfurl.

Clay had no heartbeat, but I heard his heavy footsteps. Asa's familiar rhythm soothed as he cut south. At best, the other blips I detected were rabbits or foxes. Nothing bigger than a cat. The creature, whatever it was, might not exactly be mammalian—the line blurred with fae creatures—but it ought to have a...

Ba-bum.

Ears straining to catch the sound again, I listened for a full minute with no luck.

Ba-bum.

Those beats were coming almost ninety seconds apart.

The hunter in me, that itch in the back of my throat that sensed an easy meal ahead, thrashed against its tether. There was no reason not to kill the creature, to plunge my taloned fingers into its chest and rip out its pulsing...

I swallowed the saliva pooling in my mouth and fixed a mental picture of Colby in my head.

If I came home smelling like black magic, she would be terrified of me.

And the loss of her trust, however deserved, would break my black heart.

The smart thing to do was text the guys and request backup now that I had a general location.

Ba-bum.

The slow beat caused my stomach to spasm in hunger.

Ba-bum.

Pretty sure that wasn't ninety seconds.

Ba-bum. Ba-bum. Ba-bum.

Nope.

Not ninety seconds.

And the tripping pulse was heading this way.

Fast.

Chirping rose from the pasture to my left, and I pivoted to triangulate the noise as I drew my wand.

Phone in hand, I used voice commands to dial Asa, who didn't answer, and then Clay. "Little help here."

After I opened my big mouth, giving the creature my location, it lunged across the road with more of those whistle-chirps.

"What in the...?" I gawked as it flew at my head. "This is wrong, on so many levels."

A thick red arm smacked the furball out of the air with a meaty thwack before I could zap it.

During the few minutes where I quit listening for Asa, the daemon had stolen control and come for me.

"Careful, Rue." The daemon pointed at the crumpled beast. "Poison."

Forget the dobhar-chú, I heard only my racing heart. "It didn't get you, did it?"

"No," he said smugly. "I too fast."

The urge to roll my eyes was strong, but he had protected me, and so I let it go.

Leaning around him, I got my first good look at the creature. "How is it so *adorable*?"

"Not adorable." He curled his lip. "Mean." He sniffed. "Ugly too."

"You're right," I said dryly. "There's nothing uglier than a giant otter."

Pleased by the sarcasm that flew over his head, he pressed his hair into my hand. "Pet."

"We need to make sure it's dead." I hated to do it, but it was a threat. "We need to dispose of it too."

On the edge of my vision, I spotted the twitch of a plush paw and almost caved to a catch and release. His tail swished next, and I waffled on how dangerous it could possibly be to round him up and relocate him.

Its liquid eyes opened, glistening and full of the kind of cute memes are made of, but then it bared its teeth.

The inside of its mouth was a cavern of horrors that reminded me of a payara, whose six-inch incisors had earned it the nickname vampire fish. Except on this already oversized otter, they were more like twelve. It must have negative spaces in the upper portion of its skull to accommodate those saberlike chompers. Otherwise, it couldn't sheathe them without lobotomizing itself.

On its right ear, I spotted a black disc, too glossy to be natural. I inched closer, and it did *not* like that.

With a shrill chirp, it shoved to all fours and arched its back like an iconic black cat on Halloween décor. I lifted my wand, ready to strike when it got near, but my jaw fell open when spikes pierced its spine in an alarming threat. Nictitating lids slid into place over its eyes, turning them opaque, and its tail plumped at the end, fattening into a club that it swished back and forth in agitation.

"You didn't mention it was half porcupine," I squeaked at the daemon. "Tell me it can't—"

A grunt of effort sent four quills flying, aimed straight at us, and the daemon moved to intercept.

"No hurt Rue," he bellowed and charged the creature. "Now you die."

Since he hadn't warned me how it administered its venom, quills or teeth, I sprinted after him.

"Don't touch it." I skidded to a halt when he leapt on its back. "The poison…"

Heavy footsteps thudded behind me as Clay caught up to us, and he whistled at the brawl.

"He said it's venomous." I ducked under his arm, waiting for my opening. "How venomous?"

"Not too bad."

"Oh good."

"Unless it hits you with multiple quills, which are like mini hypodermic needles."

As I performed a quick count, the daemon tried to rip out the monster's throat. The dobhar-chú twisted at the last second, giving the daemon a mouthful of quills for his trouble. Already his cheeks bloated, and his eyes swelled. Now he couldn't talk except to yell his incoherent fury.

"I'm going in." Clay set off at a run. "Come behind me and vaporize the sucker."

The poison wouldn't hurt Clay. The monster otter would have to scratch his *shem* to cause him any harm. He would have been the ideal candidate to wrestle the creature, but it hadn't been interested in waiting around for Clay to show.

"Okay." I pushed out a slow breath, gave him a head start, then followed. "Here we go."

Clay joined the dogpile with a whoop of what sounded suspiciously like glee. He got his hands around the dobhar-chú's throat and squeezed while it fired quills in all directions. The daemon got elbowed aside by the golem and slumped onto the road to catch his breath.

"Now." Clay pinned the beast on its back. "Watch the tail."

Dancing around the swishing appendage, I jabbed its hide with my wand and murmured a quick spell.

Magic ignited in its veins, setting it alight, and it burst into ash, leaving Clay to thump onto the flaky pile.

Relief gusted past my lips, and I sagged on my bones. Control used to come as easy as breathing to me, but that wasn't the case anymore. Or it hadn't been until Colby began exercising our familiar bond. The odds of me zapping the dobhar-chú, and that charge transferring into Clay, were still higher than made me comfortable, but I was getting there.

"Well, that was fun." He climbed to his feet. "I wish I had gotten here sooner."

"Me too." I scrabbled to the daemon's side. "Hey, big fella. You with me?"

"One, four, six." He smiled, his teeth on display. "So many Rue." He waved a hand. "Hi, Rues."

"He's delusional." I pressed a hand to his forehead. "Help me get him home."

"He'll have to shift." Clay glanced behind us. "We parked in town, remember?"

"Can you shift?" I scratched the daemon's scalp with my fingernails. "I'll wash your hair tomorrow if you do."

"Brush?" The daemon purred for me. "Braid?"

"Yes," I promised. "Wash, brush, braid. All of it. If you shift now so we can get you both help."

"You two and your kinks." Clay shook his head. "Where did I go wrong?"

The daemon, pleased with our deal, allowed Asa to claim his skin, which only highlighted his injuries.

"I'm certain that spending my formative years with a golem who tucks his wigs in at night had nothing to do with who I ended up with romantically." I checked to see if Asa was conscious, but he was out cold. "I really don't want to do this, but we need to get the worst of these quills out before he wakes."

"I don't tuck them in." Clay reached up to pat his brown curls. "I box them in. Totally different."

"Mmm-hmm."

With gentle hands, I worked on Asa's face, which plumped under my fingers to an alarming degree.

"Not everyone can pull off a wig," Clay extolled, allowing me to do the heavy lifting—yanking?—while he watched our backs. "It takes a connoisseur's eye to select the finest cap and hair, and then you have to know how to style it. You must invest in wigs. Buy quality. Spend the time maintaining them."

Familiar with how he spent his downtime washing, brushing, and taking them on "walksies," I zoned out.

And yes, he really called wearing his wigs, particularly ones that hadn't been worn in a while, *walksies*.

"Done." I sat back on my haunches. "Lift him, and let's go."

Once the golem had his partner in a bridal carry, we began the long walk back to the parking lot behind my shop, where I had parked my SUV. Halfway there, I texted Colby a heads-up. Healing made her nervous, and with good reason. She still heard the Proctor grimoire speaking to her on occasion, offering tips, tricks, and helpful suggestions.

Every time I muffled its voice, it found a new way to be heard, and I had to plug that hole.

Honestly, it was a lot like playing whack-a-mole. Or patching leaks in a dam that was about to burst.

By now, I should have had the grimoire memorized and been ready to toss it into the backyard firepit. But it was a tricksy old book. A sentient one too. It kept hiding the chapters on Colby, on *loinnir*, and producing new material relevant to my past interests.

Melissa Rivers, Clay's ex-lover turned pile of ash, had been right when she claimed I couldn't read the book. But it wasn't about lack of power, as she had implied. It was the will of the book that I absorb it, that I covet it, that I begin to care more about it than my mission to protect Colby.

As much as I hated the idea of dispatching knowledge that might help me protect her, I was close to saying the heck with it and roasting s'mores over the book's smoldering pages.

Clay, unable to fit in the copilot seat even if he wanted to, climbed in the back to hold Asa.

"He's trying to kill me." I stomped on the gas. "Death by heart attack."

"The daemon thinks with his fists," Clay joked. "When it comes to you, he doesn't think period."

Hands tight on the wheel, I gripped harder. "I don't like this feeling."

"Love," he said, meeting my gaze in the rearview mirror, "is practically the same thing as terror."

From life with Colby, I knew what he was telling me to be true, but Asa was twice as killable, in a way.

"He can't keep throwing himself between me and danger."

"Hey, you don't fuss when I play shield for you."

"You're indestructible." I shot Asa a glare over my shoulder. "He's not."

"He could heal this on his own, Rue. It would take a while, and it would hurt, but it's hard to kill him."

After our last case, I had two words for him. "Cold iron."

A deformed bullet, one of many Colby and I forced out of Asa, sat heavy in my pants pocket. I had been carrying it around since that night, and I couldn't let go of the reminder of the fragility of happiness.

"He has the weaknesses—relatively few I might add—of his mother's people, but so do you."

"It's not the same," I protested. "I'm not…"

"You're not what?" Clay loomed behind me. "Careful how you talk about my best friend."

"He's good," I said softly. "He doesn't have to stop and think *before* he does the right thing."

"His upbringing was vastly different from yours. Neither of you had it easy, but half his childhood was as idyllic as it gets for fae." He didn't go into detail, in case Asa could hear. "Not to take anything away from him, but he was taught knee-jerk responses for right and wrong. He acts on those, without thought, in an established pattern. He uses his mother as his own moral barometer. You don't have that."

"Gee, thanks."

"What I'm saying is, you work hard to be *good*. Your own version of it, anyway. Your actions aren't automated, they're deliberate. You make a choice, every day, every time, to make the right call." He patted me on the head with his wide palm. "That makes you pretty remarkable in my book."

"You're just saying that because you hope I'll stress bake during his convalescence."

"Two things can both be true at once." He hesitated. "I was considering brookies."

"Double the batter, double the fun."

"What's not to love about brownies and cookies stacked together in nature's perfect square?"

"Not sure how much nature had to do with that."

"Don't miss your turn."

"What?" I jerked to attention. "Goddess bless, I'm a mess."

He had distracted me too well, and I overshot the turnoff to the house.

"Warn a girl next time."

"I did."

"Before we sail past my driveway."

"It's not my fault you were daydreaming about brookies and forgot about Ace."

As I twisted in the seat for a better view backing the SUV down the road, I was tempted to smack him.

Sadly, it would only hurt my hand, and it wouldn't teach him a lesson.

Asa wasn't the only one who came with preprogrammed responses. Clay's had been molded into him. It meant more to have him praise my choice-making abilities, given how few he had in life. Not that he was a robot, by any means, but he operated with the knowledge his freewill could be snatched from his fingers at any moment. One order from his master, and he lost any objections to his task.

No.

That wasn't right.

He retained the ability to object, to decide for himself it was wrong, but he could be forced to act against his conscience.

We reached the house as the front door swung open. Colby zipped out in a tizzy and made loops above our heads after we entered the wards with Asa.

"Tell me what to do." Her eyes hardened with determination. "We got this."

A swell of pride pushed against my breastbone at her rising self-confidence, despite all the hiccups along the way. The fact she included me, how she always made us a team, was its own peculiar morale booster. I had had partners in the past. Clay, obviously, had been my favorite, but the bond between Colby and me transcended even that, and I was proud of how far she had come.

"Let's get him in." I waved them toward the house. "We'll put him in the spare room."

Arms full of poisoned dae, Clay lumbered past and beat us to the bed where he set down his partner.

"Ready." Colby lit on Asa's shoulder and rubbed her hands together. "Let's do this."

Amusement quirked Clay's lips at her enthusiasm, but she was eager to redeem herself in my eyes, as if I was anyone to impress. I worried she might never forgive herself for allowing the grimoire to creep into her thoughts and channel our familiar bond into searing magic that almost burned me alive.

Yet another reason why it was critical she learn to harness her power.

And protect her mind from outside influence.

Which would be easier if I could flambé that grimoire.

Hand on Asa's shoulder, I reined in our familiar bond. "We do this slow and easy, okay?"

"Slow and easy." She rubbed her temples. "I got it."

Closing my eyes, I opened myself to our bond, pulling on her magic to supplement mine into a steady flow. Together, we fed power into Asa until viscous black fluid dripped from his pores, evaporating on his skin. He began to glow, and I don't mean with health. Colby was a beacon, shining bright and banishing the darkness in his blood, and Asa glowed alongside her.

Within a few minutes, he finished purging, and his eyelids began to flutter against the light.

"Hold still," I chided him. "We're almost done."

As soon as Colby gave me the nod, I scooped her up and severed contact with Asa to let him settle.

Residual magic fizzled between us, and she glided to Clay to break our familiar bond clean.

"The light show is impressive." Clay began to clap. "You guys should take your show on the road."

"Very funny." I flicked my wrist at him. "Shoo." I brushed the hair off Asa's forehead. "He needs to rest."

A thump on the window left me crossing my fingers Mrs. Gleason hadn't come to investigate our shenanigans. She was used to lights being on in the house at all hours. She knew I was an insomniac. But she was a night owl herself. She might have noticed Aedan before we relocated him and decided to slink around and catch him on her land. She might have used the glow as an excuse to interrogate me so late.

A webbed hand lifted in a wave when I peeked through the blinds, and I swore under my breath before remembering Aedan could hear every word. Since the wards weren't blaring at his intrusion, he must have tossed a pebble against the glass to get my attention rather than knock.

"New plan." I released the blinds to snap back into place. "Draw the curtains, Clay, and guard Asa."

"Rue," a groggy voice protested from the bed. "Stay."

"I won't be long." I leaned over and kissed Asa's forehead. "Be a good patient for Clay while I'm gone."

The press of my lips to his skin set him purring, confusing me all over again, but I had no time to linger.

A daemon was outside the house, one who had issued a challenge to Asa, who might now be aware that he was in no shape to fight. It would be simple for Aedan to take advantage to save his own hide, after I hit him with that pep talk earlier.

Way to go, Rue. Convince him to fight for his life then top it off with letting him glimpse Asa unconscious.

With a grim set to my jaw, I exited the house to determine whether I had to kill Aedan myself.

4

"I saw the light," Aedan said by way of explanation, when I stepped outside. "I thought there might be trouble."

"There's no trouble." I took the stairs and joined him in the yard. "Why leap to that conclusion?"

"You're harboring me?" The slits opened on one side of his neck, the other was caked with poultice. "I don't want to bring trouble to you."

"Oh." I waved away his concern. "I forgot about that."

In an adrenaline-fueled rush to determine whether I had to kill you to protect Asa.

"You...forgot?" He laughed softly. "Life with Astaroth must be some kind of adventure."

There was no good answer for that, so I spun it into a question. "What do you know about dobhar-chú?"

"They're adorable when docile and vicious when riled." He cocked an eyebrow. "Have you seen one?"

The internal debate on how much to tell him waged only for a few seconds.

"One attacked an animal in town." I watched for his reaction. "I killed it tonight."

"Pity." He rubbed his nape. "They're not a bad sort..." He dropped his arm. "You saw one *in town*?"

"Yes." I tracked the play of emotions across his face. "What of it?"

Others were much easier for me to read than the clutter of *feelings* looming when I turned my gaze inward.

"They're comfortable in rivers and lakes, but you don't have more than the creek out back and one hole I noticed local humans swimming in. Dobhar-chú come inland to birth their pups, but not for much else. It wouldn't have come to a landlocked place like this of its own choice. It's most vulnerable out of water, and several pups would have died on the trip back to the river."

"How do you know about those waterways?"

"These aren't to enhance my good looks." He flexed his healing web fingers at me. "Do you think I would travel to a landlocked area without mapping all escape routes first?"

A smile crept up on me. "Escape routes?"

"I came to challenge the high king's son and heir." He huffed. "Only a fool wouldn't come prepared."

"So..." I crossed my arms. "You came to die, but you wanted to know where to run."

"I..." A frown knit his vibrant-blue brow. "It's habit."

That much was probably true, but I suspected more. "Or you didn't really want to die."

"No one wants to die." His confusion evaporated. "I see what you're doing."

Good.

That made one of us.

A low rumble that promised violence poured into the night behind me.

"Um." I lifted a finger. "Hold that thought."

One of these days, I would remember that the instant Asa went under, the daemon clawed his way up.

"Rue," the daemon snarled as he stomped toward us, *"mine."*

"Ace," Clay yelled from the porch. "Get your butt back in here."

Legs braced apart, I waited for the daemon to reach me, the better to shield Aedan from him.

"Hey." I snapped my fingers in the daemon's face. "I'm not a chair. You can't own me."

"Rue not chair," he agreed, baring his teeth over my shoulder at Aedan. "Rue *my* chair."

This time I didn't resist the urge to smack my forehead with my open palm.

"I mean no harm." Aedan raised his hands on my periphery. "I will leave, if you allow it."

The daemon took one step, as if to pursue him, but I grabbed him by the hair to hold him back.

"No." I jerked hard. "Aedan is my guest, the same as you."

"Not same as me." He pounded his fist against his chest. "I yours. He not yours."

"This is better than *First Date Bake Off*." Clay rubbed his hands together. "Where's the popcorn?"

"I will pour steaming kernels down your nostrils in your sleep if you don't help me."

Not that Clay slept, exactly, but I wasn't above erasing his *shem* to pay him back.

"Hate to break it to you, but he doesn't listen to me."

"Aedan, back away slowly." I twirled the daemon's hair around my finger. "I'll distract him."

"This ought to be good," Clay muttered under his breath, aware I would hear him.

"Come back to the house," I coaxed the daemon. "I owe you a brush and braid, remember?"

"I remember." He snatched me off my feet and into his arms, then he smiled down at me. "Hi, Rue."

Unable to stop my smile, I let him hold me. "Hi, pain in my butt."

"Rue like me." He preened. "Rue like my hair."

"I do like you, and your hair, but you're still a pain in the butt."

The daemon carried me onto the porch, where I kicked Clay in the shoulder hard enough to rock him.

"Help Aedan get back to the creek." I narrowed my eyes on him. "Or I will substitute salt for sugar in everything I bake for you until your tastebuds give up on life and your tongue crawls out of your mouth to escape."

"That is, and I say this as a friend, the threat of a deeply disturbed mind." A shudder rocked him from head to toe. "You win."

Once I had the daemon through the door, I nudged it shut with my toe. He knew the way to the former home of Hollis Apothecary, and he headed straight for the sink. The portable sink I had disconnected when the girls and I moved the shop to downtown. It was on wheels and connected to a waterline, like the ones installed for washing machines. But, thanks to the daemon's agreement to act as a guinea pig for a haircare line, I had dusted it off and rolled it back to its former spot in the corner weeks ago.

While I got to work on washing his hair with a lavender-and-chamomile blend shampoo bar, I waited for Clay to report back.

"Smell good." The daemon gave me two thumbs-up. "Like this one."

"I'm glad you approve." I glanced up to find Clay watching us. "Well?"

"I tucked him back in, but we might have a problem."

"We always have a problem. Usually more than one." I blew out a sigh. "What is it this time?"

"He's convinced the dobhar-chú came inland to birth pups. He says it wouldn't have hunted in town if it hadn't required an easy meal to feed little mouths."

"We decided it got dumped," I reminded him. "Why else would it be so far from water?"

"I told him we suspected it was a gift, and he clammed up until I reminded him of guest rights."

"That's a fae thing."

"It's a white witch thing too."

"You're making that up." I rinsed the daemon's hair. "You are, right?"

"It's very much a white witch thing. They offer weary travelers succor, they establish and maintain neutral grounds, and they're often selected as arbitrators." He smirked. "You've got a lot to learn."

Guest rights meant Aedan was safe from harm on my property. Even Asa couldn't touch him. Unless he wanted to go through me to get to him.

"Right now, I'm more worried about not eating people." I shrugged. "Etiquette lessons can wait."

"You're further along than that," he scoffed. "Don't sell yourself short."

Done rinsing the suds, I began toweling the daemon's hair dry. "Back to the issue of pups."

"Too bad they're not like possums," he mused. "We could have wiped it and its young out in one go."

"Life is never that simple." I started brushing to keep the daemon occupied. "Besides, they're babies."

"Aedan says they're born the size of corgis. They might be babies, but they could eat someone's baby."

"True."

"Point of interest." He lifted his index finger. "It might not have been pregnant when it was caught."

"Um, okay?"

"Aedan says they can reproduce via parthenogenesis, an asexual form of reproduction. Confinement on land might have been enough to trigger, or confuse, its natural instincts and result in a pregnancy."

Remove the possibility the creature acted on instinct, thanks to a preexisting condition, and our dumped theory rocketed back to the top of the list.

"Hmm." That kind of insider info was handy. "Do you think we could convince him to consult?"

"Since this isn't an official case, which means we can't officially hire him, sure. Why not?"

"I need to finish up here." I accepted the hairbands the daemon passed me. "Can you ask?"

The mention of our *un*case reminded me I had to pack a change of clothes for after work.

Monster hunting in kitten heels, pressed slacks, and a nice blouse was a fast way to ruin a wardrobe.

"Uh, no. Hard pass." Clay backed away slowly. "Wait until Asa comes back from la-la land and ask him."

"Ask him to do it, right?" I narrowed my eyes on him. "I'm sure you didn't mean ask his permission."

"Night, Rue." He pivoted on his heel and headed down the hall. "See you in the morning."

"Chicken," I called after him then settled in to pay my dues in the form of two tidy braids.

5

The day after our grand reopening was not the time to take a sick day.

Particularly the morning after a gruesome event occurred a stone's throw from the shop.

Especially not when word spread that five pets—two dogs and three cats—had been reported missing during the early morning hours.

The three hours of sleep in my tank would have to hold me over until I could get horizonal again.

Lucky for me, Clay and Asa were free to work the *un*case while I was otherwise occupied at the shop.

Gritting my teeth and pouring on the charm for customers, I clocked eight hours and not a second more.

"You and Asa still on the outs?" Camber hugged me from the side. "You've been in a mood all day."

"We're fine." I leaned my head against hers. "We both suck at relationships, but we'll figure it out."

Eventually.

"You're worried." Arden squeezed me from the other side, sandwiching me in a hug. "About us."

The edge of guilt in her expression, as if any of this were their fault, cut me to the marrow.

"There's a big difference between a psycho who kidnaps girls and a wild animal who munches on pets."

"She's right." Camber withdrew and locked the door. "We're not at risk more than anyone else."

Because I loved them, they were in more danger than anyone else in town, but maybe not this time. Unless they wore raw steaks as necklaces, everyone's odds of a dobhar-chú attack were about the same.

"Mom and Dad have already forbidden me to go outside after dark." Arden started cleaning. "Even Gran called to threaten me. She's not leaving her house until whatever it is gets caught."

"Bojangles had a litter," Camber explained. "Eight puppies."

Miss Dotha was Camber's grandmother, but the girls both called her Gran. She bred gorgeous Cavalier King Charles Spaniels. Once upon a time, she would have invited me over to play with the newest litter. But after the girls had been taken, Miss Dotha had retreated from our friendship. I couldn't blame her, but it still hurt. And it was inconvenient, especially during the holiday season.

Sooner or later, I would have to hire an extra set of part-time hands to fill the void she left.

"I don't blame her." I smiled through the twinge in my chest. "I would keep them close too."

Both girls gave me a look that told me I had a crap poker face when it came to them.

"Gran will get over it," Camber promised. "She's not mad at you. She doesn't blame you. She's just..."

"She has a right to her feelings." There was that pesky word again. "I don't hold it against her."

"Do you want to come over to watch *Murder in Munson* with us?" Arden grinned. "It's a total gorefest."

"This is your reaction to Dasher?" I had taken the coward's way out and let the local news break the story to them while I was out monster hunting. "Watching *more* horror?"

A knock on the door drew my attention to a tall man in his early twenties.

With piercing, unearthly turquoise eyes.

"Oh crap," I muttered, shocked to see Aedan, both in town and in glamour. "I need to get this."

He looked like Santa and his team had run over him a few times in the sleigh, but he was handsome. The shoulder-length blond hair was sun streaked, and his skin was tan. He wore jeans and a clean tee with a pair of scuffed sneakers. He was playing surfer boy to the hilt, and it worked for him.

"Get...?" Arden's mouth fell open. "Who is that?"

"No one." I nudged her toward the office. "Count the till."

Camber beat me to the door and twisted the lock. "Hi."

"Hello." Aedan slid his gaze past her to me. "Can I speak to Ms. Hollis, please?"

"Sure." Camber stepped aside, welcoming him in. "There are chairs in her office."

"Thank you, but no." He shook his head. "It's a private matter."

"I'll handle it." I met Aedan at the threshold then turned back. "You two lock up, and you can go."

"What's your name?"

We all jerked at the question, but Aedan was staring at Arden like an art collector spotting a Monet at a garage sale. Not a print. The real deal.

"Arden." A hiccup jostled her frame. "That's my name." *Hiccup.* "It's Arden."

"*Ardere.*" A flirty smile spread his cracked and scabbed lips. "It means 'to burn.'"

A flush lit her cheeks as her hiccupping turned staccato, and Camber had to escort her to the back.

That...was a line. One wasted on her. But not on me. Fire and water. He was telling her opposites attract.

Nope, nope, nope.

"Let's go." I shoved him out the door then shut it behind us. "What was that about?"

"Your human?" Aedan glanced back, just once. "She's beautiful."

"You're too old for her." We walked the empty sidewalk. "Quit being Frenchy with her. Girls love that."

"I know." His smile revealed a dimple in his left cheek. "And I'm not that old."

"How old is *not that old* for a daemon?"

"Twenty-five."

A crack in the pavement tripped me, and I would have gone sprawling if he hadn't caught me. *"What?"*

The alienness of his appearance, and the fact he had challenged Asa, a death sentence, had convinced me he was older, more worldly. Aedan had conducted himself with such poise, I never once considered his age. The stilted language and his rigid formality let me believe he was an adult. I suppose he was, technically, but still.

"Twenty-five," he repeated. "How old is Arden?"

"You're a *baby*." I leaned against the brick wall for a beat. "Why on earth would you challenge Asa?"

The assumption he was a contemporary of Asa's was my fault, but Aedan was a kid on a suicide mission. The knowledge he was so young, so burdened, unlocked a protectiveness in me I had experienced only once before.

"I'm an adult of the species." He frowned down at me. "Arden smells sexually mature."

"Don't." I held up a hand. "Don't smell her." I rubbed my hands over my face. "Goddess bless."

"Would you prefer I come back later?" He angled toward the shop. "Do you need a moment?"

"Why did you come?" I forced my feet to hold my weight. "What did you need?"

"I made you this." He held out a carved river rock. "You can use it to call the dobhar-chú pups."

"*If* we find any."

"If," he agreed, smiling.

"Daemon sure are crafty." I turned it over in my hand. "I had no idea."

And I didn't mean crafty as in wily, I meant crafty as in arts and crafts.

"This is a tool." He was quick to dismiss his talent. "No different than a knife or a hook."

"Agree to disagree."

"Do you think Arden—?"

"Look." I had to nip this in the bud fast. "Arden has been through a lot, and all of it was my fault."

A brief rundown of what David Taylor did to the girls was enough to leave Aedan with clenched fists.

"She must be terrified of water." He sawed his molars together. "And men."

Her comments about Louis gleamed in my memory, cast in a whole new light.

Maybe she had told the truth, and he did get weird. Or maybe, just maybe, the opposite was true.

"I wouldn't go that far, in either direction." I wouldn't lie to get my way. "But she's still healing."

"I can respect that." He tensed at motion on the corner. "I ought to be going."

Lifting the stone, I twisted it in my hand. "How do I use this thing?"

"This won't end well," he murmured then took three wide steps back.

"What won't?" I craned my neck to see what set him off and found Asa. "Oh, hey."

Gone was sexy Scrooge. He was back to Black Hat agent tonight. Dark suit, neat braids, and simple studs. The piercing in his septum was more interesting, a mandalalike fan of silver filigree that sat above his lip.

A very kissable lip.

Bad, Rue. Focus.

"Clay is waiting in the car." Asa noted what I held, and his expression turned thoughtful. "A *scairt*."

"You know how to use it?" I tightened my grip when he reached for it. "You're not going to break it, are you?"

"Why would I do that?" He pried my fingers, one by one. "I am capable of reining in my baser impulses."

That sounded a whole lot like Clay hadn't told him the daemon had taken over last night.

The daemon had zero impulse control, which was the opposite of Asa's buttoned-down vibe.

Almost like what instincts Asa refused to act on, the daemon reveled in, balancing them out as a person.

"This is a fine piece of craftsmanship." Asa ran his thumb over the stone. "Aedan made it?"

"From a rock in the creek." Aedan kept his hands loose by his sides. "I got bored."

"Would you like to help us hunt the dobhar-chú pups?"

The invitation shocked Aedan and me into silence, and we exchanged a wary glance that Asa noticed.

"Did I interrupt something?" He checked with us. "I can go back to the car."

"No." I took his arm. "Let's walk and talk." I called back to Aedan. "Give us a five-minute head start."

Aedan's sense of smell was keen enough he could follow our path to wherever Asa had parked his SUV.

Once we got far enough away from Aedan, I leaned in close. "Your other half was ready to tear him a new one."

"Last night?" Asa absorbed the information in stride. "I did warn you rapid transformations were likely to happen as we progress."

According to him, the daemon would claim his skin more often to ensure I cared about them both.

"I don't mind him visiting." It sounded odd but felt right. "But he can't kill everyone who talks to me."

"Any *man* who talks to you," he clarified, as if that made all the difference.

"Yes." I pinched his side. "He needs to learn how to behave."

"He doesn't want to lose you."

I heard what Asa left unsaid, that he didn't want to lose me either. "He won't."

A twitch in his neck warned me he wanted to look back at Aedan. "Are you certain?"

"Did you know Aedan is in his twenties?" I jerked on his arm to stop him. "He's a *baby*."

A short laugh huffed out of him. "Daemons mature at accelerated rates."

"He's a third of my age, Asa. I have zero interest in him. Besides, he flirted with Arden."

Tension knotted his shoulders as his protective instincts kicked in. "That is not advisable."

"I warned him off her." I rested my head on his shoulder. "She's not ready, I don't think."

"And, perhaps more pressing, she doesn't know daemons exist."

"That too." I buried my face in his suit jacket and breathed in his green apples and cherry tobacco scent. "Ain't love grand?"

"Yes." He appeared to give it serious consideration before smiling down on me. "I believe it is."

The way my throat swelled shut convinced me I would never breathe normally again.

"I gave you five," Aedan said from behind us. "You kind of stalled out, and I didn't know what to do."

A grateful laugh unglued me, relief a giddy thrill in my middle, and I latched onto the interruption.

"You're fine." I pulled back from Asa. "We got distracted."

The glamour suited Aedan, but I could tell he didn't interact as a human often.

"What's that smell?" His sharp inhale flared the sides of his neck. "Can we...?"

"Your, um, gills are showing." I ran a finger down my throat. "You might want to fix that."

"You forgot your bag."

The voice drew my attention back toward the shop, which was barely in sight.

"Rue." Arden lifted the duffle in question. "Wait."

Part of me felt vindicated for my earlier clumsiness when she tripped on the same notch in the sidewalk, then I watched, helpless, as she took the same tumble. I ran to help her up and dust her off, but Aedan beat me by a mile.

Oh, yeah.

Definitely not used to acting human.

His speed was blinding.

Arden didn't hit the sidewalk, she came close enough to squeeze her eyes shut, but impact never came.

Because Aedan scooped her into his arms, where she stared adoringly up at him.

"You're fast." She hiccupped. "*Really* fast."

"I ran track in high school," he lied while gently setting her on her feet. "Must be muscle memory."

"Someone ought to fix this." I kicked the loose concrete. "I tripped here earlier."

Inspiration struck, and I brought out my phone to snap a few pictures I then sent to the mayor.

That would put a bee in her bonnet.

I wouldn't be surprised if she mixed her own concrete to patch the spot overnight.

A dark gleam caught my eye, and I covered it with my shoe before glancing up—but nope. Arden hadn't noticed what I found. She was too absorbed by Aedan's turquoise eyes to do more than stare up at him.

"Thanks for bringing me my bag." I pried it from her clenched fingers. "You need to get home."

"Yeah." She blinked, seeming to notice her surroundings. "It's getting dark, and Camber is waiting."

"See you tomorrow." I slung on my duffle, gripped her shoulders, and aimed her toward the shop. "Bye."

Curious about the commotion, Camber met her on the sidewalk with a concerned frown.

"What were you saying before? About a smell?" I jerked my attention back to Aedan. "Are you hungry?"

"Nothing." Aedan stared after Arden, nostrils flared, as if he couldn't get enough. "I'm good."

The girls caught us looking and waved before crossing the street to the diner parking lot, where Camber parked with the owner's permission. Thanks to that whole no-second-parking-spot thing.

"Okay." I lifted my foot. "Do you see what I see?"

The odds of any imperfection marring the streets of downtown Samford were always low, especially prior to an event that might result in injuries if someone fell, and that should have occurred to me.

"A claw." Aedan bent to retrieve it. "How far are we from the kill site?"

"Not far," I allowed, "but I doubt the mayor missed anything in her initial evaluation."

She was the sort to set up orange cones and yellow police tape to keep citizens from stubbing their toes. Except during festival season, when the almighty dollar held her allegiance over us mere shop-keepers.

That meant the dobhar-chú had come back, probably searching for the carcass of its kill. It was no longer a problem, but its trips to town would have laid a scent trail its pups could follow. That might explain the disappearance of smaller prey animals. Then again, we had no real timeline for when the pets had been taken, only when their owners noticed them missing. The difference between the two could have been hours.

"Let's get to the car." I waved them on. "Clay will come looking soon."

We hustled to the Black Hat-issued SUV the guys had been patrolling in and piled in with Asa behind the wheel and Aedan in the back with Clay. Asa pulled out and started driving toward the outskirts of town.

"Hey, Dollface." Clay stuffed a cookie in his mouth. "That took forever."

"I see how you suffered." I flicked a glance up and down him. "You're covered in sprinkles."

And facial hair. A full beard and mustache. Bushier eyebrows. The wig alone belonged on the set of *Vikings*.

"We ate a late lunch at the diner." He grinned. "Ms. Hampshire set these aside for me."

Given the time, it was closer to an early dinner, but that wouldn't spare me from feeding him later.

"They're from yesterday." I stuck my tongue out at him. "She probably couldn't sell them."

That was a lie, and we both knew it. Ms. Hampshire didn't bake often, but she was fantastic at cookies.

"Jealous I sampled another woman's cookies?" He clucked his tongue. "That's beneath you."

"Give me a cookie," I bargained, "and I'll take it back."

"Ha." He crammed another one in his mouth. "I'm rubber, you're glue—"

"—I'll bounce my fist off your face if you don't give me a cookie."

"That doesn't even rhyme." He ate a third. "Try again."

"Clay, you had a dozen." Asa trained his gaze on the rearview mirror. "You can't spare one?"

"Nope." He frowned at Aedan. "What's the daemon doing here?" He snorted. "You building a harem?"

A low growl poured from the driver's seat, and Aedan flattened his spine against the door.

The threat of the daemon bursting from his skin was very real, and I could strangle Clay for putting us in this position in such a confined space. "I am never baking for you again."

"I was joking." Clay hit me between the eyes with a cookie. "Slobber on that and calm him down."

A snort burst out of Aedan that no one believed was the coughing fit he faked afterward.

Chomping down on the cookie, I resolved to beg, borrow, or bribe my way to this recipe.

"Take a bite." I held it an inch from Asa's lips. "You know you wanna."

As soon as I said it, I had an epiphany that kissing Asa would be that much more intimate than us sharing food. That part wasn't the revelation. The curiosity sparked from wondering if the same instincts that drove us to eat after one another would prompt us to exchange saliva more often to get that same dopamine hit.

And I really had to stop obsessing over kissing Asa to the point where I daydreamed about saliva...

The rumble of sound quit, and he sank his teeth into the soft treat, his eyes on mine the whole time.

"This is a good cookie," he said, once he finished chewing, "but it's not as good as yours."

Pleased warmth suffused me, and I didn't care if my drool made the cookie more delicious to him or not. It was sweet of him to side with me against Clay, who deserved a swift kick in the pants for being a sugar hog.

Little wonder he and Colby were thick as thieves.

"Since Clay is dead to me, you get to pick tonight's dessert." I nibbled the edge. "Here."

Feeding Asa worked wonders on his temper, which, same. And now it was time to focus on the problem.

"Where are we going?" I recognized the area, but it was pasture-land. "Did you find the nest?"

I left the question open for either guy who wanted to answer.

"No." Clay grew serious. "We found confirmation the mamma didn't get here under her own steam."

A minute later, Asa pulled the SUV onto the shoulder of the road and parked.

"This is where we get dirty." He eyed my tidy outfit from work. "I can carry you, if you like."

"I brought clothes." I held up the bag. "I can swap out in the back."

The plan had been to close shop, send the girls home, and change at the shop. Aedan's unexpected visit derailed that to the point I wouldn't have my spare clothes if Arden hadn't noticed I forgot the bag.

The more often the two halves of my life intersected, the worse I became at dealing with the traffic.

"Your creek cuts across this property." A distant expression clouded Aedan's eyes. "I smell it."

"You can tell that from in here?" I saw only a sea of grass through the windshield. "Impressive."

"The spring that feeds it carries a sediment imprint similar to a fingerprint."

Who knew having an aquatic daemon on your team would prove to be so useful?

"Come on, Aedan." Asa exited the vehicle. "You and I will head on down."

Aedan and Clay got out, Aedan left, and Clay leaned against the side of the SUV. I climbed over the center console, changed on the bench seat they vacated, and exited beside him.

Once I had my boots on, we ducked between the strands of barbed wire fencing and hiked a mile or two down to a copse of trees shielding a trickle of water that wanted to be a creek when it grew up, or when the next heavy rain fell.

Parked across it was a white pickup from a national car rental company with a heavy-duty metal cage tethered in the bed.

No sign of Asa or Aedan, which concerned me, but they must have gone to investigate upstream.

"Did you dust for fingerprints?" I circled the vehicle, stopping at the tailgate. "We've got blood here."

Given our last two cases involved rogue agents, I was willing to bet the driver was in our database.

"Why would I dust for fingerprints if I don't have anywhere to send them for processing?" Clay joined me at the open cage door. "Same goes for blood or tissue samples." He crossed his wrists. "You've tied my hands, Dollface."

A growl to do Asa proud rattled in the back of my throat. "What do you want me to do?"

"Accept this as proof your enemies are coming out of the woodwork, with or without Samford on the books." He tugged me against his side in a one-armed hug. "This isn't what you wanted for the town, I know, but you struck a deal with the director to stay here. You're invested. You've put down roots. You've made your stand. Now it's time to back it up, or else, I hate to say it, you need to move on."

Colby and I could resume the nomadic lifestyle most agents embraced to cut down on entanglements. As a young agent, I hadn't minded frequent changes of scenery, but it had gotten old there at the end.

Colby might live a largely virtual life, which meant travel would be easier, but she had settled into calling Samford home. She liked the girls, our neighbors, the town, and its endless flow of activities. Her relationship with those things was removed, her experiences often secondhand, but did I want to force her to give up on the one stable thing in her life? Aside from me, she had no other constants.

"I'll think about it."

"You already said that."

"Fine." I huffed. "I'll actually think about it instead of blowing you off with a nonanswer."

"Thank you." He kissed my temple. "And, because I love you, I sent those samples to a private lab."

"You're the best." I squeezed him. "A cookie hog and a bully, but still pretty awesome."

"If I had blood," he said, pulling back to fan his cheeks, "I would be blushing from such high praise."

Knocking his hands down, I hauled him back on track. "How long until we get those results?"

"You're overlooking a teeny problem." He pinched two fingers together. "Without the Kellies, we can't compare what we find to bureau records."

I wasn't so sure about that, but I had to speak to our resident Kelly first.

"Where did Asa and Aedan go?" I scanned the soft earth for footprints. "You don't think Asa...?"

"Lured Aedan off to murder him?" Clay pretended to consider it. "The daemon would in a heartbeat."

"That's not comforting."

"Oh, I didn't realize you wanted me to lie." He cleared his throat. "Ace would never! How dare you even think slander about my honorable partner who's in fascination with you and is basically a murder spree waiting to happen and would view any male daemon as competition until he makes sweet love to you. The gall. The *nerve*. The balls on you must be bigger than my head."

"Clay..."

"Asa wouldn't murder him." His eyes crinkled at the corners, then he muttered, "Not where you would catch him."

Annoyed with my former partner, I stalked off in the direction the footprints indicated, listening for heartbeats to guide me. I picked them out soon enough and homed in on their location.

"Do you hear that?" Clay caught up to me. "It sounds like baby chicks."

As I absorbed that, I noted a skyrocketing pulse in one of the daemons ahead and broke into a run.

"Oh, crap." I splashed through the trickle of water, mud sucking at my boots. "They found the nest."

"Go help." Clay slowed to a walk. "I'll be right back."

"Are you serious?" I yelled over my shoulder. "This is not the time to BRB, Clay."

The golem spun in the direction of the truck, and I let him go without a fight. I could no longer hear the daemons over the thudding of my heart in my ears, and a metallic taste flooded my mouth. I pushed myself harder, faster, leaping a rotting fence to reach the daemons battling in an old cotton field.

Hard to miss the turquoise guy running circles around a huge crimson and black dude who laughed uproariously while blowing a tune on the stone Aedan had fashioned as a dobhar-chú call.

"Rue." The daemon waved to me. "We found babies."

"Little," Aedan panted and kept sprinting, "brats."

A short distance away, I hesitated to join them. "Why are you running?"

"He taste like fish." The daemon threw his head back, bellowing with mirth. "They want to eat him."

"This isn't funny." Six dog-sized otters bounded after him. "Zap them, Rue."

As much as I begged to disagree—it was hilarious—I pitied him. He and Asa had been gone a while, and Aedan was still recovering from his wounds. He must be getting tired, and the daemon was no help. Between bursts of laughter, he kept blowing on the stone, which agitated the pups even worse.

"Okay, okay." I debated my options. "I've got something that will knock them out."

"I don't care if you kill them." Aedan craned his neck to yell at them. "You're all hats. All of you. Hats."

Not sure monster otter fur hats were a thing, but maybe it was daemon high fashion.

Smothering a laugh, I entered the fray, which sobered the daemon in a blink.

"Rue," he warned. "Fluffies bite hard." He pointed to Aedan's bleeding calves. "Big teeth."

"I have to touch them with my wand." I patted his cheek. "Guess you'll have to protect me."

"Always," he promised, fist over his heart. "Rue mine."

"Keep telling yourself that, big guy."

"Okay." He brightened at the permission. "I will."

Good thing there were no trees around, or I might have been tempted to bang my head against one.

"Remember me?" Aedan zigzagged toward us. "The guy being eaten alive by mini dobhar-chú?"

"Let's start from the end and work our way up to that chubby guy." I waited until Aedan ran past, jogged to catch up, then tapped the straggler. It stiffened and fell sideways with a gasp. "One down, five to go."

With the daemon running interference, I took them out without getting bitten. He didn't have much work to do, though. The pups were too invested in Aedan. Fishy or not, he must taste good.

"I see the party started without me." Clay's voice rang out. "I brought a present anyway."

On my periphery, I noted the cage he hauled alongside him. "Look at you, Mr. Softy."

"I feel bad we killed their mom." He plunked it down. "I figured we could relocate them in her memory."

"Very noble of you." I hid a smile. "You better hurry, though. They won't stay down long."

A burst of colorful swears brought my attention back to Aedan and the pup attached to his calf.

"Vicious little beasties." Clay gathered the unconscious pups. "They're cute, though."

Until their momma decided to use the daemon as a pincushion, I thought she was too.

With Clay cleaning up behind us, I focused on the remaining pup. "Circle back, Aedan."

Daemons had incredible stamina, so I knew the loping-limp Aedan had adopted was due to injury.

Poor guy. I owed him another poultice or ten after this. Maybe a tub to soak in too.

When Aedan got close, the daemon grabbed for the pup and yanked, which made Aedan roar.

"If we don't get it off you," I explained through a wince, "you'll get zapped too."

I was improving with practice, the same as Colby, but I wasn't proficient with my new magic yet. It threw me curves on the regular. Better to let him think the worst outcome was a certainty rather than to admit I had performance issues. That would only freak him out more.

"I don't care." He kicked his leg, but the pup clung to him. "Get it off me."

Dialing down the intended jolt, I tapped Aedan, the bigger target, with the wand. "Sorry in advance."

His spine bowed, knees collapsed, and he faceplanted in the dirt before anyone could reach him.

The stubborn pup's eyes rolled back, but it had locked its jaws, and it hung from his mangled calf.

"Its teeth are still in his muscle." Clay grimaced. "Maybe they're not as cute as I thought."

"Having second thoughts about your rescue mission?"

"No," he said after a moment where he clearly sifted through second and maybe third thoughts.

"I stick finger in mouth," the daemon offered. "It let go then."

"You'll break its jaw." I patted his arm. "I'll do it."

Kneeling beside Aedan, I wedged my fingers into the pup's mouth, pried it open, and removed it.

"There you go." I tossed it to Clay. "Lock it up while I patch Aedan's leg."

Thanks to my practice with Colby, I was getting better at healing. Superficial damage, like this, while painful, was easy to mend. Aedan would be sore tonight, but he would be good as new tomorrow.

As I stood, I stowed my wand in my pocket and faced the daemon. "Would you mind carrying Aedan?"

"Leave him." The daemon curled his lip at Aedan. "No one like him anyway."

Laughter shook Clay, and I fought not to chuckle too. The daemon was cute when he was being bad.

"If you do, I'll let you cook s'mores over the firepit," I tempted him. "You love how marshmallows burn."

"No." Clay slashed a hand through the air. "Absolutely not."

The daemon's enthusiasm got away with him the first time, and he flung molten marshmallow from the end of his stick right into Clay's hair. The way Clay shot up, smacking his head and howling, I thought he was on fire at first. But no, he was just being a drama king. The goo washed out of the wig no problem.

Delight brightened the daemon's face. "Deal."

Without another complaint, he fisted the back of Aedan's pants and lifted him like a sack of groceries.

"That's not what I…" I bit the inside of my cheek. "Never mind."

Aedan hung low enough for grass to tickle his nose, but I was sure he would be fine.

"I'll get the cage." Clay locked it tight. "Don't want these little fellas to escape."

"No," I agreed. "We don't."

We backtracked to the pickup, where I waffled on my options.

Had this been an official case, I could have had an agent come out, pick it up, sanitize it, and return it. But, as Clay was fond of reminding me, this wasn't an official case. That meant one of us got the honors.

A call had Clay shoving the cage back into the truck bed, leaving more scratches and dings.

"Kerr." He sat on the tailgate, and the truck creaked. "What's up?"

To give him privacy, I turned to check on the daemon. I found him standing with his arm relaxed, which dunked Aedan's face in the piddly creek and held it there.

"You know that won't kill him, right?" I folded my arms across my chest. "He's aquatic."

"He like water." The daemon tried for innocent. "I give him drink."

The line was delivered with an air of benevolence, which I might have believed if I hadn't seen him sigh when I informed him cosmetic alterations to Aedan's appearance didn't change his fundamental self.

He might no longer have blue skin or visible gills, but they were only a layer of magic away.

"You're a brat." I really had to stop finding his shenanigans adorable. "Put him in the truck, please."

The daemon lifted Aedan, cocking his arm, and I leapt in front of him with my arms outspread.

"In the cab," I clarified, which earned me a grumble. *"Gently."*

"Bad news." Clay tapped my shoulder. "Ace and I have to roll out."

The daemon finished his task and returned to my side, stuffing his hair into my hand. "No go."

"You have to go." I smiled at the show of solidarity. "It's your job."

"Pet." He gave me more hair. "Maybe I go then."

"Are you—?" I gawped at him. "You're blackmailing me?"

"Asa get in trouble if I not go," he said thoughtfully. "That bad."

Karma for pocketing that fake camera to hold over the mayor's head was swift in revisiting me.

"Why you little..." I yanked on his hair. "That's not nice."

"Your boyfriend is a toddler." Clay snickered. "He's going to tantrum any minute now."

"Don't give him ideas." I shoved Clay. "What's the case?"

"I don't know if I should share intimate details with a part-timer," he began. "This is real agent work."

The low-key bullying to return to active duty never ended with Clay. He wouldn't be happy until we were partners again. But, as I liked to remind him, he already had a partner. He didn't need another. Our team dynamic worked well for us. Plus, it allowed me to live a somewhat normal life between cases.

Colby deserved to enjoy her endless childhood without the constant reminders of how she came to exist thrown in her face with each new case. I wanted to give her time to *forget* the darkness. Just for a little while.

"Keep your secrets." I cut him a smug grin. "Colby will tell me after you leave."

Clay, to make Colby feel like a valued member of the team while keeping her out of the field as much as possible, decided to teach her how to access the Black Hat Bureau database under my accounts.

She could contact the Kellies. She could download case files. She could make work-related charges to my shiny new black card.

Colby could do *anything* at my security clearance level. As me. But, for a curious moth, that hadn't been enough. She dug and dug and dug until she hacked the system. She learned paranoia at my knee, and she had become vigilant when it came to skimming for any blips that mentioned either of us.

I was proud of her. *So* proud. But hers was a dangerous undertaking for anyone, let alone a kid.

Knowledge was power, and too much power was poison.

"That girl." He shook his head. "How did you get so lucky?"

"What happened to her was as unlucky as it gets." I leaned against the truck. "But she...saved me."

"Don't give her all the credit." Clay ruffled my hair. "You had to already be standing on the cliff for her to tip you over the edge."

For whatever reason, Clay had always believed the best in me. I still didn't understand it. I was grateful for it, but it confused me then, and it baffled me now. How was he so sure of me? What did he see that I didn't? And was it real? That was what concerned me the most. If I hadn't known him pre-Colby, I would have worried he saw me following my Good Person Guide and bought into the act.

"Anyway." I forced my thoughts back to what mattered. "The case?"

"A kelpie." He watched the pups snoozing in a pile. "Three towns over."

Kelpies were ethereal horses, truly gorgeous fae beasts, who lived in bodies of water. They walked the roads near the waterways, tempting the unwary onto their backs. Once they had a rider, they galloped back to their home and drowned their victim before devouring them whole.

They targeted humans. Specifically. Most fae were too smart to fall for their tricks.

"What?" I glared at his phone like it might tell me different. "That can't be a coincidence."

Two aquatic fae breeds reported in the same area? Alabama wasn't exactly a hotbed of fae activity.

"No," he agreed. "It can't be." He frowned. "You understand Samford might get pulled in by proximity?"

Better to be crime scene adjacent than crime scene central. "Do your best to keep our problems quiet?"

"You really have to ask?" He thinned his lips. "You know how kelpies are, though."

"Spook it in the wrong direction, and we'll have a kelpie."

"Exactly."

Angling toward the daemon, careful to keep stroking his hair, I asked, "Can I see Asa before you go?"

"You smell mad at him." He snuffled me. "You never mad at me."

"I wouldn't go that far," I said dryly. "Please?"

"Fine," he huffed but gave himself over to Asa for my sake.

Influence over a daemon of his stature was terrifying for a person raised to hunger for power.

Asa, and his daemon, were temptations in more ways than one.

"Walk with me?" Asa held out his hand. "I would like a moment with you before we go."

The certainty that the sucker cleaning up this mess was *me* left me tired before I started.

As our palms slid together, he exhaled a breath that mirrored the one parting my lips.

Whatever this was between us, it was getting stronger, kiss or no kiss, and I couldn't deny that.

We walked the creek bed, the water a faint suggestion the farther we traveled from the truck.

"You want me to kiss you."

"Um." I planted my feet like that would throw on the conversational brakes. "Well…"

"That's why the distance," he said, as if analyzing the problem. "I asked for your permission, but I didn't follow through."

"The distance is because I want to give you as much space as you need to feel comfortable."

There.

That sounded confident and concerned, not like a woman who fell asleep dreaming how he might taste.

"I should have explained myself." He angled in front of me and slid his hands over my waist. "I was…"

"Nervous?"

"Yes." His thumbs smoothed across my hipbones through the denim. "I've never kissed anyone."

The air punched out of my lungs, and I couldn't swallow enough oxygen to reinflate them. *"What?"*

"You're aware of the limitations on my person." He eased farther into my space. "There hasn't been a woman I have given such permissions to, only you, and I didn't want to disappoint you."

"I thought you changed your mind, or that you didn't want me." I leaned forward, resting my forehead on his chest. "I didn't want to throw myself at you, but I was getting close."

"You've had sex."

Sweat slicked my palms, and I was glad he was no longer holding my hand. "Yes."

A lot of sex. All of it meaningless. Except the first time. But that act was borne out of necessity.

He sought my chin, tilted my head back, and forced me to hold his vibrant stare.

"Teach me," he murmured. "I want to know how to pleasure you."

Heat curled through my middle as a blush painted my cheeks with a stinging brush.

"Here," I croaked like a laryngitic frog, impossibly sexy. "Now?"

"Not unless..." A curious glint lit his eyes. "Do you enjoy sex in mud?"

"No." I flicked muck off my boot. "Mud is not great." It got in too many places. "Water is okay."

The mention of water sent his gaze skating past my shoulder toward the truck and Aedan.

"I meant to say that water is terrible." I gripped his shoulders. "No one should even drink it."

A smile quirked his lips that brought my attention zinging back to his mouth.

"Will Aedan stay with you?"

"Yes." I thought about the damage he had taken today. "He's banged up, again, and I owe him."

The three of us could have rounded up the pups without his assistance, but he took the hurting for us.

"He's a good man." Asa slid his focus back to me. "He won't survive long without you."

"Your other half would be thrilled to hear it."

A soft huff of laughter was his only response.

"Do you think you'll be home—back?—tonight?"

Home was too presumptuous, even if it felt that way with him and Clay, but there was no taking it back.

"No." He caught my hands as they eased down his chest. "We'll stay in Munford until we corral the kelpie."

"I figured." I toyed with the buttons on the front of his shirt. "Keep me in the loop?"

"Of course." He leaned down until his warm lips pressed against my forehead. "Will you think of me?"

Without further ado, he turned us around, and we began the short walk back to Clay. No doubt, Asa had wanted to give me a second to compose myself before I answered him, since I had trouble articulating mushy stuff in the best of times.

"I always think of you when you're not here." The honesty left me raw. "I like having you around."

The slow grin that spread across his face was radiant, and I wanted to stop and stare.

Like a creeper.

Or a lovesick fool.

I wasn't sure which was worse.

"I would like to take you on a date when I return." He flashed me a smile. "Will you go out with me?"

"Hmm." I scrunched up my face, pretending to think about it. "Depends."

The tiniest line appeared between his brows. "On?"

"Whether Aedan has dragged me beneath the waves to his undersea kingdom to be his bride."

"I would kill him." Asa brought my hand to his lips. "I wouldn't be able to help myself."

"The first part I believe." I held out a hand and wobbled it side to side. "The other part..." It hit me then, what he meant. "You mean the daemon would kill him."

"He would do anything for you. Name it, and it will be yours. Ask it, and it will be done."

The way his mouth lingered on my skin made me bold. "What would *you* do for me?"

"There is nothing I wouldn't do for you." His teeth scraped my skin. "I am utterly fascinated by you."

The tightness in my throat made it hard to swallow. "Same."

"Truly?" He jerked his head up to study me. "You mean that?"

"I am utterly fascinated by you too."

And I was afraid of what I might do for him, if he asked me, if he needed me to do it.

I had been a creature of bloodlust with flesh between her teeth, a monster with no morals or cares. That vicious, craven thing had been driven by her own selfish needs and wants. Imagine what I might do to protect those I loved, to keep them safe.

For Colby, I had sacrificed that power, stepped out of that darkness.

For Asa, I would paint my face in crimson and prowl back into the void.

"I wish you two would mate already." Clay wrinkled his nose. "This lovey-dovey crap gets old fast."

"Your ex-lover tried to kill us all last month," I reminded him. "You've got no room to talk."

"I have bad taste in women." He shrugged. "That doesn't mean you don't also have bad taste in men."

"We're getting sidetracked." I massaged my temples. "You two are leaving, yes?"

"Yeah." Clay turned serious. "I hate to ditch you with a mess, Dollface."

"It's fine." I wasn't totally up a creek, well, yes, I was, but anyway. "Aedan can help."

Clay cocked an eyebrow at Asa. "That cool with you?"

"Rue makes her own choices," he said wisely then glanced at the cage. "She'll need help with us gone."

"Okay." Clay lifted his hands. "It's not you I'm worried about, if you catch my drift."

"It won't be a problem." He rubbed a hand across his chest. "I think."

The daemon had trouble staying away when Asa was nearby, but maybe he would behave this time.

What did it say about me that, deep down, I held my breath in the hopes he would be a brat as usual?

"We'll burn that bridge when we get there." I checked, and the truck keys were in the ignition. "When do you expect those lab results?"

"Maybe tomorrow." Clay scratched his head. "I'll check in with Lindy and see."

Lindy.

I filed the name away, but off the top of my head, I didn't recall having met a Lindy.

Anyone with a private lab was worth remembering.

"See you in a day or two." Clay dragged me in for a hug. "Make my apologies to Shorty."

"I will." I walked into Asa's arms and rested my cheek above his heart. "No pony rides, okay?"

"I will do my best to resist." His arms came around me. "I expect to be wined and dined when I return."

A surprised laugh shot out of me, which must have been his intention, given his grin.

"I see how it is," I teased. "Spoil me with cupcakes to lure me in then turn the tables."

"I couldn't help overhearing." Clay wiped a smile off his mouth. "Rue doesn't have a romantic bone in her body. You know that, right? Are you really leaving a date night up to her?"

"I can do romantic." I honed my glower on him, my competitive nature rising. "I *will* do romantic."

The joke was on him. I had read enough romance novels to plan a date night in my sleep. It might not be tailored to Asa and me, the way perfect moments unfurled in books, but I could do generic. No problem. All thanks to the education Clay foisted upon me when he stuck the first romance novel in my hand.

"I trust her." Asa stroked his hands up and down my back and whispered in my ear, "You've got this."

That he was cheering me on made me feel like a bad bet and more determined than ever to figure out a way to repay his thoughtfulness for the cupcakes he still sent daily whenever we were apart. He hadn't fixed the quantity either, so I got mountains of baked goods to remind me of him whenever he was away.

The girls thought it was swoony. I did too. Even if I fussed about the expense, I was pleased he felt I was worth it.

"I appreciate your faith in me." I breathed him in once more. "Drive safe."

Asa pressed his warm lips to my temple and shut his eyes. "I hate this."

"Me too." I stepped away, forced my hands not to reach for him. "Okay, I need to get to work."

The night was wasting, and I had a shift at the shop in the morning.

I climbed into the cab, and Asa shut the door for me while I strapped in. I cranked the engine, happy to hear it rumble to life with no problem. I hadn't been certain the truck was abandoned on purpose, or if it suffered a malfunction during its ordeal with the pissed-off soon-to-be-momma dobhar-chú.

Clay and Asa began their walk back to the SUV they would drive to their next assignment.

Me?

I elbowed Aedan until he cracked open one bloodshot eye, then began the slow process of unsticking the heavy truck from the mud gripping its tires. I wasn't sure how the driver had gotten into the field. There was no obvious damage to the fence. He must have spotted a gate or road and used that.

Which meant now I got the fun of backtracking to cause as little damage as possible.

No Black Hat backing meant any repairs came out of my pocket.

"I should have let Astaroth kill me," he mumbled. "It would have hurt less than this."

"It wouldn't have felt like anything at all," I countered, "and you never would have felt anything again."

A quiet settled over him, but I couldn't tell if he thought that was a good or bad thing.

With a long night ahead of us, I put my temporary partner to good use. "So...where are we going?"

That jarred him out of his head. "What do you mean?"

"These pups have to go somewhere that's not here. Where do you recommend?"

"Coastal would be ideal." He pushed himself up straight. "I have a friend who can take them to Florida."

"The Everglades?"

Lots of paras called it home, and they were all invested in spooking off humans who got too close.

"Yeah." He stared out the window. "Lots of river otters there too."

Thinking of how cute actual otters were, I had to ask, "Do they like to play together?"

"I can make a call," he rushed out, "and get my friend here tomorrow morning."

With sinking dread, I grasped what he didn't want to say. "They *eat* them?"

"They'll eat anything they can take down." He winced. "They just really like otters."

"Cannibals," I muttered. "I think I hate dobhar-chú."

"Most people do." He rubbed the side of his throat. "I need to get in water soon."

Faint bluish spots began to show beneath his skin. "Are you wearing a glamour or...?"

"Or," he said with a grin. "Definitely or."

Since he was the man with a contact, I had to lean on him. "How do you want to handle this?"

"We should go back to your place. I'll bring the cage down to the creek to make the pups comfortable." He frowned at his flaking skin. "I can carry it to my friend when he arrives in the morning. He can park in the driveway, right? Without affecting your wards?"

"Yes." That meant giving out my address to a stranger, but it was unavoidable. "That'll work."

"Do you have a phone I can use?" He picked at the seam on his jeans. "I tossed mine."

Because he didn't think he would need it after he showed up on our doorstep.

"Aedan..." I struggled for a polite way to ask. "Do you have any resources?"

"I have contacts, a few friends who won't kill me on sight, but I don't have any money. I signed it over to Delma before I left. She didn't want there to be any unpleasantness about who received my portion of our inheritance."

"Your sister sounds like a piece of work."

And smart to play on his good heart to lure him to her under the pretense of signing paperwork so she could beat him within an inch of his life to ensure Asa finished the job for her. As dedicated as she was to wiping out her siblings, she had no reason to care about splitting hairs on Aedan's share when she stood to be the sole inheritor of their father's holdings once she finished killing off her relatives.

Either she was that vicious, or she was that petty, and I wasn't sure which was worse.

"Have you met any daemonesses?"

Aside from the one I potentially saw in the mirror each morning? "No."

"Delma is no better or worse than most." He stared out the window. "I'm the anomaly."

"Asa isn't a frothing monster either," I pointed out, so he felt less alone. "You two can start a club."

Wild laughter pinged around the inside of the cab, and Aedan doubled over with it, unable to breathe.

"What?" I slammed on the brakes. "You didn't get hit with any quills, did you?"

Plenty of young had potent venom. One tiny quill might have turned him delusional.

Long moments later, he leaned back and stared at the ceiling. "You think he's tame."

"No." I had only to picture the daemon in battle to know better. "He's just not an indiscriminate killer."

"Do you know how many challengers he's killed?"

"Do you know how many hearts I've eaten?"

The amusement melted off his face. Pretty sure I felt a bump as I ran over it.

"He has no choice but to defend himself, or he dies." A fact that disturbed me, more and more as time went on. "I wanted power. I didn't *have* to kill. I *wanted* to do it. I did it for my own selfish reasons. I am the frothing monster in our relationship. He doesn't hold a candle to me." I cut my gaze to Aedan. "Remember that. I'm not tame either."

In a soft voice, barely a whisper, he asked the universe. "What do I do if he doesn't kill me?"

"You live." I clasped him on the shoulder. "Less glorious than death in battle, but still pretty awesome."

"I don't have anyone who..." He made a faint gesture with his hand. "How will I survive?"

Goddess bless, what I mess I was about to make of both our lives.

"You'll stay with me until you get your feet under you. I'll help you get a job in town." Not one at the shop, where he could make goo-goo eyes at Arden, but somewhere. "Once you save up enough money, I'll help you find an apartment. After that? We'll see how it goes." I turned my focus back to the road. "You're only out of options when you're dead."

The trip home earned me three calls from concerned neighbors, one of which left me with cold sweats.

"There's an intruder," Mrs. Gleason informed me. "White pickup. Big metal cage in the bed. Bet you it's more of those heartless bastards who dumps weaned pups in the country to avoid vet bills. They're headed your way. I've got 'em in my sights. Want me to blow out a tire?"

"No." I gripped the steering wheel harder. "It's me." I shot frantic glances down the road. "Don't shoot."

"Oh." Her earlier excitement turned to disappointment. "What are you doing with a cage and a truck?"

"A friend of mine is relocating a dangerous animal. He got hurt earlier, so I'm driving his rental."

"He caught what ate old Terfel's reindeer?"

"Not yet," I lied. "He's working on it, though."

"Don't let him have all the fun." Her enthusiasm returned. "I've been tracking it."

Why was I not surprised to hear her say so? "You have to be careful, Mrs. Gleason."

"Bam-Bam and I are plenty careful, don't you worry."

"Call if you need backup, okay?"

"Sure thing."

The call ended with me more certain than ever that her backyard was a graveyard.

"That's the old woman with the gun." Aedan recoiled from the phone. "She's scary."

"She's good people. She's just also a good shot." I bit the inside of my cheek. "At people."

"She almost caught me out of the water. I don't know what tipped her off, but she knew I was there."

The offhand comment told me he had other glamours, or means of camouflage, than his human guise.

"She's got a sixth sense when it comes to people on her property."

As I said it, I got a hunch. Between the years she spent on that land, and the blood she had shed there, she might have bound herself to it. It was witch magic, but I already knew the town had multiple witch bloodlines. None of them were powerful, as I hadn't wanted a challenge on my hands. Most of them had more human in them than witch these days, but that didn't mean there weren't the odd outliers.

Arden and Camber had enough magic to work in my shop, to imbue the proper intent into our products.

Mrs. Gleason might be touched with a little bit extra too.

"She patrols." He shook his head. "Humans are so odd."

The behavior was peculiar, but I had chalked it up to the eccentricities allowed to all of us as we age.

Maybe, now that I had access to bureau resources again, I ought to dig deeper into the locals' histories. I would love to have an extra hand at the shop. Right now, sick days and vacations days were a luxury. We had to replace Ms. Dotha, and soon. Especially with me taking on a heavier Black Hat workload.

Midnight loomed by the time I parked at the house. Aedan could leave the wards without help, but I had to let him back in. He set off toward the creek with the cage, and I—after making certain I was alone—let magic unspool from my wand toward the truck, cleansing it inside and out of any damning evidence.

The rental logo was a familiar one, and I called the national hotline.

"Hi." I put on my best concerned citizen voice. "I found one of your rentals abandoned on my road. I was afraid someone would steal it, since the keys were in the ignition, so I drove it up to my house."

After answering a barrage of questions, I left the keys on the front seat and lumbered into the house.

"What's with the truck?" Colby dropped from the ceiling onto my head. "I saw Aedan with you."

"The truck was used to bring those killer otters to town, but whoever rented it dumped it in a field."

"I miss all the fun." She heaved a sigh. "I should have gone with you."

"Eh." I patted her head. "You had more important things to do."

"The guild is on break until New Year's." She glided into the kitchen. "I'm officially on family time."

"Excellent." I rubbed my hands together. "Christmas movie

marathon?"

I wasn't a huge fan of Christmas movies, but she loved the classics. We had a list to work through for the twelve days of Christmas, but it had kept growing until the month of December was packed with them.

"Clay said he wants to watch *The Santa Clause* with us." She glanced at the door. "Hey, where is he?"

As much as I hated being the bearer of bad news, I had to fess up to her. "He and Asa left for a case."

"He left?" Her antennae drooped against her back. "He didn't say goodbye."

"He's in Munford, so not far. Someone turned a kelpie loose there, so the guys had to leave fast."

"A kelpie." She touched down on the bar. "He knows not to ride it, doesn't he?"

Colby, like all the Silver Stag's victims, had been a fae girl, one well versed in her species lore by her concerned parents.

"I warned him." I poured her pollen granules in a small dish. "Whether he listens..."

"We need to call him." Her wings twitched in agitation. "He can't drown, but he—"

"I'm joking." I stroked her back until she calmed. "Clay can be reckless, but he's not careless."

"I'm going to call him anyway," she mumbled. "He thinks he can't get hurt."

"I'm sure he would appreciate any tips you can give him."

With me as her only point of physical contact, she and I had been joined at the hip. Clay and Asa gave her a second and third choice for personal interaction when she wanted variety. I was thrilled for her, if a smidge jealous she preferred Clay these days, but I couldn't fault her good taste.

He had been my first real friend, still was my best friend, and I was glad they got along so well.

Sadly, Asa was so adept at cramming himself into a box, making himself smaller, easier to be near, that Colby hadn't gotten to know him as well. He watered himself down for her, trying to protect her against the predatory calling in his blood that spooked most people.

I wasn't most people. Neither was Colby, after what she had endured in her short life. But that was why Asa never wanted to give her a reason to fear him, to worry he might ever hurt her. He was earning her trust by degrees, and I was determined to let the two of them sort it out.

And, selfishly, her attachment to Clay gave me more time to spend alone with Asa.

Lucky for me, Clay solved the problem of a babysitter on the night I picked for my date with Asa.

Not that Colby required one—she entertained herself—but it made me feel less guilty if she had company.

Guilt.

Another of those new and pesky *feelings* that left me confused about the hows and whys of it.

"Movie or no movie?" I was tired, but I wasn't sleepy. "Your call."

"Pass for tonight," she decided. "I want to warn Clay about kelpies."

"Okay." I left her with her pollen and her phone. "I'll be in my room, reading."

"Kissy stuff?" Her voice drifted to me. "For Asa?"

"I wish." No improbable shifters for me, though I had a cobra and mongoose romance calling my name. "Research."

"Rue?"

"Yeah?" I paused outside my bedroom. "What's up?"

"I'll help you bake when you get done."

The olive branch she extended was better than a movie. "Thanks, smarty fuzz butt."

Once I heard her voice mingling with Clay's, I let myself into my room and shut the door.

I wasn't surprised to find the Proctor grimoire waiting for me on my pillow.

6

"Looks like it's just you and me." I sat next to the Proctor grimoire. "What's on tap for tonight?"

The best routine for my mental health involved reading the cursed book for thirty-minute stretches. The odds of it worming into my head, the way it had with Colby, were low but never zero. Plus, it had a knack for making me reflect on what I had done—and might still do—with the power on offer.

Which, honestly, was proof it *was* seeding my subconscious with its macabre delights.

I had to figure out how to get to the good stuff, memorize that, and then torch this pesky book. It wasn't a leap to assume it knew that was the plan, which was why it kept thwarting me at every turn. It didn't want to die, and it was doing everything it could think of to prevent that outcome.

The fact its sentience allowed it to fret over its demise was, yes, another sign it needed to go.

First things first, I set a timer on my phone to ensure I didn't fall down a rabbit hole.

After I settled on the bed, legs crossed, back against the headboard, I opened the book on my lap. At the top of the page, in bold letters, were instructions on how to call otherworldly creatures to do your bidding.

"You've been eavesdropping again, I see." I flipped forward and then back. "You're on a roll tonight."

Aside from popping up all over the house, the grimoire didn't move that I had ever seen. It didn't riffle its own pages or leave itself open on passages for me to find. It was much worse. The book was in absolute control of its contents. It could show me what it wanted on any page I chose, which meant it didn't need those parlor tricks to get its point across.

Had I not skimmed the information on Colby that first night the grimoire was in my keeping, I might never have known. Then again, now that I knew the book better, I suspected it had been baiting me, even then, with the knowledge I wanted in exchange for its continued existence.

The timer went off before I made any inroads, and I put the grimoire back in the safe with other artifacts that had no business in the world. Until this grimoire, I hadn't believed a book could be smug, but it pulled off self-satisfied well.

Sleep proved more elusive than usual on nights when Asa was away. He and Clay more or less lived with Colby and me between cases, and the roommate life was working out for all of us. She and I enjoyed the company, and they enjoyed having a *home* to come home to.

About to check on Colby, see if she wanted to bake Mexican wedding cookies with me, I got a call from Asa.

"Hey, you." I swallowed the pounding of my heart. "Miss me already?"

Hmm.

That almost sounded flirty.

Maybe I was getting the hang of this.

"Yes, but—"

A groan poured out of me, along with my newfound confidence. "But what?"

"Javelle has reported a vodyanoy."

Javelle was a town above Munford, but a vodyanoy? "That's the least dangerous one yet."

Vodyanoy were stooped-back creatures with froglike heads. Their long beards reached their knees, and I remember hearing something about scales. They resembled old men from a distance, and they weren't malicious. Still, they had no business so far from water.

"It killed a lifeguard at the municipal pool."

"Clearly, I shouldn't make sweeping statements without fact-checking myself first."

Most towns surrounding Samford were just as teeny as ours, and none had the resources for a municipal pool. Javelle orbited those towns, but I hadn't realized it was that much bigger or it had the disposable income to burn on maintenance and lifeguards.

No wonder the mayor was always in a tizzy. Her competitive streak must be a mile wide.

"I didn't mean to come off as chastising."

"You're fine." I flopped back on my pillow. "I just finished up with the book, so my brain is mush."

His silence reinforced his opinion that we should damn the contents and destroy the grimoire.

I was slowly leaning in that direction too, but my witch nature made me too curious for my own good.

"What are the odds," I asked into the quiet, "these other locations aren't related to Samford?"

As much as I didn't want to hear it, I required confirmation he was thinking what I was thinking.

"We have three aquatic fae creatures known to kill humans dropped within a fifty-mile radius."

"Do you think an old acquaintance of mine was trying to locate me within a general area?"

Dump a bunch of monsters and see how long it took me to put in an appearance, that kind of thing.

"That seems to be the likeliest scenario. It was pure luck they hit Samford first."

From the moment I accepted the director's deal, I had known the risks involved in me returning to active duty, even as a consultant, while remaining stationary. Eventually, my enemies were bound to find me. And discover Colby. But I hadn't expected the bottom to drop out this fast.

"Why aquatic fae?" I watched my ceiling fan spin. "That's not exactly subtle."

"If we're right, they weren't going for subtle. They chose species who would react with extreme aggression under the right conditions. A fae dependent on water to survive who wakes up in the middle of a landlocked area is going to panic and jump straight into survival mode."

"They'll head for the nearest body of water," I mulled it over. "The creek here, the pool in Javelle."

"The kelpie," he filled me in, "was nesting in a water purification plant."

"That reminds me." I exhaled. "Aedan is babysitting the pups in the creek. A friend of his is picking them up in the morning. He's going to drop them in the Everglades."

"That—" he chuckled, "—is the equivalent of a parent telling a child flushing a goldfish sends it to heaven."

"Do I want to know what you're trying to tell me, or do I want to plead ignorance?"

"Dobhar-chú pup fur is valued for its softness, and their meat for its tenderness."

So, Aedan hadn't been kidding about the hat thing. Good to know.

"What is wrong with people?" I shot off the bed. "I'm going to tear him a new one. Want to listen in?"

"They'll die without their mother," he told me, voice soft. "You can't foster them. Other females will eat them. You can't bottle-feed them. They can only tolerate the unique secretions of their mother for the first six to eight weeks, and no one in their right mind would attempt to milk a dobhar-chú anyway."

The fight drained out of me, and I slumped back onto the bed. "Well, that's depressing."

"I wasn't sure, or I would have mentioned it earlier. I made some calls on the way here to verify."

"I can't believe Aedan lied to me." I had to set ground rules. "That's not acceptable."

"I wouldn't be too hard on him."

"Really?" I scoffed at his gentle rebuke. "This coming from you?"

"He didn't want to upset you with knowledge that won't change anything. I can appreciate that."

"I'm sure you can." I shut my eyes. "Please tell me you don't withhold information *for my own good*."

"There are topics of a personal nature I find difficult to discuss," he confessed, "but I'm working on it."

"Does this mean I'm one step closer to receiving a copy of *Dating Dae for Dummies*?"

His soft laugh went a long way toward melting my anger. Dang it. I had to learn to be tougher on him.

"I don't make this easy on you, do I?" His voice lowered. "It's all so new, and confusing."

"Confusing, yes." I latched on to that common ground. "I have all these thoughts and *feelings*."

"I have all these thoughts too," he rumbled, the sound clenching my abdomen. "And urges."

"What kind of urges?" Oh, yeah. I was definitely flirting with him. "And do they involve your horns?"

His groan met my ears and curled my toes in my socks. I was playing with fire, and I didn't care if I got a burn or two or fifty if it meant I got to hear that low sound of need from him again. This was a different kind of power than what I was used to, but I enjoyed it humming under my skin all the same.

"Unless you want me at your door at dawn, we need a new topic."

A flush spread down my body, and I had to force the mental picture of him in my bed away. I didn't have a teacher kink that I was aware of, but it was dizzying to think Asa was entrusting so many of his firsts to me. I was equal parts afraid I would botch it and relieved he didn't have a leg up on me. The mechanics, I could handle. It was linking emotion to action that worried me. Our mutual inexperience was a blessing.

Short of jumping under an icy showerhead, I had one surefire mood killer. "I told Aedan he could stay."

"Stay?"

Yup.

The mood was dead as a doornail.

That was all it took to convince me horn play was the last thing on his mind now.

"We have a full house, so I'm going to pick up a tent, an inflatable mattress, and some camping supplies. He'll be happier closer to a fresh source of water, I think, and he'll be safe as long as he stays on my property." It was a gamble, but I was trying to trust these new, more merciful instincts. "I also said I would help him find a job, just not at the shop."

A flicker of worry struck me that Asa would forbid it, or try to, and that would cost him points with me.

"My only concern is for Colby." He took care with his words. "The longer he stays on the property, the more likely he is to notice her and ask questions."

That bit of caution I could respect, as it mirrored my own thoughts. "I'm debating how to handle it."

"You trust him, and you're a good judge of character."

"But this is Colby," I breathed. "I can't risk her safety."

"Did you know that when a daemon claims a territory, they're allowed to bind other daemons to them with a blood oath, basically deputizing a select few to help maintain the peace and enforce the rules?"

"I did not know that." A thread of tension wove through me. "Are you suggesting *you* claim Samford?"

"I'm not the daemon I had in mind."

"Oh." I got a headache from the very idea. "That would cause more problems than it solved."

Despite not claiming me publicly as his granddaughter, the director felt he had every right to weigh in on my life and the choices I made. To come out as the quarter daemon we suspected I might be? It ensured he would never acknowledge me as family. Then again, that made the notion more, not less, tempting.

"You don't want anyone to know you have daemon blood."

Eyes slamming closed, I should have seen this coming. "I don't know for certain that I do."

Asa fell silent, and I had no idea how to restart the conversation without making it worse.

"I should go," he said at last. "Clay and I have a few miles to cover at dawn."

"Yeah." I continued staring at the backs of my eyelids. "Of course."

We made goodbye noises then ended the call, and I knew one recipe wouldn't cut it tonight. This was a solid two-dessert night. Maybe a three.

Forcing my eyes open, I startled to find the grimoire resting inches from the tips of my fingers.

For curiosity's sake, I flipped to the middle and read what it wanted to show me.

The spell was the magical equivalent of a freaking paternity test.

"Thanks, book." I always tried my best to be polite. "But that won't be necessary."

I got up, put it away, and found Colby sulking in her rig.

"Ready to bake?" I went for upbeat and chipper, but I didn't quite hit the mark. "Cake? Cookies? Both?"

"Clay had to go." She spun her phone on her mousepad. "He and Asa had to follow a lead real quick."

Hmm.

Maybe I had been projecting. Maybe Asa wasn't mad at me. Maybe he was just busy.

Almost like he was working a case or something.

Against my better judgment, I found myself asking, "Would you like to meet Aedan?"

"You mean it?" She shot in the air. "He's a good guy?"

"He seems to be." I caught her in my hands. "We have a big decision to make first."

"Um." As usual, she hit the nail on the head. "Do we want him to know about me?"

"Yep." I snuggled her against my chest. "He doesn't have anywhere to go, so I've offered to let him stay on the property. He's about the girls' age, and he doesn't have a lot of options. His big sister is trying to kill him and his siblings to steal their inheritance. Basically, lots of daemon drama."

"It sounds like he needs us." She squared her shoulders. "You like him, right?"

"I'm getting there." I rubbed her back. "I just worry…"

"…about me," she finished for me then wriggled free. "I can take care of myself now."

The familiar bond had given her more confidence, which was a good thing, but I didn't want her getting too cocky. I also didn't want her to be afraid. Balance was hard. Trust was harder. Almost impossible.

Aedan had one big plus in his column, and that was he was a daemon, not a witch. He couldn't bind Colby to him, and he had no reason to harm her. While the paranoid part of my brain insisted he could still capture her and attempt to cash in with a black witch eager for the power boost, I hadn't gotten the impression he was the type of person to hurt kids. Just the opposite, in fact.

"Let's take it slow," I cautioned. "You can visit Aedan with me, or the guys, but not alone."

"Deal." Her whoop of joy was infectious. "Do you think he'll be my friend?"

"I'm sure he will be." I followed her out the front door. "In time."

Free to zig and zag, Colby raced alongside me as we picked our way to the creek. Aedan heard us coming from a mile away, I was sure. He was sitting in the water, back to his usual blue, when we reached him.

"Hey." He sat up straight. "Did you see that...?"

"Hi." Colby zipped right in front of his face. "I'm Colby."

Aedan fell backward with a splash, his peculiar eyes round with surprise as they shot to me.

"This is Colby," I repeated, in case he missed it. "Tell anyone about her, and I will rip your spine out through your butthole. Hurt her, and I will rip your spine out through your butthole. Upset her, and I will rip your spine out through your butthole."

"Rue," Colby whined. "He won't be my friend if you're mean to him."

A spark of understanding lit his eyes, and he shoved upright in the water. "This is your foster."

"She's my family," I corrected, "and there are no depths I won't sink to in order to protect her."

"I understand." A solemnness overshadowed his features. "You know I do."

"That's the only reason this introduction is happening." I folded my arms over my chest. "No one can know she exists. No one can know she's here. No one can know anything about her."

"Rue," Colby sighed. "He gets it." She swooped over his head. "Leave him alone."

"I have a bunch of little sisters, just like you." He held out his palm. "I would do anything to protect them too." He grinned when she lit on his palm. "Rue and I have that in common."

"I don't have brothers or sisters." Colby's antennae twitched. "Clay is kind of like Rue's brother, so he's kind of like my uncle."

"Cool." He glanced around him. "Are you okay to get wet?"

"I bathe," she huffed. "Just not as much anymore."

"I worried about your wings," he rushed to explain. "Don't moths have powder on them?"

"They're scales, actually." She flexed her wings. "Neat, huh?"

"Like a fish." He inspected her outstretched pose to her satisfaction. "Very cool."

While they chatted, I went to inspect the cage with the pups. They had dogpiled, for warmth or comfort, and the gentle flow of water appeared to soothe them. I didn't want to breach the topic of their fate in front of Colby, but I made sure to lock gazes with Aedan to let him know I was onto him.

Once Colby was chatted out, I scooped her up, said our good nights, and went in search of sleep.

7

Everyone who sampled the tea I brewed for the carolers' sore throats wanted their own bag. That became clear when the shop opened the next morning to a line down the sidewalk. The blend of peppermint, anise, licorice root, rosehips, and slippery elm worked wonders without any extra oomph. As much as I wanted to believe our goods were in high demand, Camber told me strep throat had hit local preschoolers hard.

Thanks to the rush, I got through the day with minimal curiosity about how Aedan handled the drop.

However, I wasn't too busy for my thoughts to keep circling back to my call with Asa.

"Do we have another box of that green apple lip balm?"

Yanked out of my head, I fumbled for the correct answer. "Yes."

"Where is it?" Camber eyed me with concern. "I have a customer who wants five."

"I'll get it." I squeezed her arm. "Be right back."

I ducked into the office, located the box, then rushed it to the counter and cut it open with a knife.

"I love how this smells," a woman told me as she reached in to help herself. "So biteable."

The comment drew my attention to her, and her identity clicked into place in my mind. I had never met her, or seen a photo, not even heard a description, but her eyes were identical to Aedan's.

Delma.

Whatever magic transformed him, it worked the same on her, betraying family traits.

Now that we had a lock on her face, I could ask Clay to rewatch the recording from the night Dasher was murdered to see if she had been in the crowd of onlookers, but I had to survive this first.

"You look like you've seen a ghost." She smiled, warm and inviting. "Or perhaps you've seen my brother. People tell us we look like twins all the time. I heard he was in the area too, but I haven't run into him."

"Oh." Camber joined us with a bag for the purchases. "You mean the guy—" She leapt back. *"Ouch."*

"Sorry." I gripped her shoulder. *Hard.* "The box slipped through my fingers."

Right off the counter and directly onto her foot.

Accidents happen.

"It's fine." She hefted it up in her arms. "I'll just return these to storage for now."

Before Camber could turn, the woman circled the counter. "What guy?"

Playing the part of harried shopgirl, which wasn't hard to do, she frowned. "What guy?"

"You mentioned a guy. Did he look like me? Same hair and eyes?"

"I hate to disappoint you, but I was picking up an earlier conversation with Rue. I was answering her, not you." Her smile was all five-star customer service. "We're expecting the cable guy. A new one."

Another step eased her into Camber's personal space. "What does he look like?"

"Mid-fifties, short, mullet haircut." Camber took a pointed step back. "Lots of butt crack."

Delma's smile thinned, and she pulled a card from her purse. "Call me if you see my brother."

"Sure thing." Camber accepted the card. "You'll be the first person I dial."

"For the lip balm." Delma pressed a hundred-dollar bill into Camber's hand. "Keep the change."

After she left, I waved Arden over to man the register and guided Camber to the office.

"You okay?" I held her hands, which had gone clammy. "Do you need to go home?"

"I hate this." She sat in my chair and put her head between her knees. "I used to be a badass when it came to dealing with the bitchy customers, but now I melt down at every confrontation. I'm a wimp."

"You're not a wimp. That woman was a bully. No wonder her brother doesn't want her to find him."

"The brother." Camber lifted her head. "That was him, who came to the shop, right?"

"Yeah." I leaned against the doorframe. "She's the one who beat him within an inch of his life."

As much as I didn't want to pique their interest in Aedan, I did want them to be wary that his sister had come sniffing around for signs of him. They needed to know she was dangerous and to avoid her.

"I haven't seen him around here." She chewed her bottom lip. "Who is he?"

"Right now, he's a failed attempt at witness protection."

"You met him on the job. Your *other* job." Her eyes rounded. "That makes sense. You're working abuse cases."

Until her bright mind made the connection, I hadn't considered I could hide Aedan using that excuse.

With the girls' trauma so fresh in their minds, I didn't bring up my other job often. I hadn't outlined the parameters of my consultant gig with Clay and Asa, except to say I was helping the police. That would do me a solid in this instance, where I could twist the boundaries of my duties to match the situation.

More lies, more reimagining the past, but how bad were white lies that kept them safe?

The fact it weighed on me, the lies, was worrisome given I had no choice but to keep telling them.

"He might not stay here long," I warned her, not wanting either girl to get attached to the idea.

"He'll have to leave if his sister finds him." Her gaze skated to the curtain and beyond. "Arden liked him."

"Arden doesn't know him." I bit the inside of my cheek. "I didn't mean to sound harsh. I just worry."

"I know." She shoved to her feet and came to hug me. "I'll fill her in after work."

"I would appreciate that." I kissed the top of her head. "Now scoot." I nudged her. "She's swamped."

The three of us fell into an easy rhythm, and I was grateful again for the all-consuming rush.

☽◯☾

As soon as the shop closed, I locked up and drove home, eager to put eyes on Colby. And Aedan. I must have checked my phone for camera notifications a dozen times after Delma left the shop, but no blips disturbed the surveillance area or the wards. Colby hadn't texted or called, and I was trying not to hover, but it gnawed on me, knowing Aedan's sister was on the hunt for him and had come straight to me.

The daemon community was aware that Asa and I were in fascination with one another, and she knew her brother had challenged Asa. I was the logical point of contact. But how had she found me?

Oh crap.

The dobhar-chú pups.

Aedan's friend must not be as friendly as he believed if he ratted Aedan out to Delma.

A chime distracted me while I parked, and I unfastened my seat belt before picking up my phone to see a text from Clay.

>>*Results are in. Blood on the cage was black witch.*

>*Fingerprints?*

>>*Belonged to Agent Fanny Barker.*

>*Any idea where to start looking for her?*

>>*The morgue. In Munford.*

>*The dobhar-chú killed her?*

>>*Hard to tell. The damage was extensive.*

>*Did she have a partner?*

>>*She did, but he's MIA.*

>*Crap.*

Black Hat would send a team to investigate Agent Barker, and her missing partner.

They would come to Samford. Eventually. And there was nothing I could do to stop it.

The next text I sent went unanswered, and I smacked my palm on the steering wheel before getting out.

To avoid receiving an earful later, I shot Clay a brief summation of Delma's activities before I forgot.

Worried for Aedan, I skipped the house and headed toward the creek to warn him. I found him in worse shape than when he first arrived, floating in the water on his back, and still in possession of the pups.

"Colby let me back inside the wards," he mumbled through a swollen jaw. "She only wanted to help."

Of course my brave girl would risk my wrath to help a new friend.

"Your sister came to my shop today." I sat on the bank, in the damp. "Asking around about you."

Things hadn't gone to plan, that much was obvious, but I gave him space to tell me in his own words.

"I thought I could trust him." Aedan shut his eyes. "He sold me out for a cut of my inheritance."

I ached for him, but I had bigger concerns. Selfish though it might be, Colby was always my top priority.

"Where did he go?" I hadn't killed anyone as a preventative measure in a long time. I was surprised at the twinge of remorse lodged in my chest. "Will he be back?"

"He went over there." Aedan pointed a webbed hand toward a pile of dirt. "He saw Colby." His arm fell back in the water with a splash. "I couldn't risk him telling my sister. She would sell Colby out to spite me."

The loyalty he offered Colby, that he offered *me*, with that gesture couldn't be bought. It was born of desperation and defiance, and a will to live that sprung from the desire to thrive despite his world attempting to stamp him out of existence like a weed.

"I appreciate you protecting her."

The night sky continued to hold his attention. "Do you want me to leave the pups with you?"

"What do you mean leave?" I nudged him with the toe of my shoe. "You're not going anywhere."

"I thought...with my sister..." He splashed as he jerked upright. "You're going to let me stay?"

My transformation to white witch must be complete. I was a total marshmallow these days.

A slightly murderous marshmallow, but still much fluffier than I ever had been in my life.

"I don't go back on my word." A grim purpose suffused me. "How do you feel about blood oaths?"

Maybe the key was to start small. Not claim a whole town, but a single person.

Or perhaps I was paving my way to Hael with good intentions.

"I hate to disagree," Clay said, his familiar voice a comfort over the phone. "This is bigger than Aedan."

"Black Hat involvement makes everything more complicated."

"No truer words," he agreed. "We're earning a reputation for putting down rogue agents, which doesn't help. Even the good ones will avoid us to prevent suspicion being cast their way. Chatting with us will be tantamount to tattooing *rat* on their foreheads. They'll be seen as guilty by association."

Agents would stop trusting agents, partners would stop trusting partners. Teams would fracture.

Convince everyone that everyone *else* is out to get them, and you can get away with almost anything.

Psychological warfare was a classic tactic for a reason.

"On one hand, we've got Agent Barker." I chewed on my bottom lip. "On the other, we've got Delma."

"And on the other, we've got a shit-ton of aquatic fae popping up all over the central part of the state."

"I don't have that many hands, and I was unaware you did, but yes. Some, if not all, of that must be connected."

"I'm not sure how yet, Dollface." He exhaled. "The sister found Aedan through a friend, right?"

"That's the working theory. I watched the feed during the time they were scheduled to meet." I blew out a breath. "The friend showed up with a truck. Aedan crossed the wards with the cage full of pups, greeted him with a handshake, and the friend took the opportunity to clock him while his hands were full. Aedan went down, the cage hit him in the jaw, and his friend started beating the stuffing out of him. Colby couldn't stomach the fight, so she left the house to let Aedan back inside the wards." I gave him a moment for that to sink in. "The friend saw Colby, Aedan killed him, and then he buried the scum in my yard."

"I can't leave you alone for five minutes."

"Yeah, well, some things never change." I sighed. "Anyway, the friend must have held out on Delma. She wasn't waiting for me at the house, so he might not have given her my address, but it's not like I'm hard to find. No one in town would give a stranger directions to my house, but she could find me if she looked hard enough." I switched focus. "How are things on your end?"

"The kelpie was shot, and its body disposed of." He sounded sad about that. "Beautiful creature."

"Shame it eats people."

"It's not like it chose to come here," he chided me. "They're practically an endangered species."

"What about the others?" I turned that over in my head. "Are they endangered too?"

"I'm not sure." He made a thoughtful noise. "That reminds me. It had a tag in its ear."

"Like a research tag?" A flash of memory hit me. "I think the dobhar-chú had one too."

"I'll touch base with the Kellies, tell them to dig deeper into the tags."

"The dobhar-chú tag is ash. Can you send me a picture of the kelpie's?"

"Sure." He tapped a few keys in the background. "Email sent."

"Thanks." I opened the file on my phone. "Talk soon."

We ended the call, and I went in search of my in-house Kelly.

"I have a research project for you," I called to Colby. "You game?"

Slowly, she peered around the side of her chair. "Sure."

"I told you I'm not mad." I joined her at her rig. "You broke the rules, but it was for a good cause."

And, white witch I might be, but I could still appreciate having one less enemy with my home address.

"Okay." She kept an eye on me. "What's the project?"

"Compile a list of endangered aquatic fae and where you can find them. Nesting sites, hunting grounds."

"Okay." Her wings fluttered with excitement. "Anything else?"

"I'm forwarding a picture of an ear tag on the kelpie. I think the dobhar-chú had one too."

"Someone is researching them?"

"There's a slim chance we're dealing with endangered species, so maybe?" That sparked an idea. "Check exhibits, zoos, preserves." Of the para variety. "Private collections too."

"That last one is classified, probably." Her expression sobered. "Are you sure?"

"Very sure." I patted her head. "I'm going to bang my head against the wall. I'll check in when I'm done."

That was code for spending my daily allotment of time with the grimoire.

Concern tightened her features, not for what she was about to do —the kid had no issue whatsoever with cyber breaking and entering —but for me. She was ready to be done with the grimoire too. I had decided to give it until New Year's. If it didn't give me what I wanted before then, I would find it out on my own, in my own time. Or not. But I had to remove the possibility the book could be used against us.

About the time I reached my room, I heard knocking and wondered if Aedan was checking in again.

"Are you literally banging your head against a wall?"

"No," I called back to her. "It's probably Aedan. I'll get it."

Flimsy excuse, but hey. I would run with it to avoid another session that only achieved wasting my time.

A tug in my middle told me who stood on the other side of the front door before I turned the knob.

"Asa?" I invited him into the entryway. "What are you—?"

Asa cradled my jaw in one fevered palm while stroking his hot thumb across my bottom lip.

"I thought you were Aedan," I said dumbly, as he walked me back until my spine hit the wall.

"We'll circle back to that." His laugh blew warm breath across my cheeks. "Can I kiss you?"

Hands fisting in his lapels, I anchored him in place. "If you leave me hanging this time, I—"

His lips silenced mine with gentle pressure, their caress a

tender exploration that turned my knees weak. I held on to my patience for as long as I could stand the tease, but my mouth opened, showing him what I wanted from him. He mimicked me, angling his head, deepening the kiss, and when I darted out the tip of my tongue to caress his, a growl built in his chest that rattled my back teeth. No, not a growl. Asa was purring. For me. And I wanted to purr right back. He tasted like dark roast coffee, and I drank him in with greedy gulps that shot straight to my head.

Dopamine achievement unlocked.

"Uh."

Asa drew back, his grip on me all that kept me standing, and glanced over his shoulder. "Hi, Colby."

"Well, this is awkward." She flitted back a foot or two. "I'll just, um, yeah. Go. To my computer."

Pretty sure she broke the sound barrier escaping, that or Asa was making my ears pop.

"You taste even better than I imagined," he murmured, pressing his lips against my throat.

"Ditto." I arched under the scrape of his teeth. "Are you sure you haven't done this before?"

A dark chuckle of pure masculine pride filled my ear. "I've had a long time to think about it."

"You dream about kissing women, don't you?"

"Every night since I met you."

"That was smooth." I slid my arms around his waist. "Much smoother than me."

Savoring the tingling warmth in my lips, I leaned my ear against his chest, over his pounding heart.

"I thought you were mad at me. For shooting down your suggestion I claim territory as a daemon rather than as a witch." As always with Asa, I found myself unable to hold back. The verbal diarrhea flowed and flowed. "I didn't want you to think I was opposed to the idea of being part daemon. That's not it. It's not like black witches are universally loved either. It's just...a shift in my worldview I'm not ready for yet."

"Your choice reminded me I had none in coming out as half daemon." His arms encircled me. "Father would allow nothing less. He wanted his claim public so that everyone knew he had sired another heir." He stroked up and down my spine. "I shouldn't have taken old hurts out on you."

Poor Asa.

His parents had him all twisted up about his identity and what it meant to be dae.

"So, funny story." I kept my grip on him. "I might have blood bound Aedan to me. Slightly. Just a bit."

With his clever fingers, Asa pushed up my shirt to feel skin. "I smelled him on you when I got here."

"And the daemon didn't take over." My eyebrows shot up my forehead. "I'm impressed."

"Don't be." His chest shook with laughter. "That type of bond precludes other relationships."

"Are you telling me you tricked me into swapping blood with him to make your daemon happy?"

"I wouldn't say tricked," he said, sounding for all the world like a fae.

"You planted the suggestion." I pinched his side. "You knew I would take that step to protect Colby."

"I expected you to, if you decided to let Aedan stay."

"It's a bonus you didn't feel the need to share that I can't have, what—romantic feelings toward him?"

"Sexual," he corrected me. "You can care for him, you already do, but not in that way."

As much as I wanted to throttle him, I considered how I would react if the daemon had pulled the stunt and not Asa. Then I reminded myself I let the daemon get away with literal murder and decided Asa flashing his fae roots now and again wasn't any worse. That didn't mean I wanted to be blindsided again.

"The next time you offer a suggestion, will you fully disclose its benefits and drawbacks, please?"

"Yes."

"You understand if you're not truthful with me, I can't trust you, and that if I can't trust you, you can't be in my life?" I wasn't telling him anything he didn't already know. "Between Colby and you, I will choose her all day long."

She was an eternal child, and I'd made her that way. She was my responsibility forever, or the next best thing. Asa was new. I liked him, a lot, but I wasn't sure how a relationship looked for us long term. For that reason, I couldn't prioritize him—or my hormones— over her safety and future happiness.

"I understand." He dipped his chin. "I apologize for not being more forthcoming."

"I enjoy when the fae comes out in you," I admitted, "but let's keep this thing between us honest."

"I can do that." He brushed a featherlight kiss over my lips. "Will you promise me the same?"

A prickle of dread stung my spine when his words permeated the lust fog clouding my brain.

"There are things I haven't told you." I leaned against the wall. "Things no one but Clay knows."

Asa appeared to consider that. "Who told him?"

"The director." I dropped my gaze. "He wanted to pair me with a watcher loyal to Black Hat."

Loyal to him, more like, but I would be spilling my secrets if I told Asa that much.

"Orders from higher up the chain of command supersede his freewill." He cocked his head. "I will accept an imbalance in our relationship." He drew me back into his arms. "For now." He buried his face in my neck and breathed me in. "As long as you think you can trust me one day."

I do trust you.

That was what I wanted to say, but I couldn't, not when I wasn't ready to burden him with my lineage. Or myself. That was likely the real issue. I didn't want to invite the director into my life by talking about him, remembering him. I wanted to erase the past and truly start fresh.

Impossible.

"One day soon," I promised him, knowing I would face the director before all was said and done, and I needed Asa on my side when that day came. Clay too. "You're spoiling me, you know?"

"How so?" He shut the door I hadn't noticed we left open. "And should I continue?"

"The second you finish a case, you're here."

"There's nowhere I would rather be."

Silver tongued. Oh, yeah. The man had fae blood, and he knew how to charm.

"I like it." I burrowed into him. "I've never had that."

I had priorities, but I had never been one for anyone else.

"Rue?" Colby called from her rig, far from any potential smooching. "I found something."

8

After straightening our rumpled selves, Asa and I joined Colby. Using two of her four fuzzy little hands, she shaded the side of her face. Her antennae leaned that way too, creating an impressive wall between her and us.

"What are you doing?" I leaned in front of her screen until she had to look at me. "Hi."

"I wanted to make sure you and Asa were finished swapping spit." She blinked rapidly. "My eyes, Rue. They were *melting.*"

Swapping spit? Really? I had to watch it with the spit muffin comments before this spun out of hand.

"They'll grow back." I patted her on the head. "Besides, you have two. Let's not be greedy."

"That's your argument?" She dropped her hands. "They'll grow back? That I have two?"

"I stick with the classics, as you obviously do too." I shrank onto my haunches. "I'm melting." I clawed at my face. *"Melting."*

"I'll give you two a moment," Asa said as I puddled on the hardwood. "I ought to check in with Clay."

From the floor, I scowled up at him. "You told him you were leaving this time, right?"

"I'll be in my room," he said, teeth digging into his swollen bottom lip, "making my apologies, if you need me."

Goddess bless, what a mess.

Asa couldn't even blame the daemon for the slip. He had driven here and arrived fully dressed and ready to ravish me. For better or worse, it was Asa's doing, and I savored a moment of smugness over it.

After I packed away my hormones, I got to my feet and leaned over Colby. "What did you find?"

"The list of creatures flagged on this case are all endangered fae, all aquatic, and they all match descriptions for a para-only sanctuary in northern Florida." She scrolled down. "The Devlin Wildlife Center."

Florida, with its ample coastlines, saltwater access, and marshes, was a dumping ground for many of the paranormal creatures that outgrew their enclosures, required relocation after eating a pet or person, or simply fit in nowhere else.

Not all fae creatures had come to this world from Faerie of their own choice, and most of them were stuck here. They had to make the best of it, and we had to ensure they didn't eat every poodle, tabby, or Timmy that made their mouths water.

"Good work." I made a mental note of the sanctuary's name. "Why did you zero in on them?"

"Not the tag." She clicked through a few tabs. "The numbers aren't doing anything for me."

We might need more than one to make sense of any patterns, but we didn't have that yet.

"Okay." I leaned over her shoulder. "So, what tickled your antennae?"

"The reviews on the Devlin website." She pulled up the most recent ones. "Notice a theme?"

Parts of the internet were magicked so that only paranormals had access. Others used specific codes for their otherworldly clientele. This sanctuary was a hotspot, from the looks of it. Popular with school tours and researchers hoping to observe these animals in the next best thing to their natural habitat.

The argument could be made that you could pop over to Faerie and capture, say, another kelpie pair to repopulate this world, but that would be a pure fae animal. Not the same thing at all. The kelpies, and most of their kin, had interbred with humans, animals, or other fae until it could be argued they were a wholly other species.

"The last few weeks, sightings are down." I skimmed the two- and three-star reviews. "Way down."

Endangered species would be the biggest draw, and those had earned the most complaints in recent weeks as no-shows. It didn't mean someone had pillaged their rare-species collection, but visitors were vocal about the absence of wildlife. It gave us a possible timeline, and a possible starting point.

"This means it's not Aedan's fault, right?" She kept scrolling. "If it's been going on that long?"

"It's not his fault either way." I wanted her to know I was on his side. "He didn't do anything wrong."

The click of a door in the hall warned Asa was on his way back to us.

"I have to pick up Clay." Asa slid his gaze past me to the screen. "What have you found?"

After I nudged her to take credit where it was due, Colby gave him a rundown of her sleuthing.

"Three weeks." He frowned. "If the specimens were collected in the same location, why wait?"

"Whoever is behind this wanted the creatures hungry." I talked out my reasoning. "Lock them up, starve them, then set them free in populated areas. They would fall on the first prey they came across. Most likely humans. That would get them noticed faster, and any response from me would be immediate. Less time to wait for whatever result they hoped for."

"Aedan challenged me a few weeks ago," Asa said, zeroing in on the timeline, "but he didn't show."

"He's clear," I assured him. "I interrogated him to make sure the blood oath held."

Approval brightened his eyes, and I bet anything it stemmed from me claiming my daemon birthright.

I might not be ready to shout it from the rooftops, but I wasn't ignoring it either.

Between the bond forming with Asa and the blood oath taking root, I had to accept it.

I was part daemon. A quarter, max. And I had no idea what that meant for me—or us—long term.

"His sister could have used that time to plan this." I turned it over in my head. "Aedan saw her before he came here to sign trumped-up paperwork, so she knew he was on his way to see you."

Delma had lured him in with the inheritance ploy, and he had fallen for it. Prior to that, he had kept off her radar so that he could secure his younger siblings' foster situations. She could have planned this—the timeline fit, mostly—but why? She had to know he was going to his death. So, what did she really want?

"This was good work," Asa praised Colby. "Keep digging. You might be onto something."

The flitter of her wings betrayed her pleasure at having impressed him, and I couldn't help smiling.

A ping on my phone had me reaching for it to check my texts.

Clay had finished reviewing the footage from the night of the festival.

>>*Delma wasn't there.*

Her absence lent weight to our supposition the goal had been to flush me out of hiding.

"Come on." I took his hand. "I'll walk you out."

"Yes, please." Colby shielded the side of her face again. "I've already lost two eyeballs tonight."

"Smarty fuzz butt," I muttered, guiding him outside for a moment of privacy. I followed him to the SUV, enjoying the fresh air. "Maybe next time, you can bring Clay with you and avoid making the trip twice?"

"You know Clay." Asa turned so his back rested against the vehicle, and he drew me close. "He won't leave until the paperwork clears."

"You couldn't wait twelve more hours, huh?"

"I've waited a lot longer than twelve hours for this." He lowered his head and captured my mouth in a slow kiss that melted my knees. "I have no regrets."

"Neither do I." I bit his bottom lip. "You realize I'll never hear the end of this from Clay."

"What do you mean?"

"You're the romantic in this relationship." I tingled from head to toe, addicted to his flavor after just one small taste. "I hadn't even started thinking about our date night."

"You've had your hands full."

"So have you, but you made time for me."

"I don't need you to be anyone other than yourself." He cinched his arms around me until we stood flush from hip to shoulder. "You ask nothing of me. It's not your fault if I want to give you everything."

"You can't help yourself." I banged my head against his chest. "You're perfect."

"Nowhere near it." He chuckled. "I'm flattered you think so."

The admission cost me, but I paid it. "You're perfect for me."

"See?" He kissed my forehead, my eyelids, my nose. "That wasn't so hard."

The vulnerability required to whisper sweet nothings left me twitchy. "When will you be back?"

A possessive grin curled his lips. "Miss me already?"

This flirty side of him was hard to resist, and so I didn't. "Yes."

A flicker of emotion darkened his eyes, and his smile softened. "I should go."

"Okay." I checked the position of the moon. "I should sleep." I groaned. "After I check on Aedan."

"I can do that." He laughed at what he read on my face. "I swear to you, I won't harm him."

"You still want to read him the riot act, I'm sure." I squinted at him. "Let me put a meal together for him."

The poor kid needed more poultice and pain relief too. I should have seen to him sooner, but my head was all over the place. Now that I had grown my circle, I would have to be more aware of him and his needs. Even if I hadn't offered to help him get back on his feet, the blood oath placed him under my auspices.

Thankful I always had a fridge stuffed with leftovers, I made another basket for Aedan and handed it off to Asa for delivery.

"Be nice." I rolled onto my tiptoes for another kiss. "See you tomorrow?"

Eyes closed, he appeared to savor the moment. "I'll be back as soon as I can."

Reluctant to watch him go, I forced myself back in the house and joined Colby at her computer.

"I need to crash." I leaned against her chair. "How late will you be up tonight?"

"Another hour, maybe." She glanced up at me. "It's boring with all my friends away."

"Tomorrow, I have to shop for Aedan. Tent, bed, solar lantern. Whatever else you need to camp."

"He's getting a tent?" Her eyes popped wide. "Can I help decorate it?"

"Sure thing." I tapped a knuckle on her desk. "I need you to help me write up the supply list too."

"On it." A few keystrokes later, she was browsing outdoorsy sites. "This is going to be so cool."

There was no doubt in my mind I was leaving her to dream of sleepovers with Aedan in his tent.

Something told me I would be pricing kiddie tents soon too, since it fit her woodsy-themed room.

Relieved to have an excuse to ignore the grimoire for the night, I climbed in bed and passed out.

9

Breakfast smoothie in hand, I had almost reached the shop when I heard someone call my name.

Ms. Hampshire hustled across the street, waving to make sure I waited on her.

"Good morning." I greeted her with a smile. "Does Frank need more tea already?"

Her partner, Frank, depended on a respiratory tea blend to ease his emphysema symptoms.

"No, no, nothing like that." She darted a glance up and down the street. "Can we talk?"

"Of course." I gathered she meant in private and let her into the empty shop. "What's on your mind?"

"A woman came to the diner yesterday. She told Frank her little brother ran away from home, and she's desperate to find him. She implied he's mentally ill and needs his medication. He's over eighteen, so there's nothing the police can do." She wrung her hands. "We didn't tell her anything, but I saw her making the rounds. She's hoping to buy herself information."

There were several reasons why she might expect me to get

involved, but I was curious which one had prompted this. "Why did you bring this to me?"

"The other day, I was locking up as the girls were going to their car. They were talking about a handsome stranger that came to your shop. They mentioned he was beat up, and that you spoke to him." She dropped her voice. "You work with the police now, right? On abuse cases?"

Thanks to the break-in at the shop, the whole town knew about my new part-time gig with "the police."

"I do, yes, and I did talk to the young man." I took her hands. "You were right to tell me."

"Can you help the boy?" She peered around me, like I might have stashed him behind the counter. "Can we?"

The opening was perfect for seeding an idea that would have time to blossom over the next few days.

"He might stay here. He has no other family." I squeezed her fingers. "For that to work, he'll need a job."

"We're always slammed this time of year. He's welcome to wait tables at the diner."

"Thank you." I released her. "I'll let him know about your generous offer."

"What about his sister?" She worried the tie on her apron. "What should we do?"

"Leave her to the police." I locked gazes with her. "She's dangerous."

"I'll let the others know." She set her jaw. "We don't cater to bullies in Samford."

After a quick hug, she marched out the door and into the store beside the diner.

Already word was traveling, and fast, that Aedan was to be protected, and it was a revelation to find myself on this side of the equation. Had this been what happened to me—for me?—when I first arrived? Who had taken the backstory I created and deemed me worthy of safe harbor? Had the store owners rallied? No. I hadn't been one then. My neighbors must have carried word of my situation into town, and the news spread from there.

As I stocked the shop for the day, waiting on the girls to arrive, I heard a muffled yelp and recalled the spot in the sidewalk in need of patching. I went up front and popped my head out the door to make sure no one required help and found Delma pinning Camber to the wall with a hand around her throat.

"Release her." I stepped out onto the sidewalk. "Or else I'll call the police."

"You mean the two *officers* in your pocket?" Her smile was feline. "They're an hour away."

How she knew Clay's and Asa's location, I wanted to ask, but it would give her too much satisfaction.

With Agent Barker responsible for trucking in the dobhar-chú, and Delma's appearance in town, I wasn't stretching to reach the conclusion that the rogue Black Hat agents had formed alliances with other factions to aid them with their end goal.

The rogues were all black witches, to date. With black witches and daemons so reviled, who was going to work with either of those factions except each other?

The angle was wrong for me to pry Delma's hand off Camber, so I swung my fist at the side of Delma's head. It snapped to the side, and her grip loosened. I grabbed for her thumb, yanking back until it broke, and freeing Camber, who stumbled away. Delma snarled, inhuman in her rage, and flew at me. I landed a kick to her gut that knocked her to the concrete in a sprawl.

"Get to the shop," I ordered Camber. "Lock the door behind you."

She would call Arden, wherever she had gone, and warn her off. The girls looked out for one another.

Voices carried from across the street, and I regretted the spectacle I had made of myself.

"Leave this town," I warned Delma. "I will kill you if I see you again."

"We'll see." An ugly smile revealed teeth too sharp to be human as she stood. "I'm not afraid of you."

"You should be."

"You sound just like her."

"Who?"

Friends and neighbors flocked to me as Delma retreated, her otherness no longer keeping them at bay, and I was stuck. I couldn't chase after her without appearing like the aggressor, and our conversation wasn't for human ears. She had planned her exit well. Did that mean she had engineered the confrontation too? Or had she benefited from timing and what constituted the morning rush around here?

Delma didn't answer, and if I attempted a citizen's arrest to hold on to her, it would get ugly.

As much as it stuck in my craw to do it, I had to let her go. For now. And file her parting shot until I could spare time to make sense of it.

Aware Camber was alone in the shop, I thanked everyone for their support and rushed to her.

At the door, she greeted me with heaving sobs and shaking limbs as she clung to me.

"Are you okay?" I held her tight and rocked her. "She didn't hurt you, did she?"

"I'm not scared." She turned her tear-stained face up to me. "I'm pissed off, and you know how it goes."

True enough, Camber cried when she got mad. Puffy eyes, runny nose, the whole shebang. She hated it.

"Are you sure?" I cupped her cheeks and forced her to hold my stare. "It's okay to be afraid."

"I'm tired of being scared." She gripped my wrists. "I'm not a victim."

"No." I let her read my sincerity. "You're not."

"What you did out there..." she squared her shoulders, "...I want to learn how to do that."

"That's a conversation." I didn't say no, not when it might empower her, but I had to ask, "Where's Arden?"

"She ducked into the diner to wait it out." Her lips quirked. "She's not happy about it, but she did it."

This bold streak in Arden worried me, but we all coped in different ways, and Camber had a good idea.

I never learned a fighting style. I was taught how to fight. Dirty. Takedown moves, submission holds, that kind of thing. Not that I could tell her, but Clay was responsible for most of those skills. The director confined my education to magic.

I was meant to be a well-rounded black witch, not a well-rounded person.

"What do you say we pick her up and play hooky for the day?"

"No." Camber ditched me for the register. "That woman? She doesn't get to win."

Tears pricked the backs of my eyelids. "I'm so proud of you."

"Maybe walk Arden over?" She attempted a smile. "You're a total badass. You can be our bodyguard."

"I'm happy to do it." I pushed the words out through a tight throat. "You know I love you guys, right?"

"We both know." Camber kept going with the opening routine. "We're lucky to have you."

Sadly, they were about as unlucky as it got, thanks to their affiliation with me.

But Camber had given me a way to pay back their faith in me.

I couldn't always be there to protect them.

But I could teach them to protect themselves.

☽◯☾

Before Asa could retrieve Clay, they were assigned a related case that carried them forty-five minutes to the east of Samford. About an hour west of their current location. Three hours away from Colby and me.

From our late-night shopping extravaganza anyway.

With Colby in hairbow mode, list in hand, we hit a sporting goods store the whole of downtown Samford could have fit in. As grateful as I was for convenience, selection, and pricing, I wished there was a way to prevent superstoreitis from spreading to our small town. Sadly, we couldn't remain in a bubble forever.

Normally, I would have ordered what Aedan required, but Colby could use a pick-me-up, and I could too.

We would get in late, but we were insomniacs anyway, and it wasn't like anyone would be waiting on us.

And, yeah, that sounded pathetic, even in the privacy of my own head.

"Can we stop for coffee on the way home?"

"Already on the agenda," I assured her. "Which color do you think for the tent? Red or blue?"

"Blue."

She left off the *duh*, but I heard it anyway.

"That does it." I checked her list twice. "We got everything."

The total at the register left me lightheaded, but it was hard to pin a cost on Aedan's life.

The sentiment had popped into my head unprompted, cheering me that it had been my first thought.

Second thought, if you counted the sticker shock of my receipt, but still. It was a solid top five. Go, me!

After we loaded our haul into the SUV—and by we, I mean me— we headed for an all-night coffee shop.

There were some—not many, but *some*—benefits to chain store mentality.

"What flavor syrup do you want?" I read off her options. "Let me guess...s'mores."

The mental picture of Clay battling molten marshmallows must have done its job, because she laughed.

"Can I get one shot of s'mores and one shot of cinnamon sugar?"

"Why not?" I spied glazed donut holes in the window with my name on them. "We've earned a treat."

The night was cool and still as I walked to the front entrance, Colby in my hair, but a prickle on my nape had me turning my head to scan the lot. Three other cars had parked, and five were in line at the drive-through. With this many humans around, I couldn't imagine a safer place. Until I spotted the problem.

"Colby." I froze an arm's length from the shop's front door. "We need to get back in the car."

The press of her tiny feet in my scalp warned she was about to argue, but then she froze. "Rue?"

With her riding on my head, and me facing the creature, it was no surprise she spotted him so quickly.

"It's a naga." I pitched my voice low. "The older ones have human-level intelligence."

"What about the young ones?"

"They're half man, half snake, all instinct and no vocabulary."

"That's a *big* snake."

That's what she said.

Had Clay been here, he would have been unable to resist cracking the joke, but we were on our own.

"Its skin pattern reminds me of a water moccasin." That would fit the aquatic theme. "Do you remember if they were listed as residents of the sanctuary?"

"Maybe?" A quiver threaded her voice. "There were so many, I might have forgotten."

"It's fine." I kept my pace nice and slow. "We'll check when we get home."

We reached the car, and I slid in and shut the door. Colby flitted from my hair onto the passenger seat.

"What do we do?" She worried her hands. "The naga will eat people if they get too close to it."

They were carnivorous, and if it hadn't fed in weeks, it would be looking for an easy meal.

"We're going to lure it away." I pulled out my phone. "I need to let Clay and Asa know."

A quick text spun the guys into a tizzy of worrying about us being in danger when they were too far away to help. Rusty I might still be, but I could handle this without them. I had Colby. We made our own team.

But first there was the teeny-tiny issue of jurisdiction.

A full-fledged agent could have waded in with bureau backing. A consultant? Not so much.

That meant citing special circumstances to request clearance. It would be handed upline to the director for his approval, but I wasn't worried he would say no. The deeper I dug my hole, the easier it would be for him to bury me.

>>*Can you and Colby handle it solo?*

Clay replied first, so I chose him as the point man for this conversation.

>*We can kill it.*

>>*I hate to greenlight that, but your safety is my priority. And the civilians. Sure. Those too.*

>*What do you mean you can greenlight it?*

>>*Asa is filing the paperwork to bring you on board as we speak.*

A shiver of foreboding trickled down my spine, but it saved me from interacting with the director myself. We had grounds, based on Agent Barker's special delivery, to have me brought in. Had I not insisted that we keep Samford's killer otter infestation out of the database, Colby and I would have had our team at our backs.

>*Let me know when I'm good.*

>>*Sit tight.*

>>*Won't be long now.*

Phone on my thigh, I angled toward Colby. "There's only one way we can bring it down."

The way it didn't get back up again.

Ever.

The tips of her antennae wilted, but she nodded. "I know."

"It's not fair." I reached over to stroke her back. "The naga isn't to blame."

"It would kill innocents and might expose us to humans."

"Look at you." I ruffled her fuzz. "You've been reading the company handbook."

"There is no company handbook." She swatted my hand. "I just listen to you and Clay when you argue."

"Black Hat cares about one thing, and that's keeping paranormals a secret from normals."

That was why we hunted our own when they went rogue, to protect the innocent from exposure.

"But this time, it's more than that." Her expression tightened. "People would die without our help."

"You're right." I hesitated then tied my hair up off my neck. "I want to make sure you understand."

I almost asked her if she was okay with it, a death sentence, but how could she be?

"Will we catch who's behind this?"

"Absolutely we will."

"Will they be punished?"

"To the fullest extent of the law." The law, as dictated by the director. "I promise."

"Then I'm okay. Ish. Mostly." She settled on my head. "So, we lure it away, you zap it, and we go home?"

"That's the plan." I lifted my phone when the screen lit with permission. "We're clear to engage."

The text that came after the all-clear didn't come as much of a surprise.

>>Found Barker's partner. Guy named Reems. Died from a hoof to the skull. Hippocampus style.

>Thanks for the update.

As much as I would have loved to ask more questions, I had to track the naga before it slithered away.

"Secret agent mode—" she knotted her tiny hands in my hair, "—activate."

This was the first I was hearing of a secret agent mode, but I could guess where she got the idea: Clay.

Leaving the relative safety of the vehicle, I walked toward where I spotted the naga. It had seen me too and retreated to the alley behind the coffee shop that butted up against a former toy megastore that had gone bankrupt years earlier.

I had it on good authority I remained plenty stinky from the magics I had cast in my youth. Each time Colby channeled her energy through me, it grew fainter, an unexpected and yet oddly comforting side effect of her unique power. So, yes, the naga must have scented me.

Lucky for humans in the area, I likely spooked it. Unlucky for us, that meant we got to chase it.

"You're my eyes in the sky." I pointed to a streetlight. "Perch there and help me keep a bead on it."

"Okay."

Quick as a flash, she kicked off my scalp to launch into the night sky with dozens of other moths.

Trapped between worlds as she was, Colby frightened off the others, and I heard her sigh. We learned early on that she couldn't have mothy friends. Pets? Fly buddies? Whatever their disparate sizes would have made them. They viewed her as a predator on the hunt, and they couldn't escape her fast enough.

Palming my wand, I stalked the alley, tuning my ears for the telltale heartbeat of the creature.

"Left," Colby squeaked. "Left."

Look left? Run left? I settled on darting left and flattening myself against the bricks.

As soon as my spine hit the wall, the naga sprang past me, fangs bared and clawed hands reaching.

"Be a little more specific next time." I counted on my voice to draw its attention and kicked it in the gut. "I'm sorry," I told the hissing creature. "You don't deserve this."

But neither would its victims if I let it roam a populated area.

Too young to understand or to respond, it bared fangs already crimson with the blood of an earlier kill.

That was when I noticed the black tag, almost hidden against its glistening scales. Hung from a hoodlike ridge near its earholes, the piece of plastic glinted as the naga thrashed on the asphalt.

Magic lit the end of my wand, and I funneled enough power into the naga to knock it unconscious.

With the immediate threat removed, I got out my phone and snapped photos of the tag.

Done with the easy part, I called up to Colby, "Anything else out there?"

"Nope." She launched off the arm of the streetlamp and made a lazy circle. "Do you think—?"

As her scream echoed off the buildings, I spun toward her, heart racing when I spotted a bat.

"Grow," I yelled at her. "Bigger."

The rather large moth blossomed to a cat-sized moth in the blink of an eye, and the eager bat squeaked in terror before flapping off as fast as its wings would carry it.

"Rue." Colby smacked into me, rocking me back on my heels. "It almost got me."

"Nah." I cuddled her. "You would have zapped it first."

We were working on nonlethal protective measures for her, in case the next thing that grabbed her was human or humanesque. The instinct to incinerate what frightened her was strong, made stronger by the grimoire that still eased into her head to whisper bright ideas on occasion.

That was one leak I had just about plugged, otherwise it would already be ash. I couldn't afford to let it worm its way into Colby's head. Not only was she a power, now that she was my familiar, but she was a good kid who didn't deserve bad thoughts planted in her head when the Silver Stag made sure she had enough of those to last a lifetime.

With her shaken, I made an executive decision. "You don't need to see this next part."

For once, she didn't fight me to stay. I didn't blame her. I didn't want to finish the job either.

To kill an enemy or threat in combat was one thing. To murder a creature defending itself was another.

About the time we reached the car, Colby back in hairbow mode, headlights blinded us.

"Wonder who this is," I murmured. "Hopefully not someone trying to keep us from our sweet fix."

The thing I loved best, next to a good smoothie, was a frozen coffee drink with whipped cream on top. If you asked me, Colby and I had earned an indulgence before we headed home to establish Camp Aedan.

Especially when you considered what I was about to do.

"They're in suits," she whispered. "I can see them through the glass."

A closer look proved she was right, and I braced for unpleasantness as the black SUV's doors opened.

"Ms. Hollis," a scratchy voice greeted from the driver's side. "I hear we have ourselves a naga problem."

The white-haired man's face belonged on a bucket of fried chicken, but his eyes were dark and cold.

"Handled it." I toyed with the bulge my wand made in my pant leg. "Thanks for checking in."

"I've heard about you, I have." His partner, a younger man, grinned. "Mind if I have a peek?"

"The scene's that way." I hooked a thumb toward the alley. "Have fun."

Would I get in trouble for tranquilizing it rather than vaporizing it? Yes. But it was their problem now.

"Where are you off to in such a hurry?" The older man

approached me. "It's late for you, isn't it?"

"I'm sorry." I choked on a laugh. "Are you implying I'm out past my bedtime?"

"Dench is old school," the younger man explained. "Likes his birds in their nests before dark."

"Well, good luck with that." I opened my door. "I'm grabbing coffee and heading home."

"This is out of your jurisdiction," Dench called. "Why are you in our neck of the woods?"

"You have a Sportspalooza, and I don't." I cocked an eyebrow. "Good night, gentlemen."

"Do you have kids, lovey?" The younger guy was really pouring it on. "Baseball? Football? *Real* football?"

"Quince." Dench joined his partner. "Black witches aren't maternal. She's not here for a child."

"Pity." Quince looked me up and down. "You've got childbearing hips. Anyone ever tell you that?"

"You've got to be kidding me." I pinched the bridge of my nose. "What, exactly, did you hear about me?"

"That you bang your fellow agents." Quince grinned from ear to ear. "Is there a line for me to stand in?"

A terrible itching sensation traveled across my scalp from where Colby vibrated with rage on my behalf.

She didn't get it. They weren't this thick. Someone would have killed them long ago if that were true.

They were testing me. Or distracting me. Possibly both. To see what I would do?

With a practiced move, I raked my hand through my unruly waves, readjusting my ponytail while removing my mothy hairbow. I mimed tucking Colby into my rear pocket to cover her while she crawled from my fingers under my shirt. As long as she stayed at my back, I could protect her.

"Boys, boys, boys." I clucked my tongue. "I'm not that easy."

"That's not what rumor says." Quince swaggered closer. "You

like daemon, eh? I'm a vampire. What say you and me get a room, and I show you what you've been missing? Dench here is a centaur. Just think—"

Before he could finish the sentence and scar Colby for life, I punched him hard enough to snap his head back. His fangs descended, and dark blood trickled from his nose. He wet his lips, and his smile glistened.

"I heard you liked it rough." He brought up his hands. "Me too."

He swung for my head, and I ducked, but he didn't pull his punch so much as he turned it into a grab. For my hair. He got a fistful and yanked, but his fingers caught my scrunchie and slid out without purchase.

Blood spurted, splashing hot on my face, and I stumbled back, blinded by the spray.

"Rue." Colby yanked on my hem. "His *hand*."

Using the tail of my shirt, I wiped my eyes clean. The scene before us flashed me back to the hotel Colby and I had burned to the ground outside of Chattanooga. Until that night, I had never seen a hand just…vanish…and I hadn't caught it this time either.

There was simply Quince, spinning in a circle and shouting, his stubby arm held over his head, spouting like he was a freaking water feature. And then there was his hand, on the pavement.

"This has been fun." I backed into the SUV. "Let's not do this again sometime."

I got in, cranked the engine, and spun out onto the road.

"This is so gross." Colby fluttered to the passenger seat. "So, so, gross."

Before I could wiggle my phone out of my pocket to call Asa, I heard it ring and struggled harder to reach it. I set the speaker icon then dropped it in the seat with Colby to avoid getting my phone even grimier.

"What happened?"

The demand ought to have set my teeth on edge, but I was too relieved by the lifeline. "You tell me."

"There was a..." A growl pumped through him. "I can't describe the sensation."

"What are the odds your hand-chopper-offer demon is now following me too?"

"None." He didn't pause to think about it. "However, you might have been assigned your own."

"This is *insane*." I shuddered. "A vampire just hosed me with blood."

"He touched you." The rumble in his voice deepened. "Where?"

"He grabbed my hair in a fight." I shook out my tangles.

"Father is excited about the prospect of a daughter-in-law, but this is overstepping. I'll talk to him."

"Daughter-in-law?" I had trouble unsticking my tongue from the roof of my mouth. "I..."

"We're not there yet." His rough tone soothed me. "We might never be."

"She's turning blue," Colby tattled. "I think she stopped breathing."

"You told me to be honest," he reminded me. "I'm telling you what Father has gotten into his head."

That level of interest made me paranoid his father might expect me to pop out kids for him to pit against one another. Or against their father. I wasn't sure if I wanted kids, but I refused to raise pawns.

"Rue?" Colby lit on my thigh. "You should pull the car over."

Based on the knots twisting my guts into a roller-coaster track, I had to agree.

"Good idea." I flipped on the emergency blinkers and parked on the shoulder of the road. "Phew."

"Feel better?" Colby climbed up my elbow. "You scared me."

"I'm sorry." I picked her up and squished her to my chest. "It's just a lot to process."

"Asa?" she squeaked as I held her in a bear hug. "Why didn't the daemon help sooner?"

"My hair," I realized. "Asa, why does that lesser daemon care about my hair?"

Y'nai.

That was what he had called them.

"Hair is sacred in my culture." Amusement emanated from him. "Yours is now protected."

"Why now? Why tonight?" I raked fingers through it. "Nothing has changed."

"Except you bound a daemon to you with a blood oath."

And Asa had kissed me. Thoroughly. Several times. But I refused to let this taint that memory.

"Yeah." I yanked until my scalp twinged. "Except that."

"Father must have viewed it as an acceptance of your heritage."

That, or, you know, sticking my tongue down his son's throat.

"Hey, hey, hey." I glared out the windshield. "How would your dad know about that?"

Aside from the people I trusted most in this world, I hadn't breathed a word of my suspicions that the director had decided to produce an offspring, my father, with a daemoness. Even fewer of them knew what I had done to Aedan. I knew they wouldn't have betrayed me, certainly not to Asa's father, so...

"The hand-chopper-offer." I sighed. "It spies for your dad." I thought about it. "You weren't there when I bound Aedan, so yours wasn't present. Do you think my new best friend was already hanging around?"

"I could scent Aedan on you," Asa reminded me. "The *y'nai* must have too."

So, when Asa stormed the castle to kiss me senseless, his sidekick figured its master would be interested in knowing my allies and sneaked off to confirm the bond before scuttling off to tattle about its findings. I wasn't thrilled with the reminder his dad always had eyes and ears on us.

Just like that, Colby and I got another project added to our not insignificant to-do list.

For Asa and me to ever truly have privacy, for *reasons*, we first had to determine how the *y'nai* could mimic his magical signature. How else could it be fooling the wards? It ought to be repelled at the gate, stopped as soon as it brushed against my magic, but it sailed through with Asa.

Worse was knowing there were now *two* of them. A matched set. Practically an infestation.

"Why is my life so complicated?" I thumped my forehead on the steering wheel. "Seriously?"

"You started dating," Colby stated matter-of-factly. "Clay says men are nothing but trouble, that I should trust him, because he is a man, and he knows what he's talking about."

Boys weren't an issue I expected to face when it came to Colby, and I hoped my dating Asa didn't give her any ideas. There was too much potential for heartbreak when anyone she met was bound to take issue with never being allowed to meet their girlfriend in the flesh.

"What I need to know is, is the hand-chopper-offer still here? Like in the car? With us?"

Asa didn't answer right away, which convinced me I was being spied on.

"Hold on." I set my phone down and muted it. "We're going to do a quick spell that will check for any unwanted guests we might have in the vehicle." I walked Colby through the process. "Now we wait."

Five minutes later, we saw no glowing auras that represented other creatures were present.

That got me thinking how some lesser fae were unable to ride in cars because of their low iron content. I could spare us the headache of tinkering with the wards if *y'nai* were repelled by metals, herbs, or gems. Asa would have to fill me in on their strengths and weaknesses, so I had a better understanding of them.

"Now what?" Colby fidgeted worse as the blood dried in her fur. "Can we keep him out?"

"That's the plan."

Together, we warded the vehicle, preventing the lesser daemon from joining us or listening in.

"There." I sat back, satisfied, and unmuted Asa. "We're secure."

"Are you heading home?"

"Yes." I glanced down at myself. "Colby and I require showers, stat."

"Then we're building Camp Aedan," she chimed in. "Right, Rue?"

Rue was hoping to mix up cookies, read more about a seal and great white shifter, and call it a night.

One good thing about the recent chaos? I was so tired *all* the time, I blinked out like a light when I got two minutes to rub together.

"Sure." I couldn't say no to that squishy moth face. "Why not?"

10

"You smell like vampire." Aedan greeted us at the SUV to help unload. "What happened?"

"A vampire got handsy—" I shrugged, "—then he got unhandsy."

"You mean that literally." Aedan swung his head between us. "Don't you?"

Poor kid was going to learn fast I didn't joke about amputation.

"Colby." I pointed to the house. "Go clean up, then you can meet us at the creek."

"Yes, please." She zipped toward the porch, flying lower than usual. "This is beyond nasty."

Once she closed the door behind her, I warned him, "My hair is now a sacred object."

A laugh burst out of him at the absurdity of the statement, then it sank in I wasn't kidding.

"Oh wait." He took a generous step back. "Are you serious?"

"A hand-chopper-offer daemon is shadowing me. Just be careful, okay?"

"I'm under your aegis," he murmured, "but I'll keep my distance until I can talk to Asa about protocol."

The only three people I could vouch for were Asa, who I was in fascination with, Colby, who was a child and therefore exempt, and Clay, who had no reproductive organs, thereby rendering him a nonthreat.

A rundown of who else was allowed, as well as how to prevent future incidents, was a must.

"You do not want a *y'nai* to happen to you. Seriously. They're fast and don't award second chances."

Tilting his head, he frowned. "Then why are you smiling?"

"It's like watching a horror movie that's so bad it's funny."

That might be read as an indication I wasn't as far along as I had hoped, but come on. Some days, it was laugh, cry, or ritually sacrifice that which annoys you, and my first choice was a no-go for white witches.

"You've had a long night." He modulated his tone. "I can handle camp, if you want to go shower."

"I do." I loaded him down with boxes and shoved him ahead. "But Colby won't rest until you're comfy."

Lucky for me, I was in the habit of leaving spare clothes in my vehicle, and I snagged a fresh shirt.

I'm not saying it was clean, but it was clean*er* than what I was wearing.

I changed fast, gathered the rest of the supplies, and caught up with Aedan.

Brow tight, he glanced over his shoulder at me, but I couldn't read his expression.

"Take a picture." I smiled, flashing every tooth in my head. "It'll last longer."

"I don't get it." He slowed until I caught up to him. "Why are you doing this?"

"When you've never been shown kindness, it's hard to accept it without feeling like it's charity. Charity isn't a bad thing, but pride tells us otherwise." I mulled over how to explain it to him. "I try to live by a set of clear rules that I've established over the last ten years. They were much easier to follow before Black Hat dragged me back in, but it's..." I heaved a sigh. "I'm terrible at this."

"You make a lot more sense than you might think."

"Thanks?" I laughed under my breath. "I guess I'm saying I believe in paying it forward. The people in this town bent over backwards to protect me, help my business flourish, and bring me into their community." Without those bonds, I could never have thrived here. It was witch nature to form a coven, which I hadn't known until I embraced white magic, and the human women in my life had filled that role for me. "I took a lot in those early years, and now I'm in a better place to give some back."

"And I'm the lucky recipient?"

The comment wasn't flippant, just curious, like he couldn't believe his good fortune, that there must be a hidden catch.

"Unless you don't want to be?" I bobbed a shoulder. "It's your call. I won't hold you here if you want to go. I won't force you to do anything you don't want to do. I required the blood oath for Colby's sake." At least that was the biggest reason. That it answered the question of whether I had daemon blood was the icing on the deep, dark family secrets cake. "I can't fix your life, you have to do that, but I can give you a tent over your head, a fresh water supply, and protection for as long as you want it."

"You didn't mention how a daemon blood oath works for you. You're a black witch, right?"

"I'm...complicated."

Delma's offhand comment after she manhandled Camber struck a chord with me, but whatever she knew—if she knew anything—she hadn't shared that information with her brother. If she had, under the oath, he would have been compelled to tell me.

"I'm not in a position to look a gift horse in the mouth."

"That's the spirit." I clapped him on the back, and he jumped away. "Oops."

"I don't mean to be rude, but I like having two hands."

As often as the girls hugged me, and my neighbors and friends, I required defined parameters too.

If this insanity hurt someone I cared about, I would have to hunt down Asa's father and behead him. The downside of that would be promoting Asa, which I doubted he would appreciate, and...hmm... guess that was the only negative. Other than it was wrong to murder people. Hard to keep that in mind when Asa's father wasn't the loving or nurturing type. He was one half of the reason Asa kept himself, the darker parts of himself, hidden from everyone.

Except me.

"Clay called," Colby trilled across the yard. "He's on his way."

At the edge of the creek, I knelt and washed my hands and face clean. A shower would have to wait.

"Then we better hurry." I winked at her. "We want to impress him with our manly forest retreat."

"Heck, yeah." She pumped her fist. "The lights are going to be amazing."

"Lights?" Aedan flicked a glance at my bags. "You bought lights?"

"String lights." Colby did a little dance. "They're solar, and sparkly, and so cute."

A cringe he couldn't quite hide made me chuckle. "Cute is great."

Poor Aedan.

If his sister wouldn't kill him, he would have run screaming into the night when we broke out the lawn flamingos. He was a good sport about it, and I don't think Colby noticed his thinly veiled horror when she unveiled the solar disco ball she chose to hang from the center of his tent.

That hadn't come from the sporting goods store. She ordered it online with express shipping.

All in all, I had reined Colby in, mostly, by reminding her Aedan was a *boy*. She only ever saw the girls, who shared her love for the intersection where boho met bling.

Two hours later, we had a double layer waterproof pop-up tent with a modest covered porch erected. Royal blue, of course. The inflatable mattress, with matching blue sheets, was ready.

A camp stove stood on spindly legs in one corner, and a compact cooler full of snacks and drinks sat beside it. We bought a pair of blue folding chairs for the porch, and a cheap hammock to string between two trees. Colby's idea. She wanted him to match her. Add in the disco ball that would spin tomorrow night, after it charged for the day, and the fairy light she strung between the trees, and Aedan was borderline glamping.

"Okay." I gathered all the trash and empty boxes. "That's all the damage we can do for one night."

The blood had dried in uncomfortable places and made me itch. It was time for a long, hot shower.

Colby flew ahead, eager to touch base with Clay and get his ETA, but I had a date with the trash can.

"Hey."

I called magic into my palm before I registered the voice and extinguished it just as fast. "Mrs. Gleason?"

"I noticed the lights." She jerked her chin toward Camp Aedan. "What's going on down there?"

"The wildlife trapper I told you about asked for permission to stay on my property while he hunts whatever's out there." I finished my clean up then went to meet her at the gate. "What are you doing up so late?"

To prevent her from nudging the ward, I stepped outside and pretended to need something from the car while thanking my lucky stars I had changed shirts and scrubbed up before her arrival.

"I keep hearing this noise under the floor in the kitchen." She shifted to one side, and I got an eyeful of Bam-Bam. "I got a flashlight and checked the crawlspace, but I didn't see anything."

There weren't words for how badly that could have gone wrong if one of the dobhar-chú had still been roaming.

"Probably a raccoon." I forced my frantic heart to slow. "Maybe a possum."

"Yeah." She pursed her thin lips. "Anyway, I saw your lights on and came to check on you."

"I appreciate it." I smiled at her. "You're always looking out for me."

"That's the neighborly thing to do." She fidgeted, uncomfortable with the praise. "I ought to tell you, I heard the word about your trapper in town." She cast me an unreadable look. "What's he really doing here, Rue?"

Dang it.

Aedan should have passed through, which meant my trapper story would have held water, but that was out the window now that the town had forced me into a more creative backstory for him based on their logical assumptions.

I couldn't afford for anyone to study Aedan, or me, closely. I had to fix this. Fast.

"Aedan does wildlife relocation, among other things. He's kind of a jack of all trades." I gestured toward the driveway and started to walk her home. "When he heard about Dasher, he came to see if there was work for him in town. We got to talking, and he confided in me." I kept cutting my eyes back to the lights, like I was afraid he might overhear. "He seems like a good person who needs a hand to get back on his feet. I never meant to tell anyone about his past, but when his sister tracked him down, I didn't have much choice."

"You've got a good heart." She patted my arm. "The vulnerable sense that. They're drawn to you."

The thought was a beautiful one, so I didn't protest. I didn't agree, but I added it to my goals list. To be the person others could sense would help them. To be a force for good that attracted those who had had bad things happen to them. To be...

...more than one fluke act of kindness to a small girl that resulted in a reordering of my world.

"Do me a favor and don't shoot him in the butt, okay?"

"He's got a nice butt." She clenched her fist. "He's a bit young, but that means he's firm."

"Mrs. Gleason." I spat out a laugh. "He's my guest, not a hunk of meat."

"He's a hunk all right." She grinned, revealing uneven dentures. "You better watch him around the girls."

"Oh, I plan on it." I rolled my eyes. "They saw him once, and they've been drooling ever since."

"That's all it took for you and your man." She elbowed me in the ribs. "He's pretty, but a police?"

"I know, I know." She had no love for law enforcement. "He's so…"

Kind. Thoughtful. Smart. Funny. With a side order of viciousness and cunning.

Heck of a combination. And that was just Asa. The daemon had his own quirky yet bloodthirsty charm.

"Handsome thing like that? You better put a ring on it."

Out of habit, I rubbed the bracelet on my wrist made from Asa's hair. "We'll see."

"If he gets snapped up, don't come crying to me. I'm telling you, the good-looking ones go first."

"What about the good ones?"

"Eh." She flipped a hand. "They're men. They have one job. The least they can do is look good doing it."

We reached her house, and I had to clear my throat of laughter a few times to find my voice.

"Call me tomorrow if you're still hearing the noise." I waited as she climbed the steps. "I'll wiggle under there and see if I notice anything. If it's a nocturnal animal, we might get lucky and find it asleep."

"Good idea." She clutched her gun tighter. "Send your trapper boy."

"Okay." I walked right into that one. "Sure." I smiled. "I'll ask him to swing by in the morning."

"I promise I'll keep my gun to myself."

"I'm sure he would appreciate that."

Under her breath, too quiet for human ears, she added, "But I didn't say nothing about my hands."

Shaking my head, I began the stroll home, enjoying the frog song and the sliver of crescent moon to light my path. Witches languished without a community, but we craved nature. Our gifts, light and dark, were tied to the earth. I got a boost from people, but I found soul-deep peace in the quiet night.

Halfway home, headlights washed over my shoulders, and I stepped to the edge of the road to let them pass. Instead, the vehicle stopped, the driver door opened, and the familiar scents of cherry tobacco and green apple teased my nose.

Hand on my hip, I stuck out my thumb. "Which way you headed, stranger?"

"North." His back shielded me from the brightest light. "Which way are you headed?"

"North sounds good." I played along. "Can I hitch a ride? I can pay."

"Hmm." He prowled closer. "What did you have in mind?"

A whirring noise interrupted us, and I squinted to get a peek at Clay in the backseat.

"Roleplaying is nice and all," he said, "but not in the middle of the road in the middle of the night."

Midnight was hours ago, but I was still wired from the run-in with the agents.

Asa ducked his head, and his shoulders shook with silent laughter.

A flush heated me from head to toe. "Well, that was fun while it lasted."

"It's cute," Clay continued. "Adorable, really." He kept digging the hole deeper. "But I'm hungry."

"Fine." I raised my hands in surrender. "Let's go home."

Again, that word—*home*—rang in my ears, a presumption I couldn't afford to make on their behalf.

Asa walked me to the front passenger side door, opened it for me, and stole a kiss before he left.

The sentimentalist in me swore my lips tingled from that brief contact, but that was silly, wasn't it?

"Glad to be *home*." Clay hooked his arm around me—and my seat —and kissed my cheek. "Tell me you have cookies."

The emphasis on that word calmed my earlier jitters. I was over-thinking things, reading into them. I was, maybe, I don't know, projecting my fears onto Asa and holding him accountable for what he wasn't even thinking. Something like that. I had to give Asa room to make his own mistakes, not invent them for him.

"I have more of those pumpkin spice ice cream sandwiches left over from last month."

"You don't love me anymore." He sighed in my ear. "I can tell."

"I've been kind of busy, Clay."

"If you loved me, you would make time for me." He withdrew. "This is how it always starts."

"How what always starts?"

"You fall in love, and I'm forgotten."

"I've never fallen in love or forgotten you." I twisted in my seat. "Stop being a drama king."

"Forgotten," he moaned. "Unloved." He slumped over on the bench. "Forced to live on pumpkin spice."

Asa got in, took one look in the backseat, and shook his head. "He's been like this for hours."

"A giant crybaby?"

"The oven was broken at the coffee shop near our hotel," Asa explained. "He hasn't had a single baked good all day."

"Poor baby." I reached back and patted Clay's leg. "I promise you a full breakfast in the morning."

Asa cut his eyes toward me. "You have work tomorrow, don't you?"

"Yep." I checked the time. "In about three hours."

"You don't want to nap?"

"I'm too wired." I slid my hand down one of his braids. "I might as well stay awake."

A soft purr rumbled in his chest as I toyed with the end of his hair, which reminded me.

"Aedan wants to talk to you about touching me."

Clay shot upright, leaning forward until his nose almost bumped mine. "Do tell."

"The hair thing, you pervert." I shoved him back. "He wants to know the rules."

"I'll speak with him tomorrow, but the general rule of thumb is what applies to me applies to you too."

"And when do you plan to talk to your dad and explain that what applies to you only applies to you?"

"I've requested an audience with him." Asa's fingers tightened on the wheel. "It could be a few days."

"Great."

Colby greeted us at the door, but her usual enthusiasm was absent, even with Clay's arrival.

"Everything okay?" I coaxed her onto my shoulder. "Did something happen while I was gone?"

"I cracked the code on the tags." She leaned against my cheek. "They're all registered to the Devlin Wildlife Center."

"That's good news." I scratched her back. "It means the creatures all come from the same place."

"The sanctuary is…" Her antennae rustled. "It's funded by a trust."

"Okay." I leaned back to see her better. "What's wrong?"

"The trust was established in the name of Amalthea Vonda Winterbourne."

A metallic taste flooded my mouth, and my ears buzzed with a high-pitched whine.

Clay, who grasped the heavy significance of the name, clapped his hands once, snapping our attention to him and buying me time to pick my jaw up off the floor before Asa noticed and started asking questions.

Amalthea Vonda Winterbourne.

Mom's maiden name.

What did she have to do with this? With any of this? Why hadn't I known? What else didn't I know?

Probably enough to fill my own grimoire of family secrets, spells, and speculations.

"We should go." Clay kept deflecting, like a pro. "Check it out for ourselves."

The link to Mom was one he knew I wouldn't—under the circumstances *couldn't*—ignore.

"I've been looking at flights," Colby slid into the conversation. "Hotels too."

If Asa found it odd how quick their plans came together, or the urgency behind them, he gave no sign.

"Told you so." Clay bumped shoulders with me. "She's our own little Kelly."

Except I trusted her far more than I had ever trusted either of the Kellies on Black Hat's payroll.

"What about the shop?" I slumped into a chair at the table. "I can't dump it on the girls and run."

They shouldered so much of the responsibility of running it as it was, and the holiday rush was brutal.

"Aedan could fill in while you're gone."

"No." I whipped my head toward Colby. "Absolutely not."

"You need a part-time hire, and Aedan needs a job." She crossed her arms. "Why not?"

"He likes Arden." I exhaled. "That worries me."

If they got serious, and he told her the truth, he would drop a nuke on my life in Samford. She was too smart not to make connections between me, my "ex", the daemon I hired and let live in my yard, and what happened to her and Camber.

"One day won't be enough for him to make her fall in love, agree to run away, and marry him." Clay rubbed his jaw. "It's enough for him to get her—"

"Nope." I slapped my hand over his mouth. "We're not going there, and neither are they."

Colby scrunched up her face, but she didn't connect the dots. For that, I was grateful.

"I'm going to shower," I announced loudly to clear the room. "Then I'll start on dinner."

Eager to snag her bestie, Colby lit on Clay's head and guided him to her rig where he would watch her play until he caved and brought out his laptop to log in to his own account. Then goddess help all who crossed them in the Mystic Realms. Those two were mercenary.

The path to the kitchen was clear when I emerged, scrubbed, brushed, and sporting pajamas.

"Want some help?" Asa hovered in the doorway. "Or would you prefer the quiet?"

The stress of the day, the upcoming trip, the mention of my mom, left me sagging on my bones.

"I would like a hug." I leaned my hip against the counter. "If you have one to spare."

In the past, I would have trudged to my room, burrowed under the covers, and read until my eyes hurt.

That was how life taught me to cope: Alone.

"I have an infinite supply." He came to me, wrapped me up tight, and held me. "All yours for the asking."

"Do you think it's safe to leave Aedan with the girls for the day?" I muffled the question against his shirt. "The distraction of a sparkly new coworker might work in my favor, but is it too risky?"

"You're worried his sister will circle back?"

"Yes."

"Aedan is a good fighter. He's strong, tough, and resourceful. He's built his sister up in his mind as this unstoppable force, but she hasn't been that since he was a small child." His hands stroked up my back. "He allowed her to rule him through fear for his siblings. His siblings are safe now. There are no chains holding him except the ones on his mind."

"I'll call Camber." His speech sparked an idea. "I'll ask her to pick him up and let them carpool."

"Smart." Asa pulled back. "You're giving him a mission, new innocents in need of his protection."

"Do you think it will work?"

"Now that he's blood bound?" Asa didn't hesitate. "He would tear his sister in half if she hurt them."

"But?" I got the sense there was more. "What aren't you telling me?"

"He might sacrifice himself to get the girls away from her."

"I don't think we have to worry about that." I allowed myself a laugh. "He might try it, it's a very Aedan thing to do, but the girls are worse about adopting people than me." Heck, they *had* adopted me. "They won't let him go without a fight. He'll have to leave with them or fight beside them, and I know which option he'll choose."

"It sounds like you've made up your mind."

"Yeah." I blew out a sigh. "I'll give him a trial run in the shop."

After things settled down, we could explore the offer from Ms. Hampshire further.

"This is nice." He rested his chin on top of my head. "You and me."

"I was thinking the same." I let his heat soothe me. "It's nice to have a hug dispensary on the premises."

"You should rest." He made a soft noise when his hands thrust into my hair. "You're swaying on your feet."

"You like it." I smothered my amusement as his grip tightened. "The hair thing."

"I would be lying if I claimed I don't enjoy knowing there are repercussions for others touching you."

"I would prefer repercussions for, say, attempting to murder me. The hair thing is just odd to me." I tugged on the end of one braid. "Except in your case." I rubbed the silky length through my fingers. "Your hair is gorgeous. I could get behind no one being able to touch it but me."

The longer I spent around him, the further I could get behind no one being able to touch *him* but me.

"How about we both take a nap on the couch, then I'll help you cook?"

"An hour nap isn't worth taking." I yawned. "Might as well start mixing pancake batter."

"Humor me." He linked our hands and drew me into the living room. "Climb in."

I sat on the couch then took the hint and stretched out, facing him. He kicked off his shoes as I scooted back to give him room. He joined me, our noses almost touching, and I smiled. He slid his arms around me and wedged one leg between mine to keep from falling onto the floor. He hooked my ankle with his, wrapping around me like a vine, and I curled against his chest.

In my experience, guys given the greenlight on kissing tended to expect make out sessions every time you got within touching distance of them. But those had been physical relationships, with no emotional connection. Maybe that was why it felt more intimate to snuggle with Asa, both of us dressed, with Clay and Colby two rooms away, than anything I had experienced with a man thus far.

"Sleep," he murmured in my hair. "I've got you."

Finger hooked in the front of his shirt, I smiled into the fabric. "I've got you too."

Before the comfort of darkness embraced me, I swore I heard him whisper, "Don't let go."

I won't, I almost said. *I can't.*

But to voice those things left me too vulnerable in a moment of perfect calm I didn't want to spoil.

Feelings? Those were complicated. This? This was simple.

Simple was good.

I liked simple.

I liked Asa too.

More than I ever thought possible.

11

The dueling scents of bacon and sausage roused me from a sound sleep, but I couldn't move, and that—more than the promise of breakfast—snapped my eyes open. As the night rushed back to me, I couldn't fault the view.

Asa was a dark god in slumber. Full lips slightly parted. Bright eyes closed. Errant hairs tickling his cheek.

And, yeah, I had it bad if those were the thoughts circling my head upon waking.

A twitch of his eyelids and his lashes parted, his smile slow in coming but brilliant upon arrival.

"Morning." His hands, which had migrated to my butt during the night, squeezed. "How did you sleep?"

The press of his thigh between my legs gave me hot flashes. "Hmm?"

"There are children present," Clay called from the kitchen. "Keep it PG in there."

"PG-13," Colby contradicted him, not for the first time. "I'm not a baby."

The bickering warmed me for entirely different reasons, and I nuzzled under Asa's jaw. "Thank you."

His clever fingers traced a back pocket on my jeans. "For?"

"This." I burrowed closer. "That." I slid my hand down his chest. "Everything."

"Ace." Clay flung a potholder over the couch. "Cut that out and get in here."

I bit my lip to hold in a laugh over him getting in trouble, but a second potholder hit me in the cheek.

"Rue," Clay warned, certainty I was the instigator in his tone. "That goes double for you."

Untangling required more coordination than I ought to be forced to master so early in the day. Asa got a leg out, planted it on the floor, and finished extricating himself from me. He ignored the evidence of his arousal, which made me wonder if that was a morning occurrence for him or if I was to blame.

Honestly?

I wanted the credit.

It surprised me how much.

"You let me sleep in." I wriggled upright on the warm cushions. "All part of your evil plan?"

"Yes." Clay came to check on us. "I stole his phone so you two would rest."

On reflex, Asa checked his back pocket. "How…?"

"You don't sleep well when we're away from her." He shrugged. "She hardly sleeps at all, but she'll rest if you're here. I need you both sharp for this. We can afford a late start."

"A late start?" I jumped to my feet. "How late?"

"The girls are already at work." Clay held up his hands, palms out. "With Aedan."

Scooping the potholders off the floor, I hurled them at his head. "You knew I wanted to talk to him first."

"No," he corrected me as the projectiles bounced off his face, "you wanted to threaten him."

"Same difference." I reached for a pillow on the couch and flung that too. "The girls—"

"—are going to be fine." He caught the pillow and bonked me on the head with it. "I promise. I threatened his life, his manhood, his future children. I hit all the high points."

"He did." Colby swooped into the room, and Asa sat on the couch. Quickly. "I helped."

"You let Colby threaten him too?"

The last thing she needed was to believe she could be Clay's mini-me and start intimidating people.

"Uh, no." She bristled. "I like Aedan." She cut him a glare. "I explained the shop stuff to him."

"Oh." I rubbed my face. "Sorry." I dropped my hands. "My brain hasn't caught up with me yet."

"You never hit REM." Clay chuckled. "You've got a hangover."

"Is that a thing?" I squinted at him. "And if so, how do I get rid of it?"

"I would say get more sleep, but we both know that won't happen. Food is the next best cure."

"Food sounds good." I winced. "Sorry I flaked on breakfast."

"I've gotten lazy." He blew off my apology. "I should be helping you out in the kitchen, not leaving you with groceries and a wish list." He took my hand. "Come on, Dollface. Let's eat."

He shoved me into a chair at the table then served me a pile of amorphous blob pancakes.

"These look..." I angled my plate, "...delicious."

"They're moths," Colby whispered in my ear. "Those are blueberries for eyes."

That explained the sensation I was being watched by my breakfast. "Obviously."

Obvious, if you slapped batter into the frying pan with the force of a bug splattering on the windshield.

"Actually, they're Ace's face." Clay served Asa, who sat beside me. "How do you not see that?"

"The blue eyes must have thrown me off," I said dryly. "Sorry for the confusion."

"I considered using olives or grapes to really nail the green, but then I thought—who would eat that?"

"I thought they were turtles." Asa studied his plate. "Or air balloons."

I smothered a laugh as I drowned our pancakes in syrup and speared a bite heavy with blueberries.

"These are phenomenal," I mumbled around my fork. "What recipe did you use?"

Cookbooks littered the counter, but that was nothing new. I was always on the hunt for a new favorite recipe.

"This one." Clay tapped the side of his head. "I might be willing to share, if you're nice to me."

"I make no promises." I noticed Asa watching me eat. "How is this still a thing?"

Aside from doodling in the syrup with his fork, he hadn't done more than sip his black coffee.

"You know we're compatible," I continued. "What other purpose does sharing food serve?"

"He won't get any better until you mate him." Clay sat down with a clang of silverware. "It's instinctual."

Ignoring the mate comment, I considered the issue. "I won't change on a cellular level overnight."

Compatible today, compatible tomorrow.

"Um." Clay shoveled eggs into his mouth until he sported chipmunk cheeks. "Mph-nft."

"Asa?" I sliced a wedge loaded with butter and syrup, stabbed it with my fork, and held it to his lips. "Explain this to me."

Following Clay's example, he stuffed his mouth to give himself time to ponder his answer.

Never a good sign.

"There's a biological component to mating," he said when I

didn't offer him more. "I would taste it if you mated another. That bond changes you. It would signal you were no longer available."

"You're the only guy I'm dating." I fed him more. "Why stress over swapping spit muffins with me?"

"What I know—" he tapped his temple, "—and what I know—" he tapped his heart, "—are two different things."

"You trust me." I helped myself to his stack, genuinely curious. "It's not a fidelity issue?"

Trust was a biggie. I couldn't risk letting him worm his way deeper into my life if he was holding back. He had a firmer grasp on what was happening to us, as a couple with daemon blood, than I did. Pair that with his fae ability to coax a potential mate into baring their soul, and I was at a disadvantage.

Aside from devouring his heart, I had no means of divining his truth, and murder would kill the romance.

And, you know, him.

"It's a maddening byproduct of having a daemon father." He caught my hand. "I trust you."

Unable to resist, I ribbed him. "Even with a hot, young daemon living in my backyard?"

Cackling like mad, Colby swooped overhead. "I'm *so* telling Aedan you said that."

"Crap," I muttered, remembering the other reason I had wanted to speak to Aedan this morning before he left with the girls for work. "I promised Mrs. Gleason he would stop by and check under her porch."

"I'll handle it." Clay shot me a grin. "She's a hoot." He wet his lips. "Maybe she'll want to see my scars."

"From where she *shot* you," I reminded him. "In the butt."

"Great aim," he sighed with a faraway look in his eyes. "She's one feisty lady."

"Thank you for ruining my breakfast with your bedroom eyes for Mrs. Gleason."

"You're welcome." His chuckle was evil. "Payback is a—"

Colby sat frozen, her antennae aquiver, eager for what swear bomb he would drop next.

"—blueberry," I supplied. "Payback is a blueberry."

Her sigh rustled napkins on the table as her hero failed to let her live vicariously through him.

For the sake of expediency, I traded forks with Asa and prodded him into eating his own food.

"While you were sleeping, I mapped our drive." Colby lit on Clay's head. "And I booked our rooms."

"Drive?" I sipped my coffee. "I thought we would fly down."

"Well…" she slid Clay a glance that promised trouble. "You remember those reviews?"

The ones that mentioned missing wildlife. "Yes."

"I might have posted about the pups and gotten several responses from para rescues in the area."

The next sip of my coffee choked me, and I took a second to reorder my thoughts. "You vetted them?"

Colby didn't roll her eyes, but she didn't have to, not when she was in full-on sassy mode.

"There's not much that can be done for them," Clay offered as a reminder to her not to get her hopes up, "but it's better than the alternative. At least this way, they have a fighting chance at survival."

"Can we afford to be away that long?"

The question applied to me, and my new employee, but also to them and their caseload.

"Black Hat has seven open investigations, thirty corpses, mostly human, and we have a lead." Clay bit into a piece of bacon. "Thanks to you, we've tied your naga case to our kelpie case. Circumstantial evidence points toward the dobhar-chú also being involved, not that we can use that to our advantage." He cut me a glare. "This trip is the natural progression in our investigation."

Mention of the naga reminded me of the agent my personal *y'nai* had attacked, and of Agent Barker.

"We can't log it." I held up a hand before he could protest. "We update the brass where we're going, and I bet you there'll be a welcome party waiting for us when we arrive."

"I booked the trip on Clay's personal card," Colby comforted me. "We'll leave no trace behind."

A wan smile I hoped passed for appreciation stretched my cheeks, but it was too hot in here to breathe.

Shrug as I might, I couldn't shake the sensation that the hand of fate was shoving me toward a precipice.

"Great. Perfect. Thanks." I got to my feet. "I'm going to pack."

"Already done." He and Colby high-fived. "We figured you'd be testy, so we did the grunt work."

With the perfect excuse snatched out from under me, I lined up a second-best option.

"In that case, I'll do the dishes." I cleared the table. "I want to touch base with the girls before I go."

"You do that." Clay saluted me. "I'm off to see what Mrs. Gleason has to show me."

That sounded far dirtier than a simple porch inspection, but anything I said would only encourage him.

Before Asa or Colby could offer to help, I shooed them out of the kitchen to give me a moment to think.

A fae wildlife sanctuary, funded by a trust in Mom's name, one hemorrhaging its occupants, might be key to solving this case.

Again, fate breathed hot on my nape, raising the fine hairs in a prickling wave of foreboding.

Thanks to the scarcity of marriages among black witches, their practices were archaic. Mom's belongings passed to Dad upon her death. His worldly possessions reverted to his father. Neither had left, nor could leave, anything for me. Not so much as a last wish for who they preferred to finish raising me.

I had been too young, too heartbroken, when Megara read their wills to process anything.

Clearly, I had missed things then that had come back to haunt me now.

"Rue," Camber answered the shop phone, breathless, when I had forgotten I already dialed her. "Hey."

"How are things?"

"Christmas came early." She sighed across the line. "All he needed was a bow on his head."

"And a gift tag that read *To Camber, From Santa?*"

"Sadly, no." Her exhale softened. "He only has eyes for Arden."

Hiccup. Hiccup. Hiccup.

Ah.

So that's what that noise was in the background. Aedan had given her hiccups again.

"It's weird," she mused. "I can tell he's totally into her, but he's killing me with the politeness."

The report buoyed my mood and convinced me Aedan was, indeed, one of the good ones.

Or that, at long last, someone respected me for who and what I was—or had been.

"Kids these days," I teased. "No respect for good manners."

"I'm not saying he ought to shove his tongue down her throat, but come on. Give her your number."

There had been no time to get him set up with a phone before I left, so I couldn't help there.

"Oh, I almost forgot to ask." I heard her snap her fingers. "Are we out of winter rosebuds?"

They kept disappearing from under the counter, but I had yet to solve the mystery. These days, a couple of missing flowers didn't rank on my to-do list. If they spouted fangs and started eating people? Then they got promoted to my top five.

"If they're not in the office, we're out." I finished up and dried my hands. "I've got to go. Text if you need me."

"I know the drill." She hesitated. "Have you had a chance to talk to your friend?"

For a second, I blanked, and guilt ate me up from the inside. "We're nailing down plans today, actually."

As much fun as Clay had hanging around my house, he would get bored with video games eventually. He liked to keep busy. The no-sleep thing gave him too many hours to bump around without a purpose. The stories he told about life without TV and the internet to entertain him made me grateful for the flashy distractions available to us in the modern era. I was edging toward seventy, but I had a regimented early life. Books were okay, if they were educational. TV? Internet? Video games? The director would have banned them. Only pursuit in the excellence of wielding the dark arts satisfied him as time well spent.

Even self-defense had been off the table for me. If I couldn't defend myself with magic, the director felt I hadn't earned the right to protection. Probably why I learned early to incinerate first and ask questions never.

But Clay had a knack for people. Self-defense classes in town would occupy his time and provide a valuable community service. People trusted him. He was huge, but he was kind. Gentle. He made others feel safe.

"Great." Her attention shifted to a low conversation I could barely hear. "Customers ahoy! Gotta go."

The call ended before I could decide if she was eavesdropping on Arden and Aedan or actual customers.

Zoning out, I finished cleaning while my brain gnawed over how the sanctuary fit.

Unsure how long I drifted, I jerked to attention when Clay let himself in the front door.

"Raccoons." He gestured to thin claw marks on his face. "A chonky momma with three mini chonks."

"To get that scratched up, you must have called her that to her face."

"Nah." He waved off my attempt to fuss over him. "I did, however, cuddle one of the mini chonks."

"Yeah." I dried my hands. "That was my next guess."

Only his lack of a home and the frequency of travel for work prevented him from owning a pet. Or fifty.

Before I ended up with a yard full of strays, I ought to sit him down for the *no pets allowed* chat.

"Mrs. Gleason said they can stay." He stole an ice cream bar from the fridge. "I suspect she knew what it was and just wanted an excuse to ogle Aedan's ass as he wiggled under the house. Followed by shining a flashlight on his ass while he crawled around to locate the problem in the name of being helpful."

A whistling indrawn breath forced me to groan as Colby swooped into the kitchen, delighted with Clay.

"Let's go." Colby buzzed him, pretending not to be an eavesdropper. "We have a raid in thirty minutes."

The lap desks I bought for the SUV might have been a mistake, seeing as how they led Clay and Colby to believe the backseat ought to be their sole domain, their own mobile gaming rig.

Had her eyes not gleamed so bright with her excitement, I might have fussed a reminder about life not revolving around Mystic Realms. But that wasn't it. She was thrilled to share her world with another person, to see it was okay to have friends you never met in person in places you might never go.

"Well, in that case..." I flicked water in her face, "...let's roll."

12

The drive to Davie, Florida, took ten hours. We made it in ten and a half, after a pit stop halfway to refuel. Braver than the rest of us, Clay got his lunch from the gas station. Fried chicken wings, fried okra, fried cherry pies, and French fries. It smelled deliciously greasy, but I couldn't find hunger past my dread.

As you would expect from a sanctuary home to dangerous otherworldly creatures and beasts, we rolled up on an entrance glamoured from human sight. A literal billboard filled with dire warnings in myriad languages awaited us past its open gates. The fine print read you were on your own beyond that point. The sanctuary wasn't responsible for deaths, dismemberments, emotional trauma, or lost items.

Easy to see why parents thought signing those annual school trip permission slips was a great idea.

Assuming they had too many kids and were hoping the marsh would swallow a few of the extras.

"That's downright cheery," Clay remarked. "No wonder it's such a popular spot."

"Rue would never let me come here on a field trip." Colby mashed her face to the glass. *"Ever."*

The lush green beyond the window captivated me, but I had to agree. "Never ever about covers it."

Based on the warm ripple of power that washed over us, the perimeter defense remained active.

Interesting.

"A ward." I checked with the others. "You guys feel it too?"

Jittery from the brush of foreign magic, Colby lit in my hair. "Yes."

Beside me, Asa nodded as he scanned for signs its activation had alerted anyone to our presence.

Large groups were required to book in advance. The website made that much clear. Individuals and their families were welcome to conduct self-guided tours within the posted hours. That was in bold print too. Their staffing situation should work in our favor. I doubt they kept many full-time employees, and none would stay past the time posted on the billboard out front. Not if they were only cashiers or tour guides.

"Yep." A click signaled the laptop shutting before Clay leaned forward. "Did not expect that."

"It felt old, stable." Asa reached for his handle. "Any idea how long the sanctuary has been here?"

"It was established sixty-something years ago," Colby told us. "I don't remember the year."

The ringing in my ears was back, louder than ever. This place was founded *before* my parents died. Mom had a trust *prior* to her death that funneled money into its construction. How long after they broke ground had she died?

What had they started here? And had they finished, or had it been left undone?

"I told the rehabbers we would leave the cage beside the front gate under an obfuscation spell."

With my head so full of ghosts, I hadn't given the pups a second thought since our arrival.

"I'll get them in position," Clay volunteered. "Ace, grab their bowl and a few bottles of water?"

Once the guys settled them in, they filled the oversized bowl with cold water. The pups weren't drinking, I don't think, but it soothed them. Hopefully, their ride would be here soon. There was nothing else we could do except the spell to conceal their location from predators and poachers.

A tap of my wand blended them into the scenery, cage and all, and I nodded to Colby when I was done.

"I'll shoot the rehabbers an email," Colby said. "Then it's out of our hands."

"You did good." I ruffled the fur down her back. "Now for the fun part."

If you considered strolling into the unknown fun, which we must, as often as we did it.

"There's the welcome center." Colby jarred me from my thoughts. "We can start there."

Following her advice, we walked down the short road to a squat building that blended with the landscape by design. It was old but kept in good repair, and there were what looked like miles of board-walk leading across the marshy landscape.

A grassy river flowed around bald and pond cypress trees, and under hardwood hammocks of live oak and gumbo-limbo. Here and there, cowhorn, butterfly, and ladies'-tresses orchids bloomed. The water churned with wildlife, and the air hummed with insects, their songs broken by the cries of birds.

"This is so neat." Colby dug her feet into my scalp. "And creepy."

"Here's a handy-dandy map." Clay took a folding brochure from a display sheltered by the sloping roof. "They ask for a donation of five dollars per person." He took cash from his pocket. "Looks like..." He squinted. "Okay, I don't see where to put the money, so I'm going to shove it through the mail slot and call us paid."

Curious about this place, what value it held for my mother, I took one too. A quick scan told me the thin paper held no answers. It was a generic pamphlet, not a cipher to decode the mysteries of the universe. Still, I folded it carefully and tucked it into my back pocket.

Flames licked across my periphery as Asa exchanged one form for another.

"Rue." The daemon trotted over to me. "Hi."

"Hi yourself, big guy." I gestured toward the sanctuary. "Smell anything?"

Nose wrinkling, he breathed in deep. "Water, moss, birds, alligators, fish—"

"Anything magical?" I rested my hand on his arm. "Anything unusual?"

"Maybe." He passed me a hank of his hair. "Pet."

Oh, yeah.

He was getting the hang of blackmail all right.

"Let's go for a walk." I clicked my tongue then snapped his hair. "Giddyap."

"You want ride?" His eyes brightened. "On back?"

"Uh, no." I backed away as far as I could without letting go altogether. "I don't want to poke an eye out."

The daemon touched the tip of one horn, and a frown dragged down his mouth.

I felt like the worst kind of jerk for putting that look on his face, and I rushed to make it up to him.

"All the trees." I gestured overhead to the heavy limbs, draped in curling Spanish moss. "The limbs look pointy."

When my meaning hit him, he grinned until his canines flashed. "Rue like my horns."

"I do like your horns." I shoved him. "Now, let's get to work."

Before I thought too much about how good Asa looked wearing them.

Clay let us take the lead, and Colby flattened herself against my head. I was only half kidding about the limbs and moss, and I didn't want her to damage a wing. The daemon, as long as I kept raking my fingers through his hair, honed his focus on the hunt. We came to a fork in the boardwalk, and he pointed right.

"Smell magic." He filled his lungs. "Daemon magic."

"Surprise, surprise." I gazed out into the murky water. "Anyone you recognize?"

Say, Delma, who had either taken my warning to heart about staying out of Samford or had lured us out to the middle of nowhere to monolog us to death. Me? I was leaning toward door number two.

"No." He planted his palm on the railing. "I find out."

Fist tightening on his hair like that would hold him, I gasped when it ripped from my fingers.

His beautiful hair.

He landed with a loud splash that would attract predators and stayed under.

"What is he doing?" Clay rushed up to me then yelled at nothing, "Ace, have you lost your mind?"

The daemon's head broke the surface, and he swam to an open space about the width of Tadpole Swim. He treaded water, spinning a slow circle, nostrils flaring, then dove again.

"I don't like this." I craned my neck for a better view. "Do you sense anything?"

"Magic." Clay gripped the wood until it creaked. "Tons of it."

"Um." Colby peeked over my forehead. "There are a lot of magical creatures here, right?"

"Yeah." I saw where she was headed but waited to hear her spin on it. "What are you thinking?"

"That maybe the daemon, and Clay, sense that. Maybe it's not a single big magic. Maybe it's a lot of little ones."

"Not bad, Shorty." Clay tipped his head. "It's possible."

As the daemon spent longer and longer underwater, I began to sweat, and my chest ached with strain as if I were down in the muck with him, struggling to drag oxygen into my starving lungs.

"What if there is big magic?" The tips of my nails lengthened to claws that bit into the wood. "What if the creatures, their magic, the whole sanctuary, is meant to conceal that?"

"Rue." Clay rested a hand on my shoulder. "You okay?"

Air slipped past my lips, but I couldn't breathe. "I…"

There was no internal debate. No external explanation. Only crystalline understanding.

The daemon was in trouble. *Asa* was in trouble. And I was going in after them.

I leapt over the railing into the murky water before Clay could stop me, and swam for the last place where I saw the daemon and dove. I kept my eyes open, not that it helped, and swallowed half the swamp in a scream when a clawed hand closed around my elbow.

Gentle pats on the head assured me I had found the daemon, but when I pulled on him, he didn't budge.

He was stuck.

And his grip was growing weaker with every heartbeat.

With the daemon anchoring me, I swung my free arm in a widening circle to determine the problem. I didn't brush against the expected tree or root or debris. I hit magic. Black magic. A blistering wall of it.

A hard zap left me tasting ozone as it traveled through my body, its flavor somehow familiar.

Shaking off that peculiar sensation, I homed in on the heart of the spell, identifying a potent ward beyond my skill set. Whoever crafted it was a true master. It wasn't budging unless they decided it should budge.

But I didn't need to tear it down. I wasn't sure I could, even with Colby's help. I just needed it to let go.

Hands braced on the daemon's shoulders, I fed power into him, drawing from Colby, until he glowed beneath me. The ward shied from that white magic and spat him free. The brightness stung my eyes, but in the deepest shadows, I made out bleached bones picked clean and piled high.

Nails biting into the daemon's skin, I dragged him up after me until his head broke the surface.

"Rue—" he gurgled, "—save me."

"You're going to drown if you don't shut your mouth." The dope was actually smiling, like he was having fun. "Back to the boardwalk with you." I swam with him still latched on to my elbow, and he kicked his feet to keep pace. "Clay?" I spat foul-tasting water. "Can you give us a hand?"

"Rue." Colby glided over me but yelped when a fish jumped out of the water. "I'll, uh, wait over there."

That kid would be the death of me. The more she ventured into the world, the more it tried to kill her.

"Sure thing, Dollface." He flattened his stomach on the boardwalk and reached down for my arms. "Careful."

The daemon sank up to his ears as I gripped the rail and hauled myself back over it to safety.

A few grunts, an inventive swear, and a bellow of daemonic rage later, he landed beside me.

"Do you need CPR?" Clay towered over me. "A shower? Fresh clothes? A cookie?"

"Yes," I croaked. "Minus the kiss of life. I'm good there."

"What the hell was down there?" He sat beside me. "The water lit up like the star on a Christmas tree."

"There's a graveyard." I rolled onto my side, coughing, and let him pat my back. "And one heckuva nasty ward."

Now that I wasn't in danger of drowning, I could appreciate the intricacy of the magic used in its design.

"It's self-sustaining black magic." I let him help me sit upright. "It feeds on other creatures to fuel itself."

Flames licked the air out of the corner of my eye, and tension in my muscles relaxed by degrees.

Asa was safe. He was sound. For a dae, he was also a surprising amount of work to keep that way.

"This place isn't a sanctuary," Asa said, voice low, "it's a prison."

"What did you see?" I angled to face him, and Colby lit on my head. "What's down there?"

"I couldn't see anything, but I heard her." His hair had come loose, as it always did when switching places with the daemon, and he shoved it out of his eyes. "I didn't understand the language well enough to grasp the meaning, but it was a daemonish dialect. An old one." He twisted and glanced over his shoulder. "She tried to hold on, to drown me, after you zapped her. I don't mean the ward, either. Whatever cage is holding her, she can reach through its bars."

Odd that she hadn't grabbed for me. Her hands must have been too full of struggling daemon.

"Asa," I breathed. "Your back." I flicked Colby a glance. "We need to heal this. Who knows what's in that water? He might get an infection. Those claw marks are deep."

Five long furrows sliced open the smooth skin of his back, the thinnest a hairsbreadth from his spine. His blood trickled in crimson rivulets and pooled on the planks beneath him.

An unspeakable rage suffused every cell of my body that burned so hot under my skin I had to grit my teeth or risk combustion.

Someone hurt him.

Someone *hurt* him.

Someone hurt *him*.

The mantra buzzed in my head, a swarm of bees eager to sting anyone who got too close, and I growled.

Soft lips pressed against mine, and strong arms enfolded me, drawing me onto Asa's lap.

"Shh," he whispered in my ear as he rocked me. "It's all right."

"I want to kill something," I whispered back. "It hurt you, and I want to end it."

Without knowing what it was or how it got there, I wanted it dead. By my hand. With my claws.

"I'm flattered." A purr ignited in his chest. "But I don't need you to kill anything for me."

"Our girl does not do emotion well," Clay said with affection. "Your daemon hormones aren't helping."

Pretty sure my hormones, not his, were the problem.

"Let's walk the rest of the sanctuary. We need a bigger picture of what's happening here."

"We can come back tomorrow," Asa offered, rising with me, refusing to let go. "That might be best."

"We're here now." I wriggled out of his grip. "We need to do what we came here to do."

Colby lit on my shoulder, her cheek soft against mine, and we began healing him.

From start to finish, it didn't take as long as it used to, what with all the practice we were getting lately. The second his wounds knit together, I set out with Colby to finish mapping the sanctuary in my head.

Away from Asa, from the panic of the moment, the fury I had yet to quash, I breathed easier.

"You get murdery when you love people, huh?"

Three steps after Colby's question, I managed to grate out, "I get murdery over you, yes."

"You like Asa, a lot."

"I do." That was easy enough to admit. "But I don't think I like that I like him."

"You believe it makes you weak." She tugged on my ear. "Vulnerable?"

"To love someone is to give them power over you." I scratched my wrist under the bracelet. "That's dangerous for someone like me. I don't like feeling controlled. No. I don't like feeling *out of control.*"

"You don't like feeling at all." She snorted. "You treated me like you do Asa, in the beginning. You were nicer, because I'm a kid, but you didn't know what to do with me."

"Colby..." I slowed my breakneck pace. "I'm sorry if I did it wrong."

Her velvety feet tickled as she climbed my face, forcing me to hold her stare.

"You did a great job. You just had to get the hang of it. You'll get the hang of Asa too."

Dragging her down into my arms, I cuddled her against my chest. "How did you get to be so smart?"

"Clay vents about you guys a lot." She giggled. "A *lot*." She grinned up at me. "I mostly just told you what he's always telling me. He thinks he gets it, but he doesn't. Not like I do." She turned solemn. "This stuff is hard for you. You have to work at it. More than most people."

"Thanks?"

"Nobody loves like you do." She rubbed her cheek on mine. "It's worth waiting for."

A bubbling noise drew my attention to the water in time to save me from the tears burning the backs of my eyes. A pair of red orbs set in a knotty black face emerged from the water, bubbles popping near the tip of its flat snout.

"That's a makara." She pressed against me. "They have ten legs and three mouths."

A shudder rippled through my shoulders. "Nice to know I went swimming with that."

"You went swimming with a lot more than that." Colby wrinkled her nose. "To save your *boyfriend*."

"Goddess bless, not you too."

As often as Colby traveled to work with me in hairbow mode, I knew exactly where she picked up the habit. I only just trained the girls to use Asa's name instead of calling him *Boyfriend*. I did *not* want to fight that battle on two fronts.

A quick check over my shoulder told me the guys were hanging back, giving us space to talk, which was nice. I had no doubt they overheard every second word, no matter how low we kept our voices, but I appreciated the gesture.

"Do you see that?" Colby leaned forward. "Is that a string? From a balloon maybe?"

The milky white cord was too thick for that, but it had no business out in the middle of nowhere. Though I had to admit, balloon releases were popular, and those suckers ended up as trash in the darnedest places.

"I'm not sure." I slowed as we neared where it hung over the boardwalk. "It kind of looks like…"

"Spider," Colby squeaked. *"Nope, nope, nope."*

An eight-legged nightmare the size of a small pony descended from the canopy. Its body gleamed in oil-slick colors, its eyes opaque as moonstone, and chelicerae, pincherlike appendages, extended from its mouth. They click-clacked together, dripping ichor, and its fangs gleamed.

In the blink of an eye, Colby was gone, and I was alone. "What kind of familiar are you?"

"The kind that does *not* want to get eaten by a spider," she squeaked. "I'm a moth, Rue. A *moth.*"

Even in cat-size moth mode, she was no match for this monster arachnid.

Me?

I didn't want to be a match for it. I would come back later. With a flamethrower.

"We're just passing through." I held up my hands. "No need to get twitchy."

"You are not welcome here," it whistled through a beaked opening. "Leave, and never return."

This guy couldn't be an official member of the welcome committee.

Pretty sure reviews would have mentioned this to lure in the Harry Potter crowd with Aragog photo ops.

"I'm afraid I can't do that." I spread my hands in a gesture of peace. "A case brought me here."

"Leave," it ordered again. "Never return."

"Is this how you greet all tourists, or am I special?"

The creature proved how unspecial it found me when it shot me in the face with sticky webbing. Like a total idiot, instead of reaching for my wand, I touched my cheeks on reflex, and my hands stuck fast.

"Little help," I mumbled through the glob over my mouth. "Guys?"

A bestial roar shocked birds into flight as Asa caved to his daemon half. "Rue *mine*."

Awkward his battle cry might be, but I was grateful for the thunder of his footfalls on the planks.

Pressure tugged on my skin, and I yelped when I got hauled forward a full step and bumped into the rail. I held on to it for all I was worth as the spider attempted to reel me in, face-first.

"I didn't sign up for this." Clay wrapped his arms around my waist. "I did *not* sign up for this."

Lips cemented together, I mumbled at him to hurry, hurry, hurry.

Over the course of my life, I had seen some things. This? No one should see this.

The daemon leapt up, fisted a spider leg in each hand, and yanked it out of its web. It hit him with a thud that shook the boardwalk, and the tugging sensation intensified until I bumped into Clay while fleeing what I couldn't see through the holes in my solidifying mask.

"You're going to have to cook it," Clay yelled over the din. "And quick. Before it envenomates Ace."

This was going to suck.

Hard.

The only way for me to zap the spider at a distance was to use the web smothering me as a conduit.

I could cook it, yeah, but I might roast myself in the process.

The daemon roared and ripped a leg off the spider, throwing it over his shoulder. It hit me, stuck, and orange goo dripped through the gaps in the web onto my face. As the ichor stung my eyes, I concluded I would rather melt off my face than stand around mostly blind and wholly vulnerable.

Extreme?

Maybe.

You get shot in the face with spider butt juice, and then we'll talk.

Mumbling behind my closed lips, I tried to get my point across to Clay. I rolled my shoulders to shake him free then tightened my fingers on the webbing and pushed as much magic into the fibers as I could summon without dragging Colby into the mix, since she would have to heal me solo after this.

"*Ace.*" Clay shouted the warning from behind my shoulder. "Hit the deck."

A splash confirmed the daemon was out of my crosshairs, and I dialed up the magic until it burned me.

An insectoid screech of agony pierced the night sky, and the stench of burning tires filled my nostrils.

"Stay back," Clay barked to someone I couldn't see. "It's still alive."

A slight pressure on my foot warned me Colby had landed on my shoe to help.

"I don't care." Her sass was off the charts. "I have to protect Rue."

A fuzzy hand slid under my pant leg until it touched skin. Had I not known Colby was there, I would have screamed, flopped over the railing, and risked the makara rather than discover what had tickled my ankle.

The white witch life was making me soft.

No self-respecting black witch would need to check her pants after this.

I could tell when the spider well and truly died, because Clay quit chanting "Kill it, kill it, kill it" under his breath.

What I couldn't tell was if Colby had been successful in saving my face, or if I had melted it off and was so euphoric over killing the spider—the *talking* spider—that pain hadn't set in yet. Adrenaline was a heck of a drug.

"We're done here tonight," Clay announced. "We're going to a hotel, we're all going to bathe in bleach, then we're going to shower in bleach, then we're going to skip dinner and eat dessert until we can't move. Then, and only then, we're going to pass out and forget this ever happened."

For as long as I had known Clay, I had never realized he was an arachnophobe.

Then again, until that bulbous body descended toward Colby and me, I hadn't realized I was one either.

Maybe we were situational arachnophobes. Or just in possession of common sense.

"I get Rue."

Familiar arms enfolded me, lifting me against a heated chest that smelled of barbequed arachnid.

"Hang in there, Dollface." Clay patted my knee. "We're going to get that off you."

So, I had flambéed the spider, but Colby had spared me from roasting myself.

Good to know.

"Hold on, Rue." Colby brushed my elbow. "Try not to struggle."

Until she mentioned it, I hadn't noticed I was tugging at the web glued to my face.

"You don't want to rip off your skin." Clay sounded close to tossing his cookies. "Just hold still."

The daemon loaded me in the back of the SUV then yielded to Asa, or so I thought, based on the lick of heat that flashed one side of my face. The SUV rocked when Clay joined me on the bench, but he didn't tuck me against his side like always. This time, I was pretty sure he was plastered to his door.

The door on the opposite side of the vehicle.

As far away from me as he could get.

With a sigh, I settled in and tried not to feel like the living embodiment of Edvard Munch's *The Scream*.

Acetone worked wonders on the spiderweb's stickier bits. Asa was the only one brave enough to use the supplies Clay bought from a drugstore before we hit the hotel to help me. He cut away the worst of the gunk with scissors then set my hands to soak while he daubed my face clean with cotton balls.

He worked with the intensity of a man given a task in which failure was not an option.

A slight crease appeared on his brow, and his bright eyes were narrowed in study. He didn't say much—he wasn't one for filling silences with empty words—but I did catch the slight curve of his lips now and again. Each time, he shook his head as if to rid himself of some fanciful idea.

"Are you laughing at me?"

The question brought his head up, and a flush climbed over his cheeks. "At myself, mostly."

"What's so funny?"

"I'm happy." He rubbed beneath my eye. "Being here, with you, makes me happy."

"You're sure you're not laughing at me?" I squinted at him. "Not even a little?"

"Maybe a little," he allowed. "You were willing to burn off your face to get rid of that spider."

"And I would have had no regrets. Giant talking spiders should not exist."

The crease grew into more of a crevasse. "It spoke to you?"

"You didn't hear it?" I scratched at my knuckles with my fingernails. "It told me to leave or else."

"That can't help the tourist trade." He dumped his trash. "Did it say anything else?"

"'You are not welcome here,'" I quoted it, trying to forget its beak-mouth. "'Leave, and never return.'"

"That level of sentience is unusual in a creature that would choose to live in a sanctuary."

Choose, because sentient creatures made their own choices.

Meaning it wanted to be there. Unless...

"Do you think it could have been enchanted?" I scratched my nose on my shoulder. "Black witches have been known to use creatures as messengers."

"An enchantment would explain why you're the only one who heard it. Perhaps it's keyed to witches?"

Uncertainty itched beneath my skin, but I couldn't voice my concerns to Asa. Old secrets left a sour taste in my mouth, but I had held them too tight, for too long, to let go on the spot. Even if I wanted to air out the past, and I wasn't sure I did, I had no idea how to throw open the painted-over windows to my soul.

The trust was in Mom's maiden name, but if the spider had been meant for me, then my parents had set it on its path *after* they were married. *After* I was born. That had to mean, whatever they had caged, they didn't want it disturbed.

Had Dad been the one who cast the spell? Had it been specifically targeted to me?

"Perhaps," Asa mused, "it was a security protocol activated using your power."

"To contain the creatures?" I snorted. "He was doing a fine job then, wasn't he?"

"Or to banish visitors with enough magic to cause trouble before they harm the wildlife."

"I'll say again." I laughed softly. "He was doing a fine job then, wasn't he?"

Either I got the tone wrong, or Asa knew me well enough to tell when I was deflecting with humor.

"You think it was there to send a personal message."

"Hard not to take a web to the face personally."

The bite in my voice earned me a considering look before he resumed his task.

"What are we going to do about the cell in the swamp?"

"Do we have to do anything?" I wasn't being flip. "We don't know what's in it, or who put it there."

Though I was starting to think my parents had built it and that they hadn't wanted me anywhere near it.

"A terrible power was hidden in that marsh. We don't know if Delma discovered it, or if rogue Black Hats roused it first, but we have an obligation to ensure neither releases it. The contents of that cell are what brought them here." He studied me. "The reason they brought *you* here."

A tendril of shame wriggled through me that I would run away from this mystery while he ran toward it.

The link to my mother was throwing me. *Hard.* I couldn't shake the impression of being led by the nose.

Mom was gone. Dad too. Had been for decades. They weren't leaving breadcrumbs for their daughter to follow, but someone must be, and that guiding hand wasn't letting me go until I figured out their hints.

"The thing in the cell is feeding on creatures who live in the swamp." I flexed my hands in the bowl, delighted to discover my fingers could move independent of one another again. "You saw those bones."

The wards were operational. The creatures ought to have been contained. This was no critical failure the sanctuary had to answer for. It was a deliberate trap-and-release scheme. But why? What was the point?

"I did." He lifted his gaze to mine. "I would have been one more skeleton without you."

"Your daemon thinks he's invincible." I bumped his shoe with mine. "He's got to work on that."

"He does seem to believe he's an unstoppable force lately."

"He's showing off." I read between the lines. "For me."

"He can be reckless, thoughtless, at times. He can't bear the idea of you being hurt."

True, but he had cause to think highly of his prowess.

"How can you win every single fight against every single challenger and not begin to feel invincible?"

"Challenges are about brute strength. No magic allowed. No weapons allowed. That makes it easy."

There was nothing easy about taking down a daemon, even for a black witch.

"He's not an unthinking brute." I set my jaw. "And, yes, I'm defending you against you."

"I appreciate the vote of confidence." Asa leaned forward, thought about kissing me, noticed the goop still on my skin, and withdrew. "Clay would never let us live it down if we got stuck together."

A snort blasted out of me, and I couldn't stop the laughter that followed. "That would be so hot."

The corners of his eyes crinkled. "We would be stuck together forever."

"*Stuck* is a strong word." I heard how that sounded and bit the inside of my cheek. "So is *forever*."

"I don't need the promise of forever." He resumed cleaning me. "Just let me stay for now."

"I can do that." I wiggled my fingers. "And not just because Clay is a crybaby wimp who ditched his former partner to suffocate in spider butt gunk while he rocked on the ground and sucked his thumb."

"I heard that," Clay bellowed from the living room. "Privacy is an illusion."

Among the paranormal set, yes, it was, and there was no changing that. Either you learned to live with it, or you spent the rest of your life setting circles or casting spells to ensure no one over-heard the banal parts of your day. Or the mushy ones. As much as I would love to hoard Asa's sweet words, I had been a witch too long to bother wasting magic on frivolity.

With another trek through the sanctuary on tap for tomorrow night, I was happy saving mine in case the giant talking spider had equally chatty friends.

13

I slept the sleep of the traumatized and woke up tangled in sheets my brain insisted were spiderwebs.

"Hey." Warm hands helped free me. "You're okay."

"What are you...?" I flipped my gaze down to check for decency. I passed. Sadly, Asa did too. "Did I wake you?"

"You were thrashing in your sleep." He threw the crumpled fabric on the floor. "I came to check on you."

"What's everyone else doing?" I pushed upright. "What time is it?"

"It's five o'clock." He straightened to his full height. "Clay's watching a holiday baking contest."

"Colby?"

"Asleep in Clay's room."

"Sorry I woke you." I patted the mattress beside me. "I must have been making a lot of noise."

Asa's chin drooped until it bumped his chest, and he rubbed the base of his neck. "Not really."

"That sounds like you were spying on me, Mr. Montenegro."

"I fell asleep in my bed, but I woke up outside your door."

"The daemon." I shook my head. "The spider must have freaked him out too."

"I don't mean to invade your privacy." He dipped his chin. "I can't seem to help it."

The daemon had proven he could sneak around while Asa was asleep, so I couldn't very well blame him.

"Question." I wiggled my toes on the carpet. "Will I fall asleep with you in my bed and wake to the daemon?"

"Me?" Asa swallowed hard. "In your bed?"

On more than one occasion, he and I had fallen asleep crafting together in his bed or mine, which sounded sad, even in my head. But we hadn't gotten handsy. Except with our hobbies. Our night on the couch was our longest sustained contact to date.

Unable to resist the urge to tease him, I fluttered my lashes. "After I ravish *you*, will I wake up to *him*?"

A line formed between his brows. "I don't know."

"Wait." I drew my legs under me. "I was kidding." I leaned forward. "Are you serious?"

"He's the other half of me." A shrug rolled through his shoulders. "I'm not sure what he'll do."

"He won't expect, um, the same treatment, right?"

"No." Asa's eyes sparkled at my expression. "He has no carnal tastes."

The implication, that Asa had the lion's share of carnality, tightened my abdomen.

"I've never dated two guys at once." I rubbed my forehead. "It gets confusing fast."

Truthfully, I had never dated anyone. Ever. Hookups weren't relationships.

Clay knocked, even though Asa hadn't shut the door behind him, and popped his head in.

"Ready to talk strategy?" He glanced over his shoulder. "We can order in—"

Another knock, this one more distant, drew all our attention.

"Where's Colby?" I was hazy on the layout of our rooms. "Does she need to be let in?"

"She's drooling on my pillow in a connected room." He frowned. "Be right back."

While Clay answered the door, I grabbed for my wand and secured it in my pajama pants. As I prepared for a confrontation, Asa hunched his shoulders, lowered his head, and began the process of making himself smaller, less frightening, unthreatening.

I hated it.

But it worked for him.

"Hey," Clay greeted our unexpected guests. "Haven't seen you guys in years."

"Clay," a man replied, his voice soft. "Good to see you, man. It's been too long."

"Clay," a woman echoed. "It's nice to see you."

"Come on in." He ushered them into the living room area. "What brings you to this neck of the woods?"

"Your teammate," the woman answered. "Rue Hollis."

"She attacked an agent," the man said. "Cut off his hand." He made a *thwack* noise. "The director wants her brought in for questioning."

"You've got the wrong witch." Clay kept his tone polite. "That's not Rue's style."

"His partner saw it," the woman countered. "Are you accusing him of lying?"

"We know you're close to Rue," the guy added. "You guys were partners back in the day."

"But no agent is above Black Hat law," she finished for him. "Where is she?"

"I am close to Rue, and we were partners." Clay stayed jolly. "But you're missing a key piece of information. Orion Pollux Stavros's son and heir is fascinated with her. She's been given a *y'nai* bodyguard to protect her most sacred self." I heard the smile in his voice. "When the agent attacked her, he must have grabbed her hair, and the *y'nai* took exception to that."

"We heard rumors." Her tone soured. "They're in fascination?" Her disgust was clear. "You're certain?"

After pressing a finger to his lips, Asa padded into the bathroom, flushed the toilet, then left the room.

"Forgive me," he murmured, shutting the door behind him. "I was in the bathroom."

"Agent Montenegro." A thready quality strained her greeting. "I'm Agent Mickelson, and this is my partner, Agent Ferragamo."

"A pleasure to meet you both." He remained cowed, lesser, whisper soft. "How can I help you?"

"We need to question your…Ms. Hollis…about an incident in Rainsville."

"My partner has already explained what happened and why." Asa let a tiny hint of his true power shine. "I'm more interested in why two agents tracked *Agent* Hollis to a remote location, threatened her, and then put hands on her."

"We're investigating both sides—" Agent Mickelson began.

"There is only one side," Asa cut in. "She took action to protect humans in a populated area, and two agents confronted her after the fact." A hint of temper flavored his rebuke. "They put hands on her. They were punished. No further inquest is necessary, unless you would like her to bring fellow agents up on charges of misconduct."

"Given her recent track record for weeding out rogues," Clay added, "I believe the director will rule in her favor."

There was no hiding the fact cases I had been involved in up to this point had resulted in the deaths of fellow agents. We hadn't advertised the cause behind those executions, but coups were common enough that agents would connect the dots without much effort.

"Does he know you're here?" Asa pounced on Clay's reasoning. "Does he know about the attack?"

"The director can't be bothered with every infraction," Agent Mickelson countered. "He's far too busy."

"Hmm." Clay made it sound like he was agreeing. "How about I call him, and we settle this now?"

"That won't be necessary," Agent Ferragamo assured Clay. "This was a routine inquiry. We have all the information we require at this time." The doorknob rattled. "Thank you for your cooperation."

"We'll be in touch," Agent Mickelson promised. "The director's favor is a fickle thing."

Not where I was concerned. No matter how hard I worked to get myself disowned, I failed every time. A more sentimental person might think he was desperate to hold on to the last family he had, but I knew him better than that. He was why my grip on softer emotions was slippery at best.

When the door closed and the elevator chimed in the hall, announcing the agents were gone, I stood.

"Well, that was interesting." I joined Asa and Clay. "The vampire tattled on me."

There was an unspoken rule among Black Hat agents.

Don't dish it out if you can't take it.

Common sense, really.

No one cared how agents vented their pent-up aggression, as long as it wasn't on the clock, didn't affect their case, and no one died. Unless, like Asa, a challenge was issued that stemmed from cultural mores. I was fuzzy on the details, since the *no one died* part was more of a guideline than a rule, but whatever.

To pick a fight then run to the director and cry about any resulting boo-boos was bad form.

The whole confrontation had struck me as bizarre at the time, and it kept getting weirder by the minute.

"I'm not saying it's been boring the last ten years or so," Clay began, "but you know how to shake things up, Dollface. It's like a revolution was just waiting for you to return before it kicked off."

Except the revolution had kicked off before I ever stepped back onto the field.

Had the Silver Stag wannabe not baited his trap so well, I wouldn't be here, back in black.

And, for better or for worse, I never would have met Asa.

"Yeah, well." I rubbed my arms. "Yo momma."

"That's the best you've got?" Clay scoffed. "I'm embarrassed for you."

"You're the one who taught me how to talk smack. Be embarrassed for yourself."

"That was ten-plus years ago," he defended. "Your insults are out of date."

Asa's phone rang, and he answered it in a language that chimed like bells in his resonate voice.

"We're going downstairs to grab breakfast," Clay announced, gripping my arm. "Continental style."

Asa frowned, promised to keep an ear out for Colby, but was then drawn back into his conversation.

Only after we exited the elevator, three floors down from our suite, did Clay get to the point.

"The director wants an audience with you." He headed to the *pour your own wuffle* station. "Why else would he dispatch two random agents to harass you? You barely had your clearance to act on the naga sighting. There's no way they saw a fresh case pop in the database and ran to help out of the goodness of their hearts. Black Hats don't work that way."

Most agents did their level best to avoid work, unless it directly related to their own caseload.

"He told them to provoke you but not lay hands on you," he speculated. "That way, when you beat them senseless, they had cause to bring you in, but it went sideways when one of the guys fisted your hair."

Better than anyone, Clay knew how the director thought, and his scenario made perfect sense. I couldn't even gripe that the director hadn't gone the direct route. He had called me. Repeatedly. Three times just today. I was the one ignoring him, forcing him to get creative in orchestrating our reunion.

"I came back." I picked over the toppings. "Why can't that be enough for him?"

"It will never be enough," Clay warned. "You know he won't rest until you're under his thumb again."

A chill swept up my spine to even ask, "Do you think I should set up a meeting with him?"

As much as I hated to give him what he wanted, I didn't want him to escalate until someone got hurt.

Worse than the handsy, or un-handsy, as it were, vampire.

"I do." He hesitated until I prompted him by stealing a walnut off his plate. "I also think if you're going to pit you and Ace against the world, then Ace needs to know." He smacked my hand. "Everything."

About me, about my parents, and about my grandfather. Until he knew that, he couldn't know the rest.

That the sanctuary was tied to my family, and maybe to me, in some way that might change everything.

"I need to tell him." I dreaded it, but he deserved to know. "I don't want to change how he sees me."

"Do you think for one hot second that Ace will care who your grandfather is? Who your father was?" He sprinkled chopped nuts into his batter. "His father is a king. He's used to dealing with uppity types that think they own the world and everything in it." He poured the batter. "What's really got you worried? There has to be more."

"No one knows me, the real me, except you. I have a lot of baggage to unpack."

In so many ways, the woman Colby knew as Rue was born the same night she died.

"He told you who he was, and you didn't blink. Give him the same opportunity."

"What if he does? Blink, I mean?"

I had done horrific things in my life. That I had done them under many names didn't erase the fact I was responsible for my actions. So much of what Asa did, he did to stay alive. I couldn't fall back on that. There was a survival element, sure, but I had also been a huntress. I enjoyed the kill.

And the feasting, the gorging, afterward.

"Then he's not the man either of us thought he was, and he's not worthy of you."

Bumping his shoulder with mine, I attempted levity. "I would miss his hair."

"So would he." Clay's big-brother instincts kicked in. "I would drug him and then shave his head."

Walking to the cooler, I grabbed small cartons of milk and orange juice. "And use the hair for a wig?"

"Only if you promise not to get weird about it. I don't want you following me around, touching it."

We both broke into laughter that helped ease the tightness in my chest.

Once Clay finished stacking waffles—two for Asa, eight for him, none for me—we trudged upstairs.

The meal was quiet, scraping forks and clacking spoons, and no one looked at anyone.

Busy shredding a napkin into tiny squares, I left Asa to eat without assistance for once.

All too soon, Clay invented a reason to get something from the SUV with Colby, leaving me with Asa.

"You're upset." He read me with ease. "Was I wrong to speak to those agents on your behalf?"

"What?" I caught up to his meaning a heartbeat later. "No, that was fine. Thanks, actually."

"What's the matter?" He kept his distance. "Did I do something?"

"*No.*" I tipped back my head. "I'm doing this wrong."

"Are you...breaking up with me?"

"You're not getting away that easy."

I laughed.

He didn't.

"I'm just going to lean into your fae juju and blurt it out."

"All right."

The wariness in his voice unhinged me, but it was about to get so much worse.

"Director Nádasdy is my grandfather. His son, Hiram, was my father."

A kaleidoscope of emotion, too bright and sharp for me to read, spun across his features.

"Just to be clear," he said, much later, "you're not breaking up with me?"

"No?" I wrapped my arms around my middle. "You did hear me, right?"

"Yes." His gaze found mine. "I was braced for worse."

"Worse?" I reached for his hand on reflex but withdrew before I touched him. "What could be worse?"

"You deciding I'm not worth the trouble of dating two people at once."

Wincing, I could have kicked myself. I hated that I had manifested a cloud of doom that had been floating over his head ever since I opened my mouth and let those words fall out.

"You're worth it." I forced myself to be bold, to take his hand, mine sweaty and unsure. "I wouldn't have told you who I am if I didn't want you to have all the facts."

"Clay knows?"

"Clay was planted in my life by the..." I tasted bile, "...by my grandfather, so yes. He knows. He's owned by my grandfather, which means Clay can't betray him. He was the perfect babysitter for me."

"Colby?"

"That kid is my life." I tried to get my hand back. "Do you really think I keep secrets from her?"

A thoughtful calm settled over him. "I'm the first person outside your family that you've told."

"Yes." I scowled at his grip. "Do you want a trophy?"

"Rue," he said softly, drawing me closer. "You know who my father is, and you accept me despite him. Why do you think I would hold your grandfather against you?"

"It's not him." I gave up and let him comfort me. "It's me." I sighed. "Who I was. What a did. How I lived."

"You upended your entire life for Colby. You're not that person anymore. Why would I judge you as if you are?"

"I'm one heart away from being her again." I wanted him to understand. "The craving is always there. The impulses are always there. The memory of how invincible I felt…how unstoppable I was…"

"No one is invincible." He dragged me onto his lap. "No one is unstoppable."

"Black magic says otherwise." I snuggled against his chest. "It's an unimaginable high."

"And I almost drugged you again." His tone softened. "I would have never forgiven myself for that."

Truthfully, I wasn't sure I could have forgiven him either. I wouldn't have been in my right mind. Rational thought would have flown out the window like a cartoon witch on a broom. I could taste blood in my mouth, recall the chew of the fibrous organ that contained a person's magical core. I salivated thinking about it, and my stomach cramped as old hungers roared to the fore.

"You stopped when I asked you." I toyed with the buttons on his shirt. "That's what matters."

"The director arranged for those agents to bring you in, didn't he?"

"Clay thinks so, and I agree it sounds like something he would do."

"He's that desperate to make contact with you?"

"Yeah." I showed him my phone, the blocked calls in my log. "I've been ignoring him."

"Is that wise?"

"Nope."

"What will you do?"

"Call him and set up a meeting." I steeled my jaw. "He won't stop until he gets what he wants. Right now, it's my attention. If I don't give it to him, he'll escalate until he gets it."

"Did the visit from those agents prompt this heart-to-heart with me?"

"Yes and no." I heard the ache in his voice and regretted causing it. "I've wanted to tell you for a while." I elbowed him. "Probably your faeness forcing me to blab my darkest secrets to you."

A laugh moved through his chest. "You realize, by that logic, you accept that we're soulmates."

"Logic has nothing to do with how I feel about you," I confessed. "I can't help myself."

"You don't like being helpless."

"Who does?" I pressed my palm against his chest, right over his heart. "But I like you."

"Even if you're compelled to like me?"

"Even if." I squinted up at him. "That's not how it works, right?"

"What if I said yes?"

"What if I took off my shoe and beat you with it?"

"Nothing about us is forced." More laughter shook him. "You could resist. You could tell me no."

No.

I really couldn't.

"Will you go with me?" I kept my head down to avoid reading into his expression. "To see the director?"

"I will." He covered my hand with his. "Of course, I will."

"Thanks."

I let myself soak up his steadfastness, then I pushed upright and attempted to slide off his lap. I didn't make it far, and I didn't mind. It was weird. The not minding. I didn't feel the urge to break each of his fingers for touching me or holding me or keeping me close. The keeping me part. Yeah. It was nice too.

About the time I caved to staying where he put me, Clay and Colby returned with empty hands.

"Turns out I didn't leave my bobby pins in the car." He checked us over to see if we were okay. "Oops."

"We need to discuss next steps." I strove for a professional tone. "The sanctuary is a problem."

As it happens, it's hard to appear professional when you're sitting on your boyfriend-type person's lap.

"It's hiding more than missing exhibits," Clay agreed. "You want to take it from here, Dollface?"

A subtle introduction it was not, but he wanted to verify I had told Asa, that I trusted him with this.

"The trust Colby mentioned," I began, "the one funding the sanctuary…" I struggled to locate my voice. "Amalthea Vonda Winterbourne was my mother." Asa was the only one who hadn't known. "I'll have to talk to Megara to check the details, but Mom must have known about what's in the cell. The ward was pure black magic. Dad might have cast the spell himself."

And if that were so, I wanted another look at that sliver of his mastery over the dark arts.

"The spider was a warning." I wet my lips. "For me."

"How do you figure?" Clay scratched his cheek. "It was just a spider."

"Just a spider?" Colby's wings jittered. "You asked me to sleep with you because you were scared."

"You just got demoted to third best friend," he informed her with a sniff. "How could you?"

"The spider talked to me," I cut in before the real bickering started. "It told me I wasn't welcome."

"It talked to you?" Colby's horror set her antennae on end. "In your mind or what?"

That confirmed she hadn't eavesdropped on our disturbing conversation.

"Good question." Clay leaned closer. "I didn't hear it."

Asa threw his lot in with them. "Neither did I."

"Why tell me to leave?" I rubbed the skin over my heart. "Why didn't they want me there?"

"Whatever's in that cell," Clay said, thinking it through, "they didn't want you near it."

"Someone did." I swallowed the lump in my throat. "Why else lead me here?"

Freeing the creatures in my neck of the woods guaranteed I took notice of the sanctuary.

The tie to my mom? It ensured I had to see it for myself. That I had to know. I had to understand.

Where did Black Hat fit in? Where did Delma?

"You sound just like her."

Like who? Mom? Had Delma known her? Known about this place? Known its tie to me?

"I don't know who or what brought you to this place," Asa said, "but we'll figure it out."

I attempted to inch onto my own cushion, but his hands found my hips, and he held on.

"What he said." Clay furrowed his brow. "We have to secure the sanctuary until we can get a witch in to test the wards. With the familial tie, Rue might muddy the waters if the spell reacts to her bloodline."

"I agree." Asa tightened his grip on me. "It might trigger another messenger."

The sudden quiet shouted loud and clear no one wanted that.

"Why house a dangerous creature in an area where school groups and scientists visit?" The website laid the sanctuary's mission out as one of preservation and education. That might or might not be what Mom or Dad intended. It might have evolved after their deaths, or it might be their original vision. "Think of the lawsuits, the potential for collateral damage."

"Camouflage," Asa suggested. "The safest place to hide what you don't want found is in plain sight."

"Maybe." Another worry pressed in on me. "How is Delma involved? There's a missing link between the aquatic fae turning up in central Alabama, Delma's appearance in town, and the sanctuary the creatures were taken from."

"She might have targeted a sanctuary out of convenience." Clay mulled it over. "One stop shopping."

"There are multiple lethal species on display," Asa agreed. "It would make capture simpler."

"That fits, practically, but it doesn't explain the why." I turned it over in my head. "The pretense of hunting down Aedan doesn't hold water either. He challenged Asa. He was out of her hair. She's after more."

Asa hooked his thumbs into my belt loops. "The siblings' locations?"

"Maybe?" I couldn't make sense of it. "That would make her an uncontested heir, but what do we know about her father? Or her mother? Are they likely to have more children? If the parents can reproduce, independently or together, they're moot. If the parents can't, then we might have motive."

Siblicide was her favorite extracurricular, and she struck me as a woman serious about her hobbies.

"Can we call Aedan?" Clay hit on the simplest, if most awkward, solution. "Ask him?"

"I haven't set him up with a cell yet." I checked the time. "The shop is open. I'll try there first."

"Hollis Apothecary," Aedan answered in a professional tone. "How can we help you today?"

"You sound so official." I wasn't sure how I felt about that. "Can you get someplace private?"

Human ears had limits. We could talk without fear of being overheard. If he could find a quiet spot.

"Yes, ma'am." He kept his customer service voice dialed high. "Let me check the back for you."

That was a line straight out of Camber's mouth when she wanted a minute to chat with a friend.

He was a quick study. Good for him. That would come in handy wherever he landed workwise.

"Okay," he said, lower. "That bought us some time, but not much."

"Are your parents still producing heirs?"

"Um."

"I hate to be blunt, but I need to know."

"They're dead."

"I'm sorry for your loss."

"I'm not." He rustled papers in the background. "They were pretty terrible, but then again, they did protect their line. Now that they're gone, the only thing standing between Delma and the rest of our siblings is...me."

"Can I ask how they died?"

"Delma poisoned the water in the small pond kingdom where our father was born. He went home for a visit, breathed in the poison through his gills, and died in days. Mother too. And about a dozen others."

"Fun times." I bit my tongue, but it was too late, and he did say they were terrible. "Have you ever heard of the Devlin Wildlife Center?"

"No." He sounded curious. "Should I have?"

"Your sister hasn't mentioned it?"

"The only thing my sister has mentioned to me lately is wanting me dead, so no."

"Hmm."

"You don't think I have anything to do with this? The creatures and Delma showing up, I mean?"

"No." I was quick to reassure him. "I'm just nailing down loose ends."

"Colby emailed me a picture of you covered in spiderweb, FYI."

He paused, suddenly unsure. "Hope you don't mind, I checked my account on the shop computer."

A door shut in the background, and a spurt of hiccups announced the visitor. "H-hey."

"I apologize, ma'am," he rushed out to me, "but we're out of the flavor lip balm you requested. Should I add you to a waitlist?"

"Nice save." I chuckled as the hiccupping grew more intense. "I'll be in touch soon."

As I ended the call, I joined the guys in staring at Colby where she curled on the couch in cat mode.

"You took pictures?" I grabbed a pillow. "Seriously?" I threw it at her. "You couldn't help, but you could do that?"

As I had known he would, Clay caught the pillow so it didn't ding her wings, and his smile taunted me.

"You knew she did it." I curled my lip at Clay. "Traitor." I squinted at Asa. "Were you in on it too?"

Amusement touched his mouth, but he shook his head. "No."

"I slid my phone under the door." She giggled. Legit giggled. Evil creature. "It was hilarious."

Right then and there, I plotted to buy as much silly string as I could locate to hose her and Clay with. Too bad I couldn't then send it to her buddies online so they could help me savor my revenge, but I could live with printing off the photos and then framing them. Maybe hanging them on the wall above her desk.

"I'm done with you, smarty fuzz butt," I grumbled. "I can trust you no longer."

"You *love* me," she sang as she glided to me. "You'll never be done with me."

"You're right." I squished her against my chest. "On both counts." I tickled under her wings until she squealed and shoved to get away. "*But* I also believe turnabout is fair play. Watch your back."

Her antennae shot up and quivered with excitement at the prospect of me pranking her.

"Okay." Clay didn't bother hiding his smile. "Let's get back to the problem at hand."

"Can I get a Band-Aid first?" I twisted to look over my shoulder. "For the stab wound in my back?"

Peals of laughter propelled the troublemaker to Clay's head, but she skipped off him and headed back to her laptop to play while we strategized. She was always down for an adventure, but not always up to the nuts-and-bolts part.

In short, she was a lot like me.

In fact, I might have broken her.

"Let's ignore ancient history for a minute." Clay settled in to plotting mode. "Focus on the Delma angle."

As wrapped up as I let myself get with the intrigue of my parents' involvement, he was right to shake up our perspective.

"Delma wanted to lure out Rue." Asa reeled me back until my spine rested on his chest. "She got a general area from her contact inside Black Hat, Agent Barker. Barker, and likely others, helped catch and release the creatures in a radius determined by where she tracked her brother."

"That would explain why she hit the shops asking for him," I agreed. "She must have wanted confirmation he was in Samford and not one of the surrounding areas. She wanted to ensure she was focused on the right town before she escalated."

"Okay, so, the Delma angle is flawed." Clay tapped his fingers on his thigh. "There's no way she chose to unleash creatures with tags that led to a sanctuary funded by your mother without a purpose."

"I agree." Awkward as it was to sprawl over Asa, I didn't mind it. "Why lure us to the sanctuary?"

"Her evil plan of unleashing creatures to eat you failed," Clay exaggerated, "so she decided to lure you to their den?"

"That..." I had to admit, "...is plausible." I rolled my eyes at Clay. "Not likely, but still an option."

"Delma wasn't at the sanctuary," Asa pointed out. "Why lure Rue down and then be a no-show?"

"There might not have been enough time for her to make her dramatic entrance." Clay shrugged. "Rue was busy living out a horror movie. That might have stolen her thunder."

"Or she might have been spooked by the spider. If it was there to deliver a message to me, she wouldn't have seen it prior to then and might not have known what kind of threat it posed or to whom."

Which was none, now that I had killed it. I really needed to stop incinerating all my problems.

"So, what's the plan?" I glanced between them. "Go back tomorrow, give Delma a second chance?"

"Then we do what we do best." Clay rose and clasped his hands together. "We wing it."

"Stick with what works, huh?" I shook my head. "Show up, kill some things, write a report that covers our butts, then go home."

"Exactly." His grin stretched from ear to ear. "We're old pros at crossing our fingers and hoping we don't die. Why mess with perfection?"

I couldn't have said it better myself.

14

The one area where I was never planless, never lacking, was in Colby's security.

"You stay in the SUV," I told her. "I'll leave a window cracked in case you need to make a quick exit."

"Make that two," Clay chimed in. "Four might be better."

His overprotective streak where Colby was concerned warmed my black heart. It was nice to share the—not burden, no, caring for her was a privilege—*responsibility* for her safety. Plus, he gave good advice.

"Okay," I agreed with him, "four windows will be cracked in the event you need to beat a hasty retreat."

A shudder rippled through her, quivering in her wings, and she lifted an inch from its intensity.

"I'm okay with staying here," she was quick to assure me. "I have my laptop and my phone."

"That spider freaked you out, huh?" I rubbed her back. "I'll have to remember that the next time I want you to stay put without a fuss."

"I'm a moth, Rue, a *moth*." Her fuzz stood on end. "It was a giant *spider*."

"I get it, I get it." I raised my hands in surrender. "You saw your natural predator and froze."

"Nothing about me is natural."

The comment slipped before she caught it, and I could tell she regretted it by the instant hunch of her shoulders, but it was out there. It was proof she was still fighting to love this new life, her new self. The face-off with the spider must have tapped into instincts that weren't—or hadn't been—hers. It was clear she still felt raw from the experience and didn't care to repeat it a second time.

"I want to sympathize with you," I teased, aware laughter was the best way to yank her out of her spiral, "but that thing almost ate me." I lifted a finger. "And then, *then*, you, the light of my life, took photos of my shame and sent them to Aedan. Now he's got dirt on me. He can blackmail me. How does that feel?"

Willing to be cheered, she scrunched up her face. "Not bad, actually."

"That was brutal." Clay high-fived her. "You're stone-cold, Shorty."

"Keep an eye out." I pointed a finger at her. "Call if anyone comes in from the road."

"I will." She settled in behind her computer. "How will I know if you need me?"

"How will I know you won't bring a camera?"

Dark cloud lifting, Colby laughed at my mock scowl. "I promise not to film your next walk of shame."

"Next?" I opened my door. "The nerve of that kid."

"The nerve," Clay said with a wink at Colby. "What a little terror."

We each cracked our windows then shut our doors and locked the vehicle. I left Colby with the keys. The weather wasn't too bad, but I wanted her to have the option to crank the SUV if she needed cooler air. It would draw attention to her, but I doubted Delma, or whoever showed for our rendezvous, would drive up and park beside us. More than likely, they were already lying in wait.

"She'll be fine." Asa came up beside me. "You've trained her well."

As much as I wanted to grab hold of the compliment, I never wanted her trained. I didn't want this life for her. Afterlife? Some days I wasn't sure how to classify her status. She had died. Horribly. She was a shadow of her former self crammed into a new body with untold powers and a former black witch as a caregiver. I had been the fun aunt, the good-time grownup, and I enjoyed spoiling her, but now she was my familiar. We were linked soul deep. Forever. And I was her mentor in all things magic.

Shut my eyes, and I could picture the room where I was taught as a child. Hear the crack as Grandfather's cane hit my hands and reverberated on my small wooden desk. The familiar ache in my joints had never gone away, but I wasn't sure if that was my imagination or if he had broken my fingers too many times for even magic to heal them properly after a while.

Probably it was in my head. I didn't think of it for weeks or months and then I spent days rubbing my hands to rid them of the arthritic sting.

How did a person taught as I had been educate a child like Colby without falling into the same traps?

It kept me up at night, the worry. Not that I slept much. But it drove me to distraction, the fear I would turn into my grandfather. That magic would sink its hooks in me until I shoved Colby to the brink of the same breakdowns I had suffered in order to feed that gnawing ache in my gut for *more, more, more.*

More power.

More blood.

Just *more.*

Of everything. Of anything. Of all of it.

"Rue," Asa breathed my name into my ear. "Don't borrow trouble."

Jerking back, I wiped away those dark thoughts. "Why do you say that?"

"You're chewing on your bottom lip." He bent down, kissed me gently. "You're bleeding."

The taste of copper lingered on my tongue. "Are you a vampire now?"

"I'm going to stop this right here." Clay forced us apart. "If he wants to suck your blood, or anything else, I don't want to know about it." He planted a hand on each of our shoulders, spun us around, and shoved us forward. "March."

Hand sliding down to the pocket where I kept my wand, I toyed with its grip, ready to draw.

We passed the hiding place where the rescuers had asked us to deposit the dobhar-chú pups.

For better or worse, the cage—and the pups—were gone.

It wasn't much of a reassurance to pass on to Colby, but it would have to do.

As we approached the welcome center, we lost our earlier playfulness and settled into work mode.

Clay took point, as usual, and I fell in the middle. Asa brought up the rear.

When we reached the spot where the daemon leapt the railing the night before, I couldn't help flicking a glance toward where we suspected a cell of some type concealed the true purpose for this sanctuary.

That was when I spotted her, and a spark of admiration for her dramatic flair kindled in me.

Delma stood on the back of a tortoise that might have been natural but was, most likely, fae. It sliced through the water, careful to avoid the area that had drawn my eye, and that, in itself, didn't bode well.

"Rue," she greeted, all smiles. "I'm so pleased you could join me."

"I'm always on the hunt for the best natural ingredients to use in the products in my shop." I picked at the thick green moss coating the handrail. "Thanks for the tip on a potential supplier."

"You're funny." She didn't mean it. I could tell. "That must be why Aedan likes you so much."

"Well, that, and I'm not attempting to murder him." I shrugged. "It's the little things, you know?"

"Hasn't Astaroth illuminated his potential mate on the finer points of succession?"

"From what I can tell, he schedules challenges ahead of time, allowing anyone who regrets their life choices to change their mind and skip town. There's also the tiny fact that he doesn't go around killing people for funsies, which seems to be a hobby of yours."

"He could abdicate," she offered. "Then the high king could seed another heir."

The impersonal expression of *seed another heir* raised my hackles. Asa would never encourage his father to reproduce, and it had nothing to do with losing his inheritance. Asa would fight to his last breath to prevent another woman from suffering the same fate as his mother. I would too, to avoid another child being born with a question mark hanging over their head.

His mother loved him, but she had twisted him, however unintentionally it was done.

It wasn't her fault, none of it, but it wasn't Asa's either.

"No," he said simply, and this time he did not make himself less.

"You're right." She chuckled. "Your father has firm opinions on how many heirs ought to exist at once."

From what I had pieced together, his father erased all traces of his failed heir before he *seeded* the next. He was so determined to start from scratch, he had one living child at any given time. That child must die before he began the process all over again.

Asa could have had dozens of siblings, but he would never know them. They were gone, forgotten, replaced.

As he would be, if he ever stopped fighting for his right to survive.

"It's a busy time of year for retail," I prompted her. "How can I help you?"

The tortoise stopped on cue, which all but confirmed it as fae, and Delma spread one palm above the still marsh, over the exact spot where I dove for the daemon the night before.

A column of water rose, twisting in the moonlight, glittering and entrancing, and a woman's reflection appeared within it.

She was ageless, beautiful, and something about the blade of her nose struck me as familiar.

"How I have longed to meet you." Her broad smile was radiant. "I regret the means through which I orchestrated our introduction, but I have so few options for travel these days. I'm afraid I must entertain guests at my home."

"Home?" I studied the trick, fascinated by Delma's control over her element. "And here I thought it was a prison."

"There's no cause for rudeness." Her lips thinned to nothing. "In that, you take after your grandfather."

"No," I was happy to tell her. "I don't."

Not anymore.

A coy smile flirted with her lips. "Aren't you curious how I know your grandfather?"

"If you went through all the trouble of bringing me here, I'm sure you'll tell me."

"Show some respect." Delma fisted her free hand. "Do you have any idea who you're talking to?"

"We weren't properly introduced, so no." I slanted my gaze back to the water column. "I've just been thinking of her as the woman who almost killed my..." *mate* nearly slipped past my lips, but I choked on it, "...boyfriend."

"That sounded painful," the woman *tsk*ed. "Are you so uncertain of him?"

"I'm certain I have better things to do than cough up bugs that fly down my throat."

"That's the excuse you're going with," Clay muttered out of the corner of his mouth.

After patching the wrinkles in her mask, the woman announced, "I am Calixta Damaras."

"Impossible." Asa's heat brushed against my back as he moved closer. "Calixta Damaras is dead."

"You must be Stavros's heir." She swept her gaze over him. "The latest in a long line of failures."

Poor thing thought she could wound him by taking aim at his daddy issues, well, she overshot the mark.

"I'm not up to snuff on the daemon hierarchy," I said, "so you'll have to spell it out for me."

With all the restrictions placed on royalty, I had my hands full learning the ins and outs of my fascination with Asa. I hadn't dug into daemon lore. I hadn't viewed it as a part of my world, even if it was a part of me, which was silly when you considered who I was making out with these days.

Between returning to Black Hat, the shop's destruction and its subsequent repairs, overseeing the girls' recoveries from their trauma, the familiar bond clicking into place, the grimoire toying with me, and learning I was part daemon, I had no time. Even if I wanted another burden to carry, I had to put one down first.

"I am High Queen of the Haelian Seas, Mistress of Aquatae."

"*Former* high queen," Asa cut in. "Calixta has been missing for decades, nearly a century."

"You're a member of her court?" I aimed the question at Delma. "What's your stake in this?"

"Cali is my grandmother." Delma jerked up her chin. "I am her heir, born of her direct line."

"Now that you've killed everyone related to you," Clay mumbled. "She must be so proud."

"Only the strong survive," Calixta chided him. "You who have lived for so long must know this."

"Are we about to witness a coronation?" I asked Delma. "Are we the only friends you had left to invite?"

"That's sad." Clay shook his head. "I almost feel sorry for you, but not really, and P.S. We're not friends."

"She can't be crowned." Asa tilted his head to study her profile. "As I said, there's a new queen."

"My claim to the throne supersedes the pretender's," Calixta hissed. "I will have what is mine."

"You're stuck in a cell in a swamp," I pointed out. "You're in no position to make demands."

"She is the rightful high queen." Delma's lip curled in a snarl. "Your ignorance is staggering."

"Don't stagger too much." I eyed her platform. "You'll stagger right off your float."

"Are you so ignorant of your heritage?" Calixta eyed me with sympathy. "Your grandfather has been keeping secrets." She lowered her gaze, and her impossibly long lashes swept across her cheeks. "Your dead parents too." She gave *dead* no special emphasis, but none was required to cut me to the quick. "You deserve to know the truth."

"If you mean that my grandmother was a daemon," I returned, "we figured out that much."

Her smile when she raised her eyes was downright predatory, and I knew whatever she said next would rock my world. I could read the glee in her expression, the expectation of delivering a sentence that would end life as I knew it.

"You're my granddaughter too," she ventured kindly. "Your grandfather and I…"

No, no, no.

This was not happening.

And yet, it made perfect sense. Grandfather wouldn't lower himself to bed a common daemon, but a queen? Yeah. That would assuage his ego. I could see him viewing her as the closest thing the species had to offer as his equal. But why would a queen give up the rights to an heir? A son?

The watery visage, the veil of rage shimmering through her beauty, told me the truth.

The director got what he wanted, and then he trapped her to prevent her from taking their son.

Maybe he couldn't kill her. Maybe he was sentimental. Or maybe he wanted to keep her around in case the experiment with my father worked to his satisfaction. Whatever the reason, he was a fool not to end her when he had the chance. His death was written in her eyes, in the curve of her red lips.

That scenario fit with what I knew about the director, but not what I knew about my parents.

Mom and Dad hadn't been on great terms with my grandfather. This was a big job, restraining a daemon queen. Would they have set aside their differences and worked together to contain her? For whatever reason? Had they linked the sanctuary to Mom to avoid any claim Black Hat might make on Calixta?

Except, Grandfather, for all intents and purposes, *was* Black Hat.

The Kellies knew about the tags. They would have tracked them to the sanctuary, the same as Colby. But she assured me there wasn't a hint of it in the database. Not a whisper, not a sigh, as if it hadn't happened.

"That's not a mental picture that needs painting," I cut in, leaning into Asa. "What proof can you offer?"

"You know I'm telling the truth." She hummed with approval. "I can see it in your eyes."

And just like that, I no longer questioned where the bureau intersected with Delma. It didn't. Never had.

This was the missing link.

Calixta.

My *grandmother*.

She must have made contacts within Black Hat during her affair with my grandfather that remained loyal to her. Those connections explained how Agent Barker and her partner got roped into the ill-advised fae relocation project. They were following Delma's orders, accepting her as Calixta's proxy.

But did that mean she was behind the rogue black witches? Or was this another, more personal, attack?

"Let's pretend I believe you without a shred of evidence." I was thankful for Asa's strength at my back. "I still don't get why I'm here, and please save us both time and skip over the scripted sentimental-ity. That doesn't work on me. I want the truth, and it better be worth all the lives this charade cost."

Innocents, creatures and humans alike, had died to lead me here, to this moment, to face her.

"With your wicked father dead, only a child of my line can free me."

"You have a henchwoman right there." I pointed at Delma. "She was just bragging about how she's of your line and of your blood and blah-blah. I tuned her out when she got repetitive. So, why *me*?"

"Yes, Grandmother." Delma studied the fallen queen. "Why *are* you entertaining her?"

Clearly, whatever story Calixta spun to get Delma on her side hadn't included chatting with me. But, if Calixta was telling the truth, I knew what Delma expected. She wanted to kill me. Her own...cousin?

That psychopathy ran in the family wasn't a huge shocker. That I came from murderers, liars, and great power wasn't anything new. Okay, the daemon thing? That was new. The rest? Not so much.

We were probably given knives instead of rattles, bottles of poison rather than milk, from birth.

"You know why," Calixta said gently. "A sacrifice is required."

Yep.

That fit with my expectations.

"Give the word, Grandmother." Delma bowed her head. "I will exchange her life for your freedom."

Flame licked my spine, and the daemon roared into being. "Rue *mine*."

"The life must be freely given." Calixta *tsk*ed. "She must agree."

Malice bright in her eyes, Delma smiled. "I challenge you for the position of heir of Haelian Seas throne."

"No thanks." I smiled right back. "Not interested."

"Stubborn child." Calixta gazed at me. "Perhaps this will motivate you."

From the canopy, a smaller version of the monster spider glided down on a single thread. Against its breast, a bundle of web writhed and shrieked, the voice muffled but one I would know anywhere.

Colby.

Whatever the first spider had been, this one was a henchman on Calixta's payroll.

The twitch in my limbs grew spastic, and my fingernails lengthened to talons that could pluck a heart from a chest as easily as a ripe apple from a limb. Saliva flooded my mouth as I stared at Delma, and a layer of that carefully curated version of myself flaked off to reveal the monster within me.

The shift in my demeanor registered on Calixta's face, her pride evident.

Delma, however, dug her toes into the tortoise shell like she imagined spurring a horse to retreat.

"You're dead," Clay informed her in a voice absent of emotion. "If Rue doesn't kill you, I will."

I swung my head to find him beside me, chest pumping like bellows, fists tight at his sides.

"I accept," I rasped, gold dots floating on the edges of my vision, rage a fire in my belly.

"No." The daemon smashed his fist through the railing. "I accept."

"The challenge wasn't issued to you, big guy." I kept my gaze locked on Delma. "Where and when?"

"Here and now." She prodded her ride until she could leap onto the boardwalk. "I want this settled."

"Fine." I stepped away from the guys. "Let's do this."

A familiar cold iced my chest, and my heart slowed to a steady beat. I became a creature of instinct when riled, and none of the self-improvement I had done up to this point had a place here.

"No magic." Delma dropped her glamour and flexed her clawed fingers at her sides. "Daemon rules."

"I'm not a daemon." I palmed my wand. "Not even half. Your rules don't apply to me."

Jerking her head toward the column of water, she growled, "Grandmother—"

"Allowances must be made," Calixta decreed. "She has no daemon form, as you do. She has no control of an element as you do. Would it be fair for her to defend herself as little more than human?"

Yes was written in the pinch of Delma's mouth and the spasm under her eye. "No."

"This was a setup." I fed magic into my wand as she drew a long dagger. "You get that right?"

"Obviously," Delma snapped. "I've worked on it for months."

"No." I pitied her. I really did. "She set you up to die, and you did all the work for her."

"Heirs must be tested," she gritted out, lunging for me. "I must prove myself fit to rule."

Using my forearm, I blocked her jab without her slicing me open, but her strength was immense.

To throw her off, I hit her where it hurt. Right in the paranoia. In the same mania that drove her to kill.

"Aedan never mentioned he's descended from royalty. Strange he would leave that off his application."

Aedan, who was also my cousin.

So freaking weird.

Now I felt icky for joking about him dragging me beneath the waves to his undersea kingdom to be his bride.

Icky, and yet oddly prescient.

"He believes the lie we were all told, that Calixta is dead." She spun aside, out of reach, too quick for me to get my wand involved. "Our grandfather was one of her many consorts, and they had ten children together. Calixta never married. She didn't want to share her power. But after she was declared dead, rather than passing the crown to her offspring, who were all illegitimate, the throne was passed to a distant cousin."

Delma jabbed, careful not to get too close, testing me, determining my weak spots.

"The threat of Calixta's bloodline rising against the usurper queen was too strong. The usurper queen stabbed the consorts in their hearts and slit the throats of the children. All except for my father and me. He had been loaned out to a favorite of Calixta's, a friend from another court, one who was interested in my future services as well." The next stab landed closer as she hit her stride. "When word came that Calixta was dead, that Grandfather was dead, Father and I were left with only the clothes on our backs. No one would shelter us. No one would dare. That is why Aedan didn't tell you. The shame is immeasurable."

Her reach was longer than mine, and she didn't have to worry about her weapon being cleaved in two.

Keep the insults coming, wear her out, make her sloppy.

Only then could I risk getting close enough to strike.

"So, instead of taking the out you were given, you decided to overthrow the monarchy. How predictable of you." She flinched at that, and I smiled, goading her. "Still, it's nice to have goals."

A snarl curled her upper lip, and her eyes promised my death. She was blind to all but her own ambition.

Goddess bless, I was staring at an earlier version of myself.

She was rage and fury and scorn, desperation and insecurity and hunger, and I pitied her. She lacked the pivotal moment where past and future collided in the present to shock her into the realization of

how empty the endless hunger for more had left her life. She didn't
have a Colby to act as her conscience.

And since she had dared touch Colby, she never would experience that life-altering epiphany.

I was a better person than I used to be, but I wouldn't call myself
good.

Never had I been gladder not to have reached that pinnacle of
decency.

It would have been a long fall to the bottom otherwise.

"Joke all you want." Her blade shook with her anger. "Ambition is
how I survive."

"Why now?" I got under her guard, almost thwacking her wrist.
"What changed?"

"You." Delma smiled. "That's what changed."

Aedan told me he was twenty-five. That math didn't hold for him
being Calixta's grandson. And if he was too young, then their younger
siblings weren't related to Calixta. A lightbulb flashed over my head.

"I'm the only one left." I laughed at her rage. "The only other
person alive with Calixta's blood in me."

"Father was a cousin of hers," Delma spat. "His offspring should
have sufficed."

The skeletons at the base of the cell took on horrid new dimen-
sion. Those were relatives of hers. Ours?

How long had she been doing this? Tithing to the forgotten
queen? Hoping if she killed enough, sacrificed enough, she would be
enough?

The idea was too enormous to fit in my head without leaking out
of my ears.

The fight was draining me, physically and emotionally, but
Delma wasn't slowing down now that she had me pegged. We were
at an impasse. Her dagger was only so long, and I wouldn't risk my
wand in a direct strike. I had come to rely on Clay and Asa to run
interference for me, but I was on my own in a challenge.

"You're not the heir she wants." I pricked her pride. "Why else pit us against each other?" I grinned for a beat. "She used you, Delma. She wants me, and she used you to get me here. She doesn't care if you live or die. She never did." I hit her with my black witch best, cruel and cold and heartless. "You're. Not. Worthy."

A furious roar fueled with the fear and fury I was right blasted me as Delma flung her knife.

It would have punched into my throat if I had moved a hair slower. As it was, I couldn't hear her heart over a thundering in my ears. The blade struck the rail I had been standing next to only seconds ago, and she wasted no time lunging to retrieve her weapon.

Delma was fast.

Mad Delma was a blur.

Fangs bared, she dove for the railing, for the hilt of the dagger. "I will—"

"—never finish that sentence."

I stepped in her path, gouged her side with my wand, and thrust power into her until she rivaled twinkle lights on a Christmas tree. The magic burned her, ate through her glamour, and revealed the deadly blue-skinned daemon at her core. And then she was gone, nothing but ash and bitterness.

Or maybe I was the bitter one, to have discovered I had family *other* than the director, only to learn they had been picked off by Delma, who was nuttier than the fruitcake curing on my counter back home.

"I have my successor," Calixta announced from seemingly nowhere and everywhere. "I am pleased."

The column of water had collapsed when Delma died, meaning Calixta didn't have enough juice alone to maintain the illusion. That was good. Not great, but good. Her hands were tied, magically speaking. What we had to guard against was her cleverness, her silver tongue coaxing others to lend her their strength.

And there was no putting this cat back in the bag, not with Delma involving Black Hat in her scheme.

Clay caught my eye then jerked his chin toward the creepy jailer clutching Colby in its spindly arms.

With a subtle nod, I distracted Calixta while he and the daemon plotted to free the struggling bundle.

"You have found nothing." I dropped Delma's blade with a splash. "I want nothing to do with you."

"Accept my offer, and you will be a match for Astaroth. His father can't contest your mating then."

"Choice mine." The daemon informed her, fist striking his chest. "Rue mine."

Given his impulsive nature, I wasn't sure if this was a part of their plan, or if he couldn't help himself.

"Not that we're rushing into a mating," I pointed out for everyone's benefit. "But still. Good to know."

"Upon my death," Calixta coaxed, "you may rule without a mate, as I did, be a power in your own right, as I was."

Pretending to consider her, I asked, "How do I set you free?"

"Blood would have been best," she mused, "fed into the water where the ward could taste it."

"There's no Plan B?"

"A life is the cost." She mulled it over. "Delma's ashes sprinkled above me will do."

"Clay." I swept a hand over the bulk of them. "Can you seal those in an evidence baggy for me?"

Since he swore they doubled as snack bags, he always kept a few on him in case of emergency.

"Sure thing." He used a business card to get every flake possible while the daemon padded closer to the spider. "Good enough?"

"That will do, golem." Calixta kept her voice dialed to benevolent. "Now, my darling girl, free me."

"Pass them to me?" I held the remains of my cousin, but no pity stirred within me. "Calixta..."

"Please," she demurred. "Call me Grandmother."

Thank all the gods and goddesses that my grandparents had called it quits after one child.

As alike as they were, they could have been a formidable pair, had they made a go of it.

"Grandmother," I humored her. "It was nice to meet you, but I prefer the devil I know."

The director held enough of my strings to jerk me around for the rest of his life. I wasn't about to set free a female version with untold years of experience in making others her puppets, as she had Delma. The woman was a master manipulator, even while stuck at the bottom of a marsh.

"Your grandfather will betray you," she warned. "You can't trust him."

"He raised me," I informed her. "I know how far I can trust him."

The same distance I could throw him.

A guttural shout and a squelching noise jerked my attention back to the boardwalk in time to watch the daemon yank Colby from the spider's clutches and toss her to Clay. Clay caught her with a prayer on his lips and carried her away from the swamp, back toward the SUV to release her in a safe environment.

Meanwhile, surprising no one, the daemon ripped off the spider's head, yelled down its neck, and tore it out of its web. He flung the carcass toward the spot where my grandmother's voice originated. The boardwalk rattled on impact when he landed, and the planks under his feet snapped in two. He shook it off, prowled over to me, spider head in his hand, its pinchers still clacking, and held out his arm.

"Present." He smiled, his face bright green with ichor. "For Rue."

"I..." I knew how much it meant to him that I appreciate his gifts, so I reached for the head, only for the pinchers to snap closed on my wrist. "I'll wash your hair when we get to the hotel if you can throw that farther than you threw the body." I jerked my hand free. "Deal?"

"Brush?" He cocked an eyebrow, weighing the gift in his hands. "Braid?"

"Yes." I was happy he set such a low price. "Just fling it, please?"

"Okay." He cocked his arm and hurled the trophy beyond where I could see. "It gone."

"Excellent." I patted him on the back. "Good work."

While the daemon preened, my grandmother seethed, but she was locked down tight.

"You will regret this," Calixta promised. "There will come a time when you need your family."

Thinking of Colby, of Clay, of Asa and his daemon, of all the people back home in Samford, I pitied her.

"I always need my family," I told her, looping my arm through the daemon's. "But you're not it."

He and I walked out of the sanctuary, and I made an executive decision on the spot.

"Stand back, big guy." I touched my wand to the welcome center. "We're about to get toasty."

With a little boost from Colby, I incinerated the building, sparking a fire that would eat through the twists and turns of the boardwalk wherever it flowed through the vast sanctuary. The trees and wildlife would remain undisturbed. For now. But this was a bandage on a gunshot wound, and it wouldn't stick forever.

Calixta was no longer safe here. Too many people knew where to find her. We had to fix that.

"S'mores?" the daemon asked hopefully. "Like s'mores."

"Everyone likes s'mores." I exhaled as the quick access to Calixta was ravaged. "But we'll have to make some at the hotel." His shoulders slumped, and I patted him. "We have no marshmallows, remember?"

Or graham crackers. Or Hershey bars. Or sticks I would allow to touch my food.

When we reached the SUV, Clay sat with Colby on his lap in the backseat with the door standing open.

The cocoon surrounding her had been cut in sections with the pair of scissors from my own run-in with a giant spider, but her wings were stuck in the hardening goop. She leaned against Clay, her eyes dark, but she perked when we ducked in to check on her.

"That was *amazing*." She gazed up at the daemon. "You killed it dead. Totally dead. With your hands."

"Colby friend," he huffed, scuffing his foot in the dirt. "Save friend."

"Can you sit back here with us?" She wiggled on Clay's lap. "Oh." She frowned. "What about your...?"

No further encouragement required, the daemon stuffed himself into the SUV, his horns raking the ceiling, shredding the fabric. The vehicle rocked under his weight, and I had doubts about shutting the door. I forgot those when Colby walked onto his lap, and he scooped her against his chest.

Antennae weighted with webbing, she asked, "Do you like computer games?"

"I like games." A furrow creased his brow. "Computer is game?"

The daemon tended to come out in times of stress, leaving Asa to enjoy the lulls. I wasn't sure the daemon understood modern technology, let alone gaming, but I was happy for the chance for him to bond with Colby.

"I'll teach you," she promised. "If you don't like it, I have tons of board games."

For his sake, I would purchase a few yard games, like horseshoes and cornhole, things he could excel at without feeling inadequate.

"Okay."

He grinned at her, she grinned back, and I shut the door to avoid intruding on their moment.

We made it halfway to the hotel before my phone rang. I didn't check the app monitoring blocked calls for me. I knew who it was before I answered, just as I accepted there was no ignoring him after this.

"Director," I greeted him with cool politeness. "To what do I owe the honor?"

"You are to report to my office," he snapped, "immediately."

The line recalled all those high school dramas about principals' offices I had watched with the girls.

"All right."

"You listen to—" His tirade petered out as he registered my words. "All right?"

"Sure." I twisted my hands on the wheel. "Give me two days, and I'll be there will bells on."

His silence told me my quick acquiescence had stunned him, which amused me to no end.

"All right," he echoed, intentional or not. "I'll see you then, Elspeth."

Ending the call, I felt lighter. Not sure why, given I had agreed to face the director for the first time in over a decade. Maybe because I had already decided to pay him a visit. Or maybe it was because I knew his dirty little secret about Calixta, and I was willing to exploit the heck out of it to finally get answers.

15

Our welcome home was spoiled by how the Proctor grimoire chose to greet us. It sat propped against the door leading into Colby's bedroom. The silent threat was proof my recent attempts at keying the wards to trap it in the house were successful, even when it attempted to stowaway. And it was not happy about it.

Oh-freaking-well.

"Books who threaten me end up on the DNF pile," I warned it. "You don't want that to happen, do you?"

The grimoire gave no outward signs of having heard me, but I was certain it was shaking in its binding.

"You sure showed it." Clay patted me on the head. "That book won't mess with the likes of you again."

"Shut up, Clay." I swatted him. "Come on, book." I lifted the wretched thing and headed for my bedroom. "Let's go put you back where you belong."

"Probably not a great idea to talk to the book like it's a person," he called. "You'll give it delusions of grandeur."

After spending time away, I was forced to admit what I had been ignoring. The safe full of black artifacts was fouling the air with its stink. The smell never bothered me before, but it tempted me to sneeze now. All in all, it was a good sign that meant my familiar bond with Colby was still cleansing my soul, for which I was grateful.

Though I might move the safe out of my bedroom if things got much worse. Better? It was a tossup between whether pressure-washing a lifetime of black magic off me was the wiser idea or if huddling in its thick and pungent embrace was smarter. I was safer as a black witch, but I flew just under the radar these days. Soon, thanks to Colby, my conversion to white witch would be obvious, and I would be a bigger target than ever. But I was also more dangerous than before, thanks to her purity.

Better to walk into a room an obvious threat, or to let it be a surprise?

Like so many things in my life, I had to make the call, and quick. Before someone made it for me.

A knock on the door distracted me from opening the safe. "Come in."

Asa entered the room, noticed the book, and hesitated. "Am I interrupting?"

I had a choice to make, and the repercussions pressed on me the way irrevocable decisions always did. It wasn't my best work, the way I told Asa about my grandfather. He had no way of knowing I had waged a war within myself on how or if or when I should tell him. Aside from trust, he had no reason to believe it was anything more than me blabbing my side of a truth he was about to learn anyway.

The scales between us, in my mind, required balance.

"Can you shut the door?" I set the book on the bed then patted the mattress. "Give me a minute?"

Without asking a single question, the truest expression of trust, he sat and let me go about spelling the room for privacy from any mothy or golemy ears that might overhear what I was about to reveal.

"Should I be alarmed or excited that you want to ensure no one can hear me scream?"

Heat swooped through my middle in a burning rush, and I was grateful to have my back to him.

"I'll let you be the judge of that." I picked up the book and thumped it across my palm. "There's something I want to show you."

Interest brightened his eyes, and he wet his lips. "Oh?"

"Kiss a guy once, and his mind falls into the gutter forever." Not that I had any room to talk. "Here's the thing." I took Delma's remains from my pocket. "I'm a collector." I pushed open the closet and knelt beside the safe. "I own things no one should have but that can't be destroyed."

His lips parted on the question I knew he would ask.

Does Clay know?

"Clay doesn't know," I answered him all the same. "He suspects, I think, but he's never asked, and I've never volunteered the information. Colby has an idea, but I've never explained the contents to her."

"But you're telling me."

"I am."

"You don't owe me this," he said softly, as if he could read my mind. "You've given me enough."

Too soon. It was too soon to tell him I wanted to give him everything. I wasn't sure what *everything* even meant for someone like me. I wasn't sure if the way I experienced love was the same for others. As much as I would like to blame the fae juju that lubricated my mouth when it came to my deepest, darkest secrets, I suspected I had wanted to unburden myself for a long time.

"I don't want secrets between us." I unlocked the safe, and foul magic seeped into the room. "I would rather you know the worst before we go any further." I shrugged like it didn't matter, like I wasn't doing my best to open my heart to him. "I want you to understand what I am, and what I have the potential to become."

A nightmare.

A misery.

A monster.

The safe's contents held no interest for him. "How long have you been collecting?"

"Since my first case." I tucked the bag of ashes in the back and set the book in its usual spot. "Why?"

"Did you ever use them?"

"Uh, no." I laughed as I spun the dial. "They call to me. *Loudly.* Answering seemed like a bad idea."

The whispers had only grown in the last few weeks, and I suspected the less stain on my soul, the more susceptible I would become to the persuasion of those artifacts. Yet more incentive to relocate the safe.

"You've been hiding dangerous artifacts from the world since you were a teen lost in the throes of black magic addiction?"

"I don't know if I would phrase it like that, but yes." I flicked a wrist. "That's not the point."

Who knew what my toxic brain thought it was doing? Stockpiling weapons for when I decided to burn the world to the ground? I must have had my reasons. I must have had a plan. But I couldn't tell you now what it had been. Could be I was simply too high to think straight enough to use them.

I had been shocked when I came to my senses and picked through the trove I had squirreled away with kleptomaniacal glee during my darkest years. I wanted to believe I was a guardian, and I had been, for a decade. Before that? I wasn't as sure, and I didn't want to examine it too closely.

The thing about addiction was, if you got high enough, you believed you were bulletproof.

Most likely, I had considered myself invincible. Far too mighty to lower myself to dipping into my goody stash.

"It's exactly the point." Asa took my hand and pulled me down next to him. "Even at your worst, you tried to be better." He searched my face. "You want to believe the worst in yourself, just as you want to credit your successes to Colby, but it's not that black and white. You were evolving before you met her. You were struggling to surface before you met Clay."

"You're giving me way too much credit."

In the back of my mind, I had probably been building an armory to take over the world or something equally insane.

"You're not giving yourself enough credit." He cupped my cheek in his palm. "You never do."

"One day, I'll be the person I want to be, and then we'll see."

"There is no finish line for you, Rue." The edge of his thumb brushed my lips. "You keep moving it before you cross it."

A frown pinched my mouth. "You might be right."

I wasn't ready to accept pats on the back yet, but I could see there was a problem with my goal of hitting a specific target when I kept pushing the bull's-eye farther and farther away.

"I am right." He lowered his head. "You're a good person. You have to make your peace with that."

"This cocky version of you does things to me," I admitted, sliding a hand down one of his braids. "It's sexy when you stop hiding." I flipped the end of his hair back and forth. "This doesn't count as a hair job or something equally inappropriate, right?"

Sputtered laughter rocked him back, and he couldn't meet my gaze, which was adorable.

"No." He coughed into his fist. "Hair jobs aren't a thing."

"You understand I had to ask." I kept hold of his braid. "You're purring, you know?"

"I'm happy, not horny."

Now it was my turn to snicker into a coughing fit. "You said horny."

"I'm not aroused." He frowned mid-clarification, tilted his head. "That was a lie."

"I know." I was in danger of shedding tears, and my stomach hurt. "You're always horny." I fell back. "They're always on your head, even when I can't see them."

Propped on one elbow, Asa leaned over me and watched me make a total fool of myself.

When I could breathe again, I wiped my cheeks dry and curled onto my side toward him.

"Feel better?" He stroked my hair. "I've never seen you laugh like that."

"I don't know where it came from." I chuckled again. "Maybe I'm losing my mind, courtesy of Granny."

Calixta was a high queen. *Former* high queen. And she was kept in a cell at the bottom of a marsh.

Easy to see, in hindsight, why my parents didn't want me near her or her insidious influence.

Then again, they'd made it easy to identify the trust funding the sanctuary, and linked Mom to it, so had they never wanted me to find her? Or had they wanted me to find her when it was time? When I was ready?

And now that I had the keeping of her, what had they expected me to do?

No one expects to die young, but they really should have left me instructions.

"Calixta Damaras." He shook his head. "*If* that was her, and *if* what she said was true."

"Lucky us," I exhaled. "We're going to see the one person who can confirm it either way."

♺

After I fully recovered from my giggle fit, which no black witch—former or not—should admit to, I took a walk to the creek to check on Aedan. He deserved to hear the news about his sister firsthand. As for the rest? It nagged at me, a secret that didn't want to be kept, so I would trust the blood oath. And Aedan.

"How did it go?" Aedan sat up in his hammock. "You don't look so hot."

"I have a lot on my mind." I helped myself to one of the camp chairs. "How was working at the shop?"

"I liked it." He brightened. "It was peaceful." He rolled a shoulder. "And it smelled good."

"You got along well with the girls?"

"Yes," he said softly. "I remembered our talk and behaved accordingly."

The complication of our relationship and his interest in Arden made things so much stickier.

Perhaps worse than the spider's web.

Okay.

No.

Nothing short of death was that bad.

"I'm not threatening you." I worked up a tired smile for him. "I'm genuinely curious."

"I like them. Both of them. They're nice." He ducked his head. "They also smell good."

The grin of accomplishment when he spoke about work made me curious. "Have you ever had a job?"

"I had duties to my family, but not a nine-to-five, no."

"You've never had to earn your own money?"

"No."

"Then someone is going to have to teach you how to balance a checkbook."

Now wasn't the time to bring up finances, but he was far from destitute with Delma in the grave.

"No one uses checkbooks anymore." He smiled a little. "Even I know that much."

"I didn't say it was going to be me," I joked. "Look, I'll have to talk to the girls, but *if* they were impressed with your worth ethic, and *if* they're comfortable working with you, I'll consider extending a more permanent job offer."

"Really?" His eyes brightened then turned sharp. "This isn't a guilt thing, is it?"

"No and yes and I have no idea."

"She would have killed me if you hadn't intervened." He reminded me of a lost boy. "You saved me."

He didn't have to use her name, maybe he couldn't bear to speak it, but we both knew who he meant.

So much for me spearheading this conversation. "I'm sorry about Delma, but she left me no choice."

"I know." He stared at me, expression earnest. "Probably better than anyone."

"How much do you know about your family's history, particularly your grandparents?"

Aedan blinked then folded his legs under him.

"Grandfather was a concubine in the Haelian Seas court. Bastards, even royal-born ones, were given to the harem to raise, so my father was given an education worthy of a prince. He was expected to put it to use wooing women who requested his services while spying for the crown." He gazed into the deepening night with distant eyes. "Then it all fell apart." He shook his head. "Calixta Damaras, the former high queen, went missing."

"And a distant cousin claimed the throne."

"Drusilla Ginevra." He nodded. "Everyone thought she killed Calixta, but there was no body, no evidence either way. Drusilla beat all challengers, so she's earned the crown." He frowned at my interest. "Why?"

He glossed over the executions, which made me wonder if he knew about them. Had the story been a lie Calixta used to weaponize her granddaughter, or was it a truth only whispered among the survivors?

Either way, for a young daemon who had sacrificed everything for his family, I owed him full disclosure.

"Delma was Calixta's granddaughter."

"Believe me, I know. It was all she talked about when we were kids. How things should have been."

The child had lived a fantasy in a court of splendors, and the woman had been willing to do anything to go back, this time as a queen rather than a pawn.

"I have reason to believe Calixta might also be my paternal grandmother."

And cause to wonder if the strength of that fallen dynasty, and the daemoness behind it, who refused to share her power, even with a mate, explained my powerful reaction to Asa, despite my watered-down blood.

Skin rippling to its natural hue, Aedan fell out of the hammock. "What?"

"I'll have verification soon enough, but until then, I believe the information to be accurate."

Silly of me to ever consider my grandmother might have been a common daemon when Grandfather accepted nothing less than perfection.

"We're cousins." He scrambled onto his hands and knees. "What are the odds?"

That his sister had urged him toward challenging Asa in order to set him in my path, thus granting her a valid excuse for hunting him —and me? None to none, maybe even less than that.

"We're not exactly cousins." I curled my fingers into my palms. "We're not blood related."

His burst of serendipitous happiness drained away. "I guess not, huh?"

A pressure behind my breastbone propelled me forward as he rose, and I planted my feet before him to keep from running away from what I was about to say, how much it revealed about me.

"As far as I'm concerned, I have no blood relations left." I winced as my nails bit into the meat of my palms. "Blood isn't what binds a family." I coaxed my fingers to flex. "Love and mutual respect do." I filled my lungs. "You're welcome to join mine, if you want."

The force of his hug left me certain my eyes were on the verge of popping out of my skull.

"Thank you," he murmured against my temple. "I won't let you down." I felt him smile. "Coz."

A throat cleared behind me, and I nearly twisted an ankle whirling toward Asa. "Hey."

"Sorry to interrupt." He kept his distance. "Colby needs you to finalize our travel plans."

"You're not going to punch him for hugging me when I turn my back, are you?"

"He's under your aegis. That makes him the safest daemon I know."

"That wasn't a *no*."

Asa came to me then, slid his hands down my arms. "I won't hurt him."

"Mmm-hmm." I returned the favor, smoothing my hands down his chest. "I'll be in after I finish up here."

"All right." He kissed my temple. "I'll be in my room, catching up on paperwork."

Asa could have called or texted me, but he had come down to check on me in person. I suspected it had been an offer of emotional support, but I wasn't ruling out ulterior motives. He was half fae, after all.

With the heavy lifting done, I settled in with Aedan and dialed Camber. I put the call on speaker, and the girls and I discussed his possible future at Hollis Apothecary.

I should have anticipated the squeeing.

So.

Much.

Squeeing.

16

Morning brought with it the itchy sensation of ants marching over my skin, as if the director watched my every move from afar to ensure I showed up to our agreed upon meeting. It was paranoia, probably, but I couldn't shake the sensation of eyes on Asa and me as we exited the airport and booked transportation via Swyft, a rideshare app catering to paranormals, with drivers who knew better than to ask questions.

"Breathe." Asa threaded his fingers through mine. "You can do this."

I would have preferred an SUV waiting for us to drive ourselves to the Black Hat compound, but it wasn't worth the paperwork for a few hours. I wanted to get in, get out, and get home to where I had left Colby with Clay for her own protection.

"We're about to find out." I squeezed his hand. "You sure you don't want to change your mind?"

"Unless you tell me otherwise, I won't leave your side."

The vow opened a pit in my stomach. I was about to parade Asa in front of the director. He already knew what Asa meant to me—we hadn't hidden our relationship—but it was one thing for him to read reports of me taking an interest in a dae princeling and another for him to read the lengths I would go to protect Asa in my eyes for himself.

I was prepared for threats.

I was prepared for violence.

I was prepared to kill my grandfather if he so much as looked at Asa sideways.

"This can't be a good idea." I rested my head on his shoulder. "Tell me it's the right thing to do."

"It's the right thing to do."

"Funny." I elbowed him in the ribs. "And mean it."

"I do." He stroked my arm. "You need answers. This was an avenue we didn't expect to open for you."

Megara would have puppies when I told her what I had done, which explained why I hadn't scried her for tips on how to proceed last night. I would have to confess before I asked her for the details of Mom's will.

The drive out to the compound took thirty minutes, and I was content to shut my eyes, lean against Asa, and pretend I wasn't due for a second homecoming in as many days. Minus the *home* part. The compound had never been that for me.

As the car slowed, I was drawn upright, eager to drink in the familiar landscape, curious if it had changed as much as I had since the last time I was here. The answer, unsurprisingly, was no.

"You can let us out here," I told the driver when he stopped in front of the gated entry. "Thanks."

I paid the fare before Asa beat me to it, and we exited the car on opposite sides. He gave me distance, an opportunity to allow him to blend into the background or act as a bodyguard for me. I appreciated that I had the final decision on how to play this, but I didn't need backup of that variety.

I wanted Asa. I wanted my person. And maybe I wanted to show him off a little, to prove I was loveable.

Not that Asa and I had used the L word. It was a big word. I wasn't sure it would fit in my mouth.

Which, in hindsight, did sound rather dirty. And why was it so hot all of a sudden?

Once we were alone, Asa stepped up to the intercom mounted on a metal pole and hit the red button.

"Agent Montenegro and Agent Hollis to see Director Nádasdy."

The nasal voice that replied set my teeth on edge.

"You're expected." A loud beep rang in my ears. "Proceed to the front door."

We stood back to give the gates room to swing open, and it was the oddest thing. As I started down the shale driveway, I had to work harder to drag the same amount of oxygen into my lungs. Even then, they ached as if a vise had clamped over them. Somehow, there was less air inside the property than out.

There were no wards. The constant disruption as agents came and went drained their magic too quickly. The varying energy signatures rendered them useless. Security here was of the old-fashioned variety, as in guards. Dozens of them. All races, specialties, and designations. All licensed to kill and happy for the excuse to alleviate their boredom.

"I've never walked the grounds," Asa said into the silence. "They're lovely."

A green sea spread before us, lush grass no one was allowed to walk on. Gardens popped up on the right and left, paths to them poured in the same gleaming white shells as the driveway. The house resembled, in my opinion, Glensheen Mansion, in Duluth, Minnesota. All twenty thousand square feet of it. Except it had bricks made with black ceramic oxide rather than the standard red clay. As a result, the house was a deep charcoal shade made gloomier by the black hard slate roof. Very gothic. Very on-brand.

"I used to hide in the rose garden." As I said it, my gaze was drawn in and stuck fast. "I liked the thorns."

The patterns they painted in blood as they raked across your skin, the design raised later in scabs, the irony even petal-soft flowers had sharp teeth.

"That doesn't surprise me." He grew contemplative. "There was a price for safety among them."

The words sank in, lodged beneath my skin, and stuck. "How do you figure?"

"I know you." He rolled his thumb over my knuckles. "You believe there's a cost for everything."

"There is." I forced one foot in front of the other. "However, it's rarely monetary."

Long before we reached the elegant steps leading into the imposing manor, the butler opened the door. His spine popped as he hunched over to see under the arched frame. His skin was cloudy white, his hair powdery blue, and his eyes glittered with iridescence as they narrowed on me in recognition.

Bjorn, who never had liked me much, bristled as the predator in him recognized the predator in Asa. The ends of his hair clotted and hardened into icicles, and snowflakes drifted from a corona above his head that reminded me of the aurora borealis. Either that was new, or I had never seen him truly riled.

When you considered I once set his livery on fire, while he was wearing it, that was saying something.

Though, in my defense, he had ratted me out to the director for staying in the garden after dark.

"You wait here," he ordered Asa. "You know the rules."

"Tell the director I'm here, and inform him I'm not taking a step inside this mausoleum without Asa."

With a grumble, Bjorn slammed the door in our faces and barred it from the other side.

"This is already going so much better than my last visit here," I said cheerfully. "How about you?"

"The director prefers I wait in the car when Clay and I come to call."

Prejudice or fear? With him, it was often hard to tell. His depth of emotion rivaled a teaspoon.

"He probably wants to talk to me alone." I heard a tremor in my voice and crushed it flat. "Too bad."

Ten minutes later, Bjorn returned and opened the door wide enough for us to enter. By this time, the ice on his skin had begun to harden into armor that would deflect physical and magical attacks.

"The daemon spawn isn't allowed in the director's most private chambers," Bjorn informed us, his voice a nasal whine that clashed with his size. "The director will meet with you in the library."

I took a step in his direction, not to follow his lead, but to break off a haircicle and stab him with it.

Asa set a hand on my shoulder, holding me back from a confrontation that wouldn't end well.

For Bjorn.

"Thank you," Asa said with a politeness that baffled me. "We'll show ourselves in."

A grunt was all the acknowledgment we got before the frost giant stomped back to his post.

"I've always wondered if he would turn to ash or a puddle of water if I touched him," I mused. "What do you think?"

"That you can't kill everyone who's prejudiced against daemons."

"What if I kill everyone prejudiced against *my* daemon?"

The emphasis on *my* brought a smile to his lips, and my heart couldn't decide if it ought to shrivel in embarrassment or swell with pride that I made him happy by claiming him.

"I appreciate the sentiment, but no."

Probably I wouldn't kill them. Just zap them until smoke poured out of their ears. But I was trying to be a better person, and a better person wouldn't experiment on the boiling point for brains à la cranium.

The library was, without a doubt, my favorite room in the house. Three stories tall, all leather and wood. Rather than blacks and grays, this room was done in browns and reds and golds and smelled of leather and yellowed paper, dust and imagination.

I hadn't been allowed to borrow from it. I could have easily learned to hate books by association, but no. I was a bookworm to the bone. Not even the director had managed to beat the love of fiction out of me.

That happy thought led me to a warning I owed Asa. "I need you to promise me you can handle this."

"Define *this*." His shoulders stiffened on my periphery. "What do you expect to happen?"

"When he gets mad, he gets physical." I couldn't look at him. "Don't get between us, okay?"

"That's a big ask," he growled. "I don't know if I can make that promise."

"Try?" I kept my gaze on the floor out of habit, shrinking myself as he sometimes did, and I hated it. "For me?"

"All right." He shoved his hands into his pockets to hide his clenched fists. "I'll do my best. We both will."

The daemon was the wild card. I had to trust he understood I didn't need saving. It was too late for that.

When the door swung open, a solid hour later, an unimposing man bustled into the room. Late forties or early fifties, thereabouts. I used to wonder how long he had looked like that, but I didn't anymore. Black suit, white shirt, glossy shoes. He wore the template for the Black Hat suit. Thick frames completed the look. I wasn't certain what secret purpose they served, but his vision was flawless.

Unable to resist its insidious draw, I dipped my gaze to the black lacquer cane with mother of pearl inlays and tasted bile.

"Elspeth." The director sank into a wingback chair and gestured for me to take its partner. "You're a difficult woman to get ahold of."

Neither Asa nor I sat, which earned me an indulgent smile. He ignored Asa altogether, for which I was glad.

"And you're a difficult man to avoid." I smiled too, and mine was sharper. "What do you want?"

"For you to sit, for starters." He thinned his lips. "Can you be civil for a few minutes?"

Counting back from ten, I strove for calm. "Does the name Calixta Damaras mean anything to you?"

"The former high queen of the Haelian Seas?" His cane *tap, tap, tapped.* "What about her?"

"Tell me the truth."

"I answered your question truthfully."

Gritting my teeth, I hated how easy it was to fall back into this dynamic with him. "She was your lover."

The old man went deathly still at having been called out for their tête-à-tête.

"Who told you that?" His knuckles whitened around the cane. "Did they imply—?"

Here we go.

Scorched earth commencing in...five...four...three...two...

"That my father was half daemon?" I kept my arms stiff down by my sides. "That I'm a quarter?"

"What you are," he said as cruel magic sliced through the room, "is my granddaughter."

The acknowledgment of our relationship, in front of Asa, struck with the precision of a knife.

When I recalled how he never claimed me, I was wrong. He had. Several times. In front of servants.

"Confirm it or deny it," I growled, the leash slipping on my temper, "but I want the truth."

"Who told you that?" he repeated. "Who dared breathe life into those old rumors?"

Unsure what to expect, how he would react, I touched my wand with my fingers. "Calixta told me."

Grandfather shot out of his seat and struck me with a backhand that sent me stumbling against the wall. He slapped his cane across my throat, gripped each end, and threw his weight behind pinning me. "Liar."

"Just like…" I wheezed, tasting blood, "…old times."

From the corner of my eye, I watched Asa struggle to contain the daemon, but he held himself together.

For me.

"We had a nice chat," I goaded him. "She told me I take after my grandfather."

"Stop this," he rasped. "Now."

"She would know, wouldn't she?"

The cane vanished from my throat and embedded itself into the wall beside my head. "You're lying."

As much as I wanted to rub my throat, I locked my hands down at my sides, showing no weakness.

"Grandmother wanted to meet me." I let him soak that in. "She claims I'm her heir."

When he failed to respond, aside from the ticking beneath his right eye, I kept going.

"I did have a cousin. Delma. She was the one who brought me to Calixta. She challenged me for the right to call herself Calixta's heir." I covered Aedan and his siblings with a lie. "She already murdered the rest of the family. I was all that remained between her and her goal."

"You beat her," he said, calculations running behind his eyes as he stared at me.

A smug grin curved my lips for his benefit. "I did."

"You're Calixta's heir."

The smugness of a moment ago fled and left me standing again on uncertain ground. "I am."

Grandfather lowered his gaze in thought, and when he raised them, magic sparked off his skin.

"You were never supposed to learn of your connection. Calixta is *dead.* You must not resurrect her."

What did it say about their relationship that he didn't even ask *where* I found her? Or was it a testament to my father's skill that the old man didn't bother with the question, knowing he couldn't get her free if he tried? What did he know that I didn't? How the ward worked? He taught my father. He knew how his mind worked. And by my own words, I confirmed I was the last of Calixta's line. Maybe that was why the topic held so little interest for him. He already had his answer. She was locked up tight, unless I bled out.

A life for a life.

Given freely.

Pity he didn't know about the bag of ashes in my safe. And, yeah. No. I wasn't about to tell him.

"Why not?" I fluffed up my bravado. "Maybe a throne sounds more comfortable than my recliner."

"You're *my* heir," he snarled. "She has no claim on you."

Those three words had sealed her fate, in his mind.

I was his toy, and no one else was allowed to play with me.

"I'm no one's heir," I corrected him. "I don't want your legacy either."

"You don't have a choice."

"I believed that, for a long time. I don't anymore."

For the first time, the director paid Asa a speck of attention, and I wished he hadn't.

"You are your father's heir." The director's eyes grew colder. "You understand the weight of responsibility."

"Rue is her own person." Asa's voice came out glacial. "She makes her own choices."

"The male of the species in fascination is utterly worthless," the director spat. "They're guided by one thing, and one thing only."

"I have obligations back home," I cut in. "I only came to ask you, to your face, about my grandmother."

Red mottled his cheeks, and he prepared to bluster at me for the audacity of claiming that relationship.

"You're practicing white magic." His nostrils flared. "I smell it on you." He wet his lips. "The weakness."

A predatory gleam lit his eyes, and his gaze dipped to my chest, as if imagining where my heart beat.

He could hear mine, drumming away, the same as I could hear his if I listened. I used to all the time. Listen, I mean. I couldn't convince myself he had one if he treated me the way he did. But that was before I learned the difference between the organ and the metaphor.

"Try me." I had no hope of winning against him, not without Colby, but I would fight. "Old man."

"Your attitude hasn't improved." His eyes flipped up to mine. "You get that mouth from your mother."

As much as he blamed her for my faults, every last one, I knew from Megara he was right. For a change.

Mom was a bit wild, a bit sassy, and her taste in men was definitely questionable.

"Why did you want to see me?"

There was no point in asking him if he set up those agents, one who was short a hand thanks to me. The old man would lie through his teeth to avoid admitting any wrongdoing and twist things around until the person grilling him got smoked and gave up. Grandfather was a liar. A manipulator. And a true politician.

Though I suppose I could have just called him a politician and covered the same ground in fewer words.

"You're my granddaughter."

Hearing those words fall from his lips in front of another person for a second time was as jaw-dropping as it had been the first.

"That's not an answer." I studied him for signs of his intentions. "Why did you bring me here?"

"The terms of our bargain have changed," he informed me. "You are no longer a consultant."

Tongue running across the edge of my teeth, I wished I could say I was surprised, but that would be a lie.

"You are to return to active duty," he continued, blotting his lips. "Effective immediately."

A tremor in his hand as he reclaimed his cane set me in a mind to bargain, though he was a proven liar.

"There are worse things than Calixta Damaras," he said, as if to reassure himself, the cane *tap, tap, tapping*. "A reckoning is coming."

Had I not been there, standing in the room with him, I would have missed the tells.

Sweaty upper lip. *Blot.* Trembling hands. *Flex, relax.* A tic jumping beneath his left eye. *Blink.*

My grandfather, the director of the Black Hat Bureau, the most powerful black witch alive...was afraid.

17

Salt air pricked my eyes as I balanced on the edge of the jagged stones, gazing down at the sea, watching as waves pounded the cliffside. The roar was so loud, its fury so palpable as it hammered away at obstacles in its path, I could scream myself hoarse, and no one would hear me.

No one had ever heard me.

Or they hadn't cared enough to check on me, which amounted to the same thing.

The urge to jump never manifested as it had when I was a child. I waited and waited, but it never hit. All this time I thought it was *l'appel du vide*, the call of the void, but maybe it had been more than that back then. Either way, I was grateful the only tug I felt was Asa's arm as it slid around me, anchoring me.

"Are you afraid I was going to fall?" I leaned my head back on his shoulder. "Or jump?"

"Neither." His warm lips brushed my temple. "I only wanted to hold you."

I wasn't sure if I believed him, or if he believed himself, but I wasn't self-destructive.

Anymore.

"Let's go home." I cast the ocean one last glance. "We have presents to wrap and a tree to decorate."

"Did you mean what you said in there?"

News of Calixta's reappearance had shaken the director, but he came into the room already twitchy.

Whatever was coming, she wasn't to blame for my promotion, but then again, she couldn't escape her prison without me...or the baggy of ashes in my safe. The person behind the coup? They were out there, moving freely, and making dangerous allies faster than we could stamp out their followers.

The director hadn't given me the ringleader's name, maybe he hadn't ferreted them out yet, but he was spooked.

Spooked enough to rip my consultation contract to shreds in front of me with a flick of his wand.

That was okay. I had a copy. And I had Megara, who would vouch for its contents under oath.

Given the rogue agents' involvement in transporting those fae creatures, I was willing to play along. I owed it to Samford, and its people, who had suffered losses on my behalf, to do what I could for them, to keep them safe. Because whatever was coming, it knew where I lived.

"Yeah." I puffed out my cheeks. "Colby will be thrilled. Clay too. The girls...not so much."

I had already cost them so much, and I was about to ask for more.

All that kept me from pulling out my hair right now was I had seen the fear hiding beneath the director's mask. He thought I could protect his organization, and through it, him. Why? No idea. But I got the feeling, based on Calixta resurfacing with help from the Black Hat rogues, it was all in the family. What else was out there? *Who* else?

That covetous glance he shot my heart told me he might wrinkle his nose at white magic, but he knew enough of what I was, what Colby had made me, to be tempted. Most likely, he would have killed me and taken my heart if he believed for a hot second he could transfer Colby's familiar bond to himself.

Yet another reason why she hadn't been here. He was too canny. Had she been in the room, he might have been too curious, too tempted not to make a move.

"The girls will understand." Asa took my hand and pulled me back from the edge. "You have built-in security for the girls in Aedan."

The sensation of being a pawn moved on a cosmic chessboard left my senses swimming, or maybe it was late-onset vertigo.

"Handy how that worked out." I let him guide me toward the gates. "Everything tied up with a bow."

I had my confirmation I was a quarter daemon. I had proof of my lineage. I had a distant claim to a faraway sea kingdom I would never see. I had a cousin, in a roundabout way, who was blood bound to me. One who could step into my shoes at the shop and fill in while I slid deeper into my old life.

All my problems wrapped up with a big bow, like a gift from the universe.

Merry Christmas to me.

18

"I win." Clay strutted out of his room and spun a circle. "Go ahead and crown me."

"That's bad." Colby burst into laughter at the sight of his ugly sweater. "Really bad."

His pine-green sweater wasn't terrible. The lumpy snowflakes weren't horrible either. The sparkly green garland? Wow. It was something. What? I wasn't sure. The scalloped design reminded me of mermaid scales, and each peak was accentuated with either a red or gold ornament that jingled when he moved. The silver tinsel wig really set it off, and I had to admit I was impressed he managed to style it into a star.

"But wait." He flipped off the lights. "It gets *better*."

A faint click sounded in his hand, and tiny Christmas lights blinked to life, flashing merrily.

A beat later, a wheezing rendition of "Have Yourself a Merry Little Christmas" gasped from a music box.

"I'm not sure what that qualifies as," I said, turning the lights on again, "but it's not *better*."

Someone needed to put that sweater out of its misery. Poor thing sounded half dead already.

"I don't know." Colby fluttered her green-tinted wings. "It's kind of impressive."

After careful experimentation, Clay had landed on a spray hair dye that Colby could use to color herself. Already, she had purchased a dozen new shades online. I might never see my white moth again.

"Yeah." I snickered. "Impressively ugly."

"This is an ugly Christmas sweater contest," Clay reminded me. "Don't hate because I won."

"You haven't won yet." I glanced toward Asa's room. "We have one contestant left."

"Aedan didn't want to participate?" Clay buffed his nails on his shirt. "Scared of losing to me, huh?"

"Uh, no." I heaved a sigh. "The girls took him to watch a midnight showing of *It's a Wonderful Life*."

As much as I wanted to issue a fraternization warning for employees, I signed off on the field trip. Fifteen of the girls' closest friends were going too, and they wanted to introduce him to people his own age. The real possibility he would remain in Samford long term had swayed me into agreeing with the outing. He did need friends if he wanted to build a life here, and maybe a girl—besides Arden—would catch his eye.

Plus, with Clay on board for self-defense lessons, she was sneakily recruiting others for his classes.

"Tell the truth." Clay smirked. "He glimpsed me in all my glory and ran away scared."

"Yes, Clay, that's exactly what happened." I rolled my eyes. "He begged me to save him from the shame."

"Thought so." He cast me a pitying glance. "You should have taken notes from him."

The black sweater I chose earned more groans than laughs, so I knew I was out of the running. The Santa peeing off a roof in a stream of yellow lights should have won me the vote from Clay, who loved naughty designs best, but I forgot to put in batteries. I would have sworn the label said they were included, but oh well. It wasn't the same if the pee didn't light up on cue. That was my fault for not testing it sooner.

Not sabotage from a fellow contestant—cough, Clay, cough—I was sure.

Unlike the rest of us, who had no skill in the knitting department, Asa had made his own sweater.

And he had kept it secret from the rest of us, to the point Clay had searched his room several times to gauge his competition to no avail. It was driving him crazy, which was a short trip.

"You might want to cover Colby's eyes," Asa told us from behind his bedroom door. "Just in case."

"You heard the man." I left Clay to the task, since Colby was on his shoulder. "Blindfold time."

Willing to humor Asa, Clay held his wide palm in front of her face then announced, "Ready."

Asa's sweater was less gaudy than ours by a mile, but it was also the naughtiest by far.

Laughter spluttered out of me, and Clay howled, delighted with his partner's entry.

For his ugly sweater, Asa chose a lush red with green bands up the arms. In the center, a reindeer looked out at us. But the pièce de résistance were the bold white words below the image.

Horny for the Holidays.

Once I could breathe again, I waved Asa back to his room. "I think we've seen enough."

"I haven't," Colby pouted. "What did it look like?"

"Inappropriate," Clay told her between laughs. "That's what."

"But wait..." Asa did his best Clay impression, "...it gets *better.*"

With one deft move, he pulled the sweater over his head, turning it inside out, then slid it on that way.

"Ha!" I smothered a laugh that Colby joined in, now that she could see too. "That is truly inspired."

This side of the sweater was the same green but with a golden frame and a piece of mirrored plastic.

"Aim that at Clay," I begged Asa, "and I'll vote for you all day long."

Humoring me, he turned toward Clay, who caught his reflection in the mirror. He used it as an opportunity to check his hair then winked at himself, pleased with what he saw.

Clearly, he didn't get that whoever was reflected put the *ugly* in ugly Christmas sweater.

"It's okay to be jealous." Clay blew himself a kiss. "Not everyone can look this good."

"Mmm-hmm." I shook my head. "That sweater should have been yours."

"And miss the chance to see myself?" He huffed. "What a waste that would have been."

"Colby." Asa slid past me. "Can I see you in the kitchen?"

Wings twitching with interest, she sailed over to him. "Sure."

The two of them disappeared while Clay and I exchanged a look.

Asa returned a couple minutes later, eyes downcast, and stood beside me.

"Prepare to crown your queen," Colby yelled. "Ready?"

"Ready," we all chorused, and then Clay and I waited for the big reveal.

Cackling with glee, she swooped a lap through the room then lit on her favorite perch.

"You made this," I murmured to Asa. "I want to call it ugly to fit the theme, but..."

Her entry was more of a vest, worn backwards. The design covered her stomach, and knitted straps rose from the neckline. They draped across the base of her wings and then snapped at the hem of the sweater. The yarn was several shades of green with silver threads to represent circuitry. I assumed it was circuitry. I wasn't the expert here, but Colby seemed impressed with the details.

Or maybe she was in love with the bright gold letters that spelled out BYTE ME.

With a ten-year-old moth girl, it was hard to say which part impressed her the most.

The nod to her love of computers, or the brush with profanity I was allowing to pass.

"It's ugly." Clay shot me a pointed glance. "The ugliest sweater I've seen tonight."

Taking the hint, I hurried to agree. "I was thinking along the lines of hideous."

"Time to vote." I passed around a cup and let everyone put in their piece of paper. "Now we shake."

After tossing the bits of paper around for effect, I dumped them on the coffee table, and tallied.

"One vote for Colby." I picked up the next. "Two votes for Colby." I smiled. "Three votes for Colby." I pressed the next flat. "Four votes for Colby." I found another piece. "Five votes for Colby?" I checked with each of them. "Who voted twice?" It hit me a heartbeat after I asked. "The daemon."

Asa inclined his head in confirmation, and I loved that the daemon had gotten to participate. I wasn't sure if he cast his vote in the moment, in Asa's head, or if they worked it out earlier. But I was glad all the same.

"We have a unanimous winner." Clay whooped. "What's the prize?"

"Bragging rights," I said at the same time Colby told him, "A hundred dollars."

Twenty-five bucks per person went into the pot as an entry fee to keep it fair-ish.

A hundred dollars was a small fortune to a kid, and I knew exactly where the money would go. I might as well go ahead and buy the Mystic Realms credits so she could get started designing her next character. It might go toward pets or mounts, but that kind of cash would outfit another avatar to play when she got the itch to be sneaky or to explore without her team.

Occasionally, she liked to get up to trouble on her own without it affecting her main account's stats.

With Clay around, it happened more often. A *lot* more often. Like they kept a running list of hijinks.

"Okay," I yelled over the commotion. "Who's ready to decorate cookies?"

"Me." Clay shot his arm up in the air. "What's on the menu?"

Once I got everyone seated at the kitchen table, I pulled the cooling cookies off the top of the fridge where I had hidden them. I placed the tray on a potholder in front of Clay and watched him blanch.

"That's cruel and unusual punishment." He poked one with his finger. "Why do you hate me?"

The cookies were gingerbread men, and I could tell from his expression he would never forget the time Mrs. Malone tried to feed us her version. My secret ingredient was chili powder. Hers had been human flesh.

"People cookies." Asa stared at them. "You baked people cookies."

"People cookies?" Colby glanced around the table. "We call them gingerbread."

"No people were harmed in the baking of these cookies," I promised them. "Think of this as therapy."

I returned with piping bags of icing in white, red, and green then fetched six bowls filled with a variety of seasonal candies.

"This is wrong." Clay recoiled from the cookie I placed in front of him. "It's just...not right."

"What am I missing?" Colby flexed her wings. "What's a people cookie?"

Poking one of my cookies, I assumed, to see if it would cry about it, he said, "They're—"

—not conducive to Christmas cheer.

"Why don't we skip this for now and open presents?" I spoke over him. "Yay. Presents. Fun."

Colby, being a kid, required no more prompting to blast off toward the tree and the mountain of gifts underneath. She resumed her spot on the chair perch and made grabby hands until I began sorting the presents into piles for each of us. I left Aedan's to one side, so he could open them when he got home.

Home.

The word encompassed so much, and these days, so many.

The second I finished double-checking under the tree, it was open season on gifts.

Evil laughter poured into the room as Colby held up two Mystic Realms gift cards, one from each of the guys, and twitched her wings like she might fly off to cash them in right then.

"You still have gifts left, and so does everyone else." I indicated her pile. "Keep going."

A flicker of childish petulance was all she could muster when there were more goodies to be had.

Especially when she noticed Clay reaching for the foodie gift she bought him.

The PieCaken had arrived cushioned in icepacks straight from its namesake bakery yesterday.

With pecan pie on the bottom, pumpkin pie in the middle, and spice cake on top, it was a showstopper. Add the cinnamon butter-cream layering it together and a generous scoop of apple pie filling, and Clay looked ready to cram the entire dessert into his mouth before anyone could ask for a taste.

"Shorty, if I loved this any more," Clay told her, "I would put a ring on it."

Antennae aquiver, she fluttered her wings with happiness at his praise then dove into her trove again.

"Are you serious?" Her eyes almost popped out of her head at her next big reveal. "A VR headset?"

One I special ordered six months ago in her size so she would be ready for the virtual reality features she might have mentioned once, or a million times, were coming soon to Mystic Realms.

"You're welcome." I threw a shiny bow at her. "Aren't you glad you kept going?"

"Yes," she squealed, spinning in the air with the box clutched to her chest. "Thank you. Thank you. Thank you."

Armed with a shiny new headset and with credits to burn, I might never see that kid again.

"Rue," Clay breathed after tearing into the present from me. "Are you serious?"

Aside from a full sampling of my wig haircare line, which hadn't launched yet, I had given him a dream.

"What is it?" Colby peeked over, headset in place. "Are you...crying?"

"The New York City Wine & Food Festival." He held his tickets over where his heart should be. "Intimate dinners, tastings, demonstrations, master classes." He fell backward on the couch. "I'm going to meet Giada." He shut his eyes. "Giada is going to cook for me." His lashes fluttered. "I'm going to eat Giada's food."

The love of his life, now that Julia Child was an impossibility, was Giada De Laurentiis.

Asa, not to be outdone, had booked the hotel, plane tickets, and a driver for his friend.

When Asa passed over the itinerary, I noticed he wasn't opening his gifts. He was smoothing a hand over the packages, tugging on the curls of ribbon, reading each tag, front and back.

Sinking down next to him, I touched his arm. "Do I have to lick each one to get you interested?"

"I'm interested." His gaze fell to my lips. "This is my first Christmas with...family."

Most paras didn't celebrate human holidays in any religious sense. They just liked the excuses to eat, buy gifts, receive gifts, eat some more, and spend time with loved ones. Plus, most para children attended human schools, and most paras held human jobs.

They got the time off, so why not indulge? And, you know, distract the kids with new toys while they're underfoot for two or three weeks.

"Do you want to open them later?" I rubbed circles on his back. "You don't have to be part of the spectacle."

"No." He shook his head. "I just wanted a moment."

"Let the man attempt to manifest X-ray vision." Clay threw a wad of tissue paper at me. "Open yours."

"You don't have to ask me twice." I grabbed for the biggest box, of course. "A KitchenAid stand mixer." I cuddled the box to me. "I've always wanted one of these."

They weighed a ton, so they hadn't been practical when Clay and I were first partners. Then I spent every penny I had on the house, the business, and the start of my new life. There had been no room in the budget to celebrate by purchasing a fancy-pants mixer when a generic one would do.

"Light and Shadow," Colby read off the box. "That's the color? It looks off-white to me."

"Shh." I rested my cheek on the box and stroked the side. "She didn't mean it."

The fine print called it sand-toned, and it came with a studded black ceramic mixing bowl.

"That was from me," Clay informed me. "Not that you bothered to check the tag, heathen."

"Thank you." I kept petting the box. "It's everything I never knew I needed and then some."

Before I dug the flap open, Clay yanked the box out of my arms and set it on the floor at my feet.

"Open mine next." Colby set a thin box on my thighs then zipped back to her hoard. "Go on."

The lid slid from my fingers when my gaze touched on the picture in the ornate sterling frame.

"How...?" I cleared a sudden lump from my throat and tried again. "How did you get this?"

The black-and-white photo showed my parents arm in arm. Mom was beaming from ear to ear, holding on to Dad tight. Her joy was incandescent, so bright I had to look to Dad for relief. His face was meant to wear a scowl, he was solemn by nature, but he couldn't fight his tender smile for her any more than I could battle the sting of tears behind my eyelids.

"I called Meg."

For Colby, that meant going through an intermediary. It would have emptied her savings to use a proxy, but a tithe must be paid to summon those beyond the veil, and Colby knew she was forbidden to give her blood to any working, no matter who asked her.

Even me.

Maybe especially me.

"I told her you had been thinking about your parents a lot," she continued, "and I asked if any pictures of them had survived. She reached out to her great-great-great niece and gave her permission to search her things. A few weeks later, she mailed this photo to me." Her voice softened. "It was taken on their fiftieth wedding anniversary." She scrunched up her face. "It's the only existing copy, and Meg says she will reincarnate, hunt you down, and maul you if you lose it."

"She never told me she had it." I smoothed my thumb over the glass. "I've never even seen it."

"I wanted you to have a piece of them with you, for when you miss them."

"Thanks, smarty fuzz butt." I opened my arms for her, and she slammed into my chest, knocking the breath out of me. "This is the best gift I could have asked for."

"You're welcome." She pried it from my hands then parroted to me, "You still have gifts left."

Unable to tear my gaze from the photo, I stared as Colby flew it to my room for safekeeping.

Beside me, Asa cleared his throat, snapping me out of *what might have beens*, if my parents had lived.

"This is from me." He pulled a small black box from his pocket. "If you're up to opening another gift."

Panic cleansed my palate as I accepted the token with damp palms, afraid of its contents.

"Breathe, Rue." He rested a hand on my thigh. "It's not a ring."

Embarrassed to be called out, I flipped open the clamshell lid to find…a fae wrought lariat necklace.

Five dainty sprigs of mistletoe hung suspended from a silver chain. Each vein on every leaf was as unique as a fingerprint. Clustered pearls mimicked berries, ripe and round, and two more bunches dripped from the center strand to form the classic Y shape.

"It's…" I stroked the leaves with a fingertip, their lifelike texture startling, "…beautiful."

Despite our audience, he leaned in, his lips brushing my ear. "For the times when you want to be kissed, and I'm too dim to pick up on the subtle hints. Touch the lowest sprig, and I'll know."

"So, what you really gifted me was unlimited kisses."

"As many as you wish." His teeth scraped my jaw where Colby couldn't see. "Whenever you wish." His voice dipped to a bare exhalation of breath no one else would hear. "Wherever you wish."

A giddy thrill shivered in my stomach as he fastened the gift around my neck.

"Thank you." I cradled it in my palm, amazed at its lightness. "It's—"

His lips brushed mine, whisper-soft and PG-13 appropriate.

"And it works." Clay slow clapped, proving he overheard. "Just what you two needed, a smooch signal."

"Hey, it works both ways." Colby fluttered her wings. "Now we know when to cover our eyes."

"Good point." He winked at her. "I knew I liked you for a reason."

The flicker of flame out of the corner of my eye was all the heads-up I got before the daemon ripped out of Asa. His eyes lit on the pile of presents before him, and, unlike Asa, he didn't hold back. He snapped the ribbons, tore the paper, crushed the boxes, and dumped his prizes in his lap to inspect when he was done. Only when he could find nothing else to shred did he turn his attention to the contents.

"This for Asa." He tossed aside the set of ethically sourced unicorn horn knitting needles I bought for a small fortune from a mostly reputable rarities dealer, Hendricks, who sailed under the Black Hat radar by snitching on poachers and thieves for them. "This for Asa." He dropped the six skeins of rainbow-hued Merino wool yarn Colby selected on the floor. "This for Asa." He held up a hand-stamped leather wallet from Clay. "No present for me?"

Had I not planned for this contingency, my heart would have broken on the spot. Clay hadn't believed the daemon would want to participate, since he never had during their solo years, but I had prepared for this moment.

"Your present is outside." I took his large hand. "You have to promise to be careful, though."

"Careful." He dropped my hand to swing his arm around my shoulders and squish me against him. "Yes."

"But first—" Clay rushed to get in front of us, "—protective gear."

The daemon frowned, but he didn't fuss as Clay put corks on the sharp ends of his horns. He was also outfitted with Kevlar-lined socks and Kevlar-lined gloves. His confusion was complete when we blindfolded him and led him to the backyard, which was lit by more of the solar lights we bought for Aedan, since Colby loved them so much.

"Are you ready?" I held tight to the piece of fabric over his eyes. "Are you sure you can handle this?"

"Ready." He bounced on the balls of his feet. "I can handle."

After I ripped away the blindfold, he emitted a noise dangerously close to a squee.

"For me?" He gazed at his present. "Not for Asa?"

"This is one hundred percent for you." I gave him a shove. "Go on." I nudged him again. "Go play."

For the past several hours, Clay had been overseeing a crew paid triple time to come out on Christmas Eve and inflate a wonderland for the daemon to play in. I hadn't been sure if it was too childish or just childish enough to appeal to him, but he couldn't stop his grin from spreading as he took in the slides, one taller than the house, the bouncy castle, and the ball pit. It was the kind of thing Colby would turn her nose up at and tell me she wasn't a baby. But with the daemon? She tossed all that out the window.

"Race you," he yelled to Colby. *"Readysetgo."*

"You're on." She laughed and took off like a shot. "First one to the ball pit wins."

"You did good, Dollface." Clay and I sat on the grass, shoulder to shoulder. "I've never seen him so happy."

"I'm not sure I've ever seen her so happy either," I admitted. "She loves having you guys here."

Her online friends were her mental age, and she loved them to bits, but she couldn't meet up at cons or do any of the other IRL things the other kids did together. She was forever stuck behind a screen, and I had been her only point of contact. Until Clay and Asa showed up in Samford.

"She's going to love being on the road more." He scooped me against his side. "And my stomach will be so glad to have you back where you belong."

"I hope she does. It will be a big change for her."

"I'm almost as hungry for your cooking as that kid is for life." He planted a smacking kiss on my cheek. "Plus, you have a home to come to between cases. You have roots here, and that makes all the difference."

Before I could reassure him he also had a home, with us, I received a call.

Given the hour, and the day, I was too concerned not to answer. "Agent Hollis."

"Two infants are missing," Agent Marty Talbot, my old nemesis, barked. "Get your asses to Charleston."

"Send me the details." I stared at Colby and the daemon, who had moved on to water balloon fights, and mentally began our packing lists. "We'll head out first thing in the morning."

After I ended the call, I stared at my phone, hoping I had made the right choice in the director's office.

"You never said why you chose to go active," Clay said. "I'm not complaining, but I am curious. Do you miss me that much between cases? Have you developed separation anxiety? Afraid I'll leave for a case and never come back?" He paused. "Oh, wait. That was me. After *you* left."

I got the subtext, the concern I was doing this for Asa, to spend more time with him. That was a bonus, but I wouldn't have upended my life—and Colby's—for a romance.

"I've realized something." I shoved him. "There are a lot of Colbys out there."

"And not nearly enough Rues," he agreed, sobering. "Or Asas. Or Aedans."

"Or Clays." I smiled at him. "Don't forget the Clays."

A pleased smile touched his mouth. "Should we bring in the kids?"

"Nah." I opened an email from Marty packed with attachments. "Let them play."

Tomorrow would come soon enough.

Tonight, the stars were brightly shining, and my weary heart rejoiced to be here, with my family.

ABOUT THE AUTHOR

USA Today best-selling author Hailey Edwards writes about questionable applications of otherwise perfectly good magic, the transformative power of love, the family you choose for yourself, and blowing stuff up. Not necessarily all at once. That could get messy.

www.HaileyEdwards.net

ALSO BY HAILEY EDWARDS

Black Hat Bureau

Black Hat, White Witch #1

Black Arts, White Craft #2

Black Truth, White Lies #3

Black Soul, White Heart #3.5

Black Curse, White Cure #4

The Foundling

Bayou Born #1

Bone Driven #2

Death Knell #3

Rise Against #4

End Game #5

The Beginner's Guide to Necromancy

How to Save an Undead Life #1

How to Claim an Undead Soul #2

How to Break an Undead Heart #3

How to Dance an Undead Waltz #4

How to Live an Undead Lie #5

How to Wake an Undead City #6

How to Kiss an Undead Bride #7

How to Survive an Undead Honeymoon #8

Lorimar Pack Series

Promise the Moon #1

Wolf at the Door #2

Over the Moon #3

Araneae Nation

A Heart of Ice #.5

A Hint of Frost #1

A Feast of Souls #2

A Cast of Shadows #2.5

A Time of Dying #3

A Kiss of Venom #3.5

A Breath of Winter #4

A Veil of Secrets #5

Daughters of Askara

Everlong #1

Evermine #2

Eversworn #3

Wicked Kin

Soul Weaver #1